Yours for the Asking

Kenna White

Bella
BOOKS

2009

Bella Books, Inc.
P.O. Box 10543
Tallahassee, FL 32302

Printed in the United States of America on acid-free paper
First Edition

Editor: Marissa Cohen
Cover Designer: Stephanie Solomon-Lopez

ISBN 10: 1-59493-163-1
ISBN 13:978-1-59493-163-5

Dedication

This book is dedicated to the little girl in me and in all of us that still believe in Christmas and the wonder of it. What could be more magical than waiting for Santa Claus? To see that wonder and anticipation in my grandchildren's eyes is a thrill beyond description.

Acknowledgments

A special thanks to Mom and Dad for making our Christmas memories so wonderful they will live on in my mind forever. From my first cap gun and holster (yes, I was a tomboy) to my first blue Schwinn, from my 45 RPM record player to my Monopoly game, from a house full of relatives around the dinner table to a stocking filled with candy and goodies, Christmas was the stuff of dreams and joy. May each and every one of you have a Feliz Navidad, Joyeux Noel, Boze Narodzenie, Buon Natale and a very Merry Christmas.

About the Author

Kenna White was born in a small town in southwest Missouri, but has lived from the Colorado Rocky Mountains to New England. Once again back in the Ozarks where bare feet, faded jeans and lazy streams fill her life, she enjoys her writing, traveling, substitute teaching, making dollhouse miniatures and life's simpler pleasures.

Chapter 1

Lauren Roberts yawned and leaned her forehead against the kitchen cabinet, waiting for the coffeemaker to trickle out enough to fill her cup. It was six-something Friday morning, and she wasn't usually this groggy or indifferent to her morning chores but yesterday was Thanksgiving. She had prepared a turkey and ham feast for thirty guests, cleaned up afterward, and hadn't crawled into bed until well after midnight. Sometime after one o'clock the couple in the Sapphire Room needed more towels and an extra blanket.

Plus, the periodic creaking of the bed by the honeymoon couple in the Lavender Room, the guest room directly over Lauren's bedroom, made falling back to sleep nearly impossible. Their repeated lovemaking was a testament to their youth and apparent athletic ability. She had counted four separate amorous events during the night, each one lasting nearly an hour.

It had been months since anyone creaked Lauren's bed. And even then, it wasn't that impressive. She and Jan had only been on four dates before they retired to her apartment on the first floor of the bed-and-breakfast to spend the night together. That was enough for Lauren to realize Jan's demanding ways and lackluster romp in the hay weren't what she was looking for in a girlfriend. It might have been enough when she was twenty. However, at thirty-six, she wanted more. Whatever it was, Jan was out of the picture. Lauren was alone, again. Single, independent and unrepentant.

She poured cream into her coffee, stirred it, and took a sip as she stood at the bulletin board reading today's menu. On this rainy Arkansas morning, she had two hours to prepare a fresh, delicious meal for ten guests. Her Victorian bed-and-breakfast, Gypsy Hill, had not yet come to life. The only sound in the Eureka Springs house was the ticktock from the grandfather clock in the hall, and the gentle rain against the windows. Even Cleo, Lauren's finicky, demanding, long-haired orange cat, had not yet crawled off the foot of her bed. As if testing Lauren's resolve, Cleo showed up on the front porch just three weeks after Lauren had instituted the inn with a strict no-pets policy. At first, Lauren ignored the cat. She refused to feed it, assuming it would eventually go home. For over a week, the cat wandered the grounds, sitting on the porch railing and looking woebegone. It wasn't until a torrential rainstorm turned the fluffy feline into something that looked like it had been extracted from a clogged drain that Lauren took pity and offered a bowl of warmed milk.

"One meal. That's all," she had said as the fur-matted cat lapped hungrily. "After that, you'll have to move on. I don't allow pets."

That was four years ago. Not only had the cat been given a name and offered a home, Cleo was prominently pictured on Gypsy Hill's Web Site as hostess, welcoming committee and the one and only pet allowed on the premises.

Lauren finished her coffee and set the cup aside. She knew she wouldn't get back for a second cup until breakfast was prepared and served to her guests and the kitchen cleaned. There was a thump somewhere outside, but Lauren didn't have time to see what it was. She had a breakfast strata to bake. Cleo sauntered into the kitchen and meandered between Lauren's legs, meowing plaintively.

"I filled your dish last night. Have you eaten it all already?" As she assembled what she needed on the counter, Cleo meowed again and rubbed against the corner of the refrigerator. "So you think you need milk this morning, is that it?" Lauren asked.

She had just begun pouring milk into a dish when there was a knock at the front door. She set the dish on the floor, patted Cleo, and went to answer it.

"Hello," she said to the woman on the porch. She was covered in mud and filth. There was a wretched smell hanging over her. Her brunette hair was pulled back into a ponytail. Lauren noticed the end of it was caked with mud.

"Hi," she said nervously. She acted like she was in a hurry. "I'm sorry to bother you so early. Did I get you up?"

"No. I was up. What can I do for you?" Lauren usually invited visitors to step inside but she certainly wasn't going to invite this woman in. She wasn't even sure she should have opened the door.

"I'm really sorry, but I hit your mailbox." She nodded toward the street. Sure enough, a silver Honda Pilot was parked just outside the white picket fence, on the spot where a mailbox post once stood.

"Oh my God!" Lauren said, flinging open the screen door and running down the walk. "My mailbox!" It had begun to rain harder.

"I'm so sorry. The pavement was wet and I guess I misjudged the corner. The car just slid right into your mailbox." The woman followed Lauren through the gate. "I'm afraid it's pretty much toast."

Lauren peered underneath the car at the broken post and smashed mailbox.

"You mashed it flat. How could you do that? It's a good six feet from the street."

"Talented, I guess." The woman grinned and shrugged her shoulders as if to make light of it.

"You may think this is funny but I don't. How am I supposed to get my mail today? I can't stand around in the rain waiting for the mailman to hand me my mail. I don't even think they can do that. You have to have an approved mailbox or they won't leave your mail."

"The day after a holiday is usually fairly light. Maybe you won't have any mail."

"I run a business here." Lauren scowled up at the woman. "I get lots of mail every day. The post, which happened to match the ones all the way around my porch, is broken in half. And the mailbox wasn't just any mailbox. It was hand-painted."

"I know. I saw it seconds before I hit it. It was very nice." The woman said it as if a compliment would help matters. "Look, I'm really sorry. I'll take care of fixing it but I'm in a hurry. I'd do it right now, but I've got to get to the hardware store. By the way, you don't happen to have a six-inch sewer line cap, do you?"

"No, I don't."

"I promise I'll come back and fix it. But if I don't get to the hardware store when they open at seven, I'm going to have a swimming pool in my basement." She hurried around and climbed in the driver's side. "Don't worry. I'm good for it."

"But my mail!"

The woman started her engine and pulled away.

"Sorry," she yelled out the driver's window.

"Hey!" Lauren called after her. "What's your name? I didn't get your name!" The SUV disappeared from sight. "Damn it!" she said, stomping her foot. "Come back here. That's called Hit and Run, you know!"

She had probably just been screwed. She would never see the woman again and it would be up to her to replace the mailbox and post. *I didn't even notice the woman's license plate number. If I'm asked to identify the perpetrator, I'm not sure I could because of all the*

4

mud. The only identifying thing Lauren had noticed about the woman was her compelling emerald green eyes.

Lauren didn't have time to chase down a hit-and-run driver. She had a breakfast to prepare, and was cold and wet from standing in the rain. She hurried inside to change, muttering to herself for not at least getting the license plate number. She'd worry about that later. For now, she needed a smile for her guests and a hot breakfast for their stomachs. Cleo was waiting in the kitchen for her, sitting next to the untouched bowl of milk, meowing indignantly.

"I'm not going to heat it. You can rough it this morning. I've got work to do and I'm running late." Cleo moved to the middle of the kitchen and hunkered down, closing one eye.

"I said no. I am not nuking your milk. Why don't you go sit over there?" Lauren scooted her across the floor with her foot. Cleo was undeterred. She returned to the middle of the floor, offering another demanding meow.

"Fine. Don't drink it then." Lauren stepped over the cat as she went to work on breakfast. Cleo was unrelenting. Each time Lauren crossed the room and stepped over her, she meowed. "Oh, good grief, Cleo. You are worse than a spoiled child." Finally, she snatched up the bowl and zapped it in the microwave for twenty seconds, and set it down again. "There. Now drink it and hush." Cleo circled the bowl then sat next to it. She looked up at Lauren and then closed her eyes as if the effort had been too much for her and she needed a nap.

Lauren, however, had no time for a nap. It was time to cook. She prided herself in providing an eye-appealing, bountiful and delicious breakfast. She had learned how much to make and how to serve it to ensure her guests would take home fond memories of their time at Gypsy Hill. Along with the sausage cheese strata, today's menu included homemade oatmeal raisin muffins, pepper bacon and fresh fruit. There was always granola, toast, assorted juices and coffee. Anyone could scramble an egg or microwave a strip of bacon and call it breakfast but that wasn't Lauren's way of doing business. To put Gypsy Hill above the flock and guarantee success, she knew it required lots of work, little extras that attracted attention, and a sense of pride in what she did. Lauren made all the baked goods from scratch. The bacon, ham and sausage in Lauren's freezer were grown, butchered and packaged locally. It was cheaper to buy a whole hog and have it butchered just the way she wanted it than to buy a few pounds at a time at the grocery store.

She enjoyed cooking, something she had inherited from her mother, but she hadn't always been good at it. The first few months after she bought the inn and began preparing all the breakfasts herself she had her fair share of disasters. But practice and experimentation had taught her the tricks of the trade to keep her guests happy. How the food was served became just as important. Silver coffeepots, platters and silverware, cut glass serving bowls, beautiful china, festive centerpieces and cloth napkins all contributed to an elegant and memorable experience. With antiques, stairs and limited play space, Gypsy Hill was not suitable for children. Lauren hated to limit her clientele but many of her return customers preferred peace and quiet, something small children didn't provide. This was a policy added as the result of experience. She couldn't count the number of partially flushed diapers, broken dishes and crayon marks left by little hands during her first six months when she allowed everything from infants to adolescents.

By eight fifteen the guests began filtering down to the dining room. By eight thirty breakfast was in full swing, and Lauren knew it would last until about nine fifteen. Lauren arranged the serving pieces on the walnut buffet in the dining room. Each guest filled his or her own plate and found a table in the breakfast room, a hexagonal room with tall windows that looked out into the garden. The breakfast room had originally been a sunroom off the dining room, filled with plants and wicker furniture but it worked well for the small tables that provided private and cozy seating. Lauren had always preferred individual breakfast tables instead of seating everyone at one long dining room table. The honeymoon couple didn't come down to breakfast but she wasn't surprised. The other guests were giggling about it.

"Did you hear them, Lauren?" a middle-aged woman asked, spreading jam on a muffin.

"Hear what, Mrs. Chamberlain?" she said, resting her hand on the woman's shoulder as she filled her coffee cup.

"That couple in the room at the end of the hall. I don't think they slept at all, if you know what I mean." She winked.

"No, I'm sorry. I guess I didn't hear anything." Lauren knew better than to engage in gossip about her guests.

Cleo seemed to know just when to appear and who was good for a scratch behind the ears. In spite of toxic stares from Lauren, Cleo meandered through the breakfast room, looking adorable and innocent. She was often rewarded with a bite of egg or a tidbit of meat.

"Quit being a mooch," Lauren whispered harshly in Cleo's direction as she went to refill the coffeepot.

"Here kitty, kitty," Mrs. Chamberlain called, making kissing sounds and dropping a bite of cheese on the floor. "Come get a bite, you pretty thing. Isn't she precious, George?"

"Uh-huh," he said, without looking up from his newspaper.

Cleo blinked at Lauren then sauntered over and lapped up the morsel as if she hadn't eaten in days. The woman smiled and fed her another bite.

"What is her name? It is a her, isn't it?" she asked as Lauren returned to fill empty cups.

"Cleo. You'd think I never fed her."

"She is so sweet," the woman cooed as she reached down and scratched behind Cleo's ear. Cleo sat stretching upward, purring for all she was worth as if mocking Lauren.

"I'd give her to you, but she thinks she owns the place. She'd sooner give me away."

"You don't need another damn cat, Helen," the man said from behind his newspaper. "We've already got two." He folded down the paper and looked over his glasses at Lauren. "Want another one?"

"No, thank you." She chuckled. "One is plenty."

7

"That's what I told Helen." He went back to reading.

"Don't listen to him," Helen said. She broke her last bite of bacon in half and shared it with Cleo. "He wouldn't give up either one of our cats."

"Would too." The newspaper rustled.

"Hush, George. Read your paper."

"Would you like more coffee, Mr. Chamberlain?" Lauren offered.

"Yes, please." He peered over the top of the paper. "Would there be any more of those muffins?"

"Absolutely. I'll get you one. How about you, Mrs. Chamberlain? Another muffin? There's plenty of strata as well. What can I get you?"

"I'll get it, honey," she said. "We shouldn't be hungry after that huge meal last night, but everything is so good. I have to get your recipe for the breakfast casserole."

"Right here." Lauren handed her a recipe card from the holder. "It's really simple. You can substitute Swiss cheese if you want a little different flavor."

"Look at that, George. She even has recipes set out. That place we stayed in Bentonville never had fancy recipe cards like this."

"Uh-huh."

"You want more bacon, George?"

"One."

"He'll want two," she whispered knowingly.

By eleven o'clock, breakfast had been cleared away, the kitchen cleaned, and Lauren was in her office. It had originally been a small sitting room and had a pair of tall windows that looked out onto the front porch. From her desk, she could see the picket fence, the gate and the remnants of her mailbox.

"I can't believe that woman crashed into my mailbox then just drove away," she muttered as she punched in the telephone number for the lumberyard. "Hi Margaret, it's Lauren. How was your Thanksgiving dinner?"

"Hi, honey. It was okay. Thanks for the broccoli casserole

recipe. It was a big hit. John loved it. How did your dinner go? I'm sure it was delicious. How many did you serve?"

"Thirty."

"Thirty? I like to have company for the holidays but not thirty. How can you do that?"

"Lots of coffee and vitamins." Lauren chuckled. "And it's really not that many. I'll probably have more at Christmas."

"At least you get paid for it."

"Yes, and that brings me to why I called. Do you have another one of the white turned posts I used to make my mailbox stand?"

"The pressure treated ones?"

"Yes. I need to replace mine."

"You really shouldn't have to replace it this soon. It's not supposed to rot, Lauren. I'm going to complain to the company."

"It didn't rot. It was mowed down by a kamikaze SUV."

"You're kidding?" She laughed out loud. "Someone actually ran over your mailbox? Why aren't they replacing it?"

"Because, stupid me, I didn't get their name or their license plate. It was raining, it was six o'clock this morning, and I just forgot." Dimly, in the background, Lauren heard a car pull into the driveway that circled to the back of the house. That would be Tallie, her housekeeper.

"Honey, I can order you one, but we don't have any in stock. I've had those on back order for a month. I know it won't match but could you use a plain square post?"

"I could but it wouldn't match the porch posts."

"How about an old milk can as the base? Janie Rutherford has one of those out front of the Henderson Inn. It looks really cute. She painted it green and planted flowers around it."

"Yes, I know. But I don't want to look like the Henderson Inn. I want to look like Gypsy Hill. My house and the cottage are both yellow with white trim. So was my mailbox and post. Let me do some checking, Margaret. I'll get back to you."

"Sorry, hon."

Lauren hung up and went to the window to stare out at the broken post.

"Damn woman driver." She turned on her heels and went to reheat her coffee.

"Lauren!" Tallie called as she rushed through the back door off the mudroom. "The mailbox. It's been hit. Come quick!"

"Good morning, Tallie. And yes, I saw it."

"What the hell happened? Who did it? Was it that man with the orange shirt from last night? The one who ate three helpings of turkey and belched like a caveman? He looked like he was drunk on just one glass of wine. He did it, didn't he?"

"No, he didn't. It happened this morning." Lauren sipped her coffee. It had been reheated several times and was now bitter and disgusting. She poured it out and put the cup into the dishwasher.

"Who did it? One of the guests?" Tallie demanded. "Mr. Chamberlain? He looks the type. Old and senile."

"Tallie, that isn't nice. And no, Mr. Chamberlain did not do it. In fact, it wasn't one of the guests. It was just a passing car."

"What was their name? Anyone I know?"

Tallie Mead was forty-eight-years-old and had been Lauren's housekeeper since she first opened Gypsy Hill five years ago. She was a square-shaped woman with nondescript graying hair. She had lived in Eureka Springs all her life and had been married twice, both times only briefly. She was also a born-again lesbian, as she put it. According to Tallie, her first marriage was out of ignorance and naïveté. The second marriage was to confirm her stupidity and only lasted three weeks. She had put herself through beauty school and took a job at the local walk-in hair salon. That was where she overheard Lauren say she needed a reliable housekeeper. Tallie had never worked at a bed-and-breakfast before but she knew how to make a bed and run a vacuum. She had a fundamental logic and a simple brutal honesty that both endeared her to Lauren and occasionally infuriated her. If Tallie thought it, chances are she was eventually going to say it, regardless of who it might offend. One thing she did have was a

10

solid and steadfast loyalty to Lauren and what she was trying to accomplish with her business. She came to work on time, did her job well and didn't complain. Tallie was more than an employee. She was a friend. Someone Lauren could confide in. Lauren suspected if she knew who ran over her mailbox, Tallie would be glad to pay them a little visit.

"I don't know her name." Lauren went back into her office.

"How do you know who did it then?" Tallie followed close on her heels.

"I don't. And before you ask, I didn't get the license plate number either. All I know is it was a filthy woman with green eyes and a silver Honda Pilot. She crashed into the mailbox in the rain early this morning."

"You mean you didn't even get her insurance number?"

"I didn't get anything, Tallie," Lauren said sternly, more aggravated with herself than Tallie's relentless questions. "The Crimson Room is empty. You can start there. The Rose Room is staying another night. You can knock and see when they would like to have housecleaning. The couple in the Lavender Room is staying another night but they don't want housekeeping. The Sapphire Room will be checking out." She looked down at her watch.

"Anyone coming in tonight?"

"Yes. A couple from Joplin for the Crimson Room. Lydia and Amber." She checked the card on her desk. "They were here last spring. Amber was the one with the quirky sense of humor. She told all those elephant jokes. Remember?"

"Oh, yeah. What do you get when you cross an elephant with a rhinoceros?"

"I have no idea. What?" Lauren said, sitting down at her desk.

"Elephino." Tallie laughed and headed back up the hall. "Why are elephants gray and wrinkled? So you won't confuse them with aspirin."

"Cute." Lauren was already busy on her computer. "I shouldn't have said anything."

A minute later Tallie stuck her head in the office door. She was carrying a vacuum sweeper and a plastic carrier of cleaning supplies.

"How do you know if an elephant has been having sex in the backyard?"

"I have absolutely no idea, Tallie," Lauren said, entering some figures on a spreadsheet. "And I probably don't want to know either."

"The grass is rolled flat and all the trash bags are missing." Tallie giggled and, with that, went upstairs to clean.

Egg & Sausage Strata with Mushrooms

Kenna's Mother's recipe
This is a great breakfast casserole for Christmas morning.
Make it the night before, so it can bake while you are opening presents.

Serves 6-8

6 slices of bread broken into small pieces or cut in strips
(remove crusts)
1 lb. sausage (browned, drained and crumbled)
(1 lb. cooked and crumbled bacon may be substituted for
sausage)
8 ounces grated cheddar cheese (or cheese of your choice)
6 eggs – beaten
2 cups milk
1 large can mushrooms - drained (sliced or stems and pieces)
1 teaspoon Worcestershire sauce

Line bread into buttered 9 x 13 glass casserole. Sprinkle cheese
over bread then crumbled sausage. Layer mushrooms over
sausage. Beat eggs and add milk and Worcestershire sauce. Pour
over sausage and mushrooms. Refrigerate overnight. Bake at 350
degrees for 45-50 minutes. Let stand 5 minutes before serving.

Chapter 2

"Thank you, Angie. I've got the reservation all set for you." Lauren cradled the telephone under her chin. "Yes. I'll be here. Just call if you think you're going to be later than nine o'clock."

"Which room?" Tallie whispered, looking in from the hallway.

"Sapphire," Lauren mouthed in her direction.

Tallie made a ghastly face and shook her head.

"What's wrong?" she asked, covering the mouthpiece.

"Toilet is clogged. I've worked on it for a half hour but I can't get it to flush."

Lauren rolled her eyes and held up her hand for Tallie to wait.

"That's great, Angie. We'll see you then." She hung up and wheeled around in her chair. "How bad is it?" she asked, racing for the door.

"I've got towels down everywhere. It's contained to just the bathroom but I can't start cleaning it up until it'll flush." Tallie followed her upstairs. "You're probably going to have to call a plumber."

"Let me take a look. What is the deal with plumbing problems today?"

"What do you mean?"

"That woman who ran over the mailbox this morning drove off because she had some kind of sewer trouble. I bet she just didn't want to pay to fix it." Lauren pushed up her sleeves as she tiptoed over the sopping wet towels strewn around the bathroom floor. She grabbed the plunger and began pumping at the toilet.

"At least it isn't gross," Tallie mumbled as she looked on. "It's just water."

Lauren gave it her best effort, pumping frantically until she was out of breath. She stood up and watched. The water lowered only an inch.

"Be right back," she said and trotted downstairs. She returned with an opened wire coat hanger and began fishing around in the toilet for the possible clog. "Aha," she said, feeling something in the line. She withdrew the wire, bent a hook in the end then reinserted it. Like a surgeon working delicately around an important blood vessel, she maneuvered the wire deeper until she felt the clog. She rotated the wire and began pulling it back.

"Have you got it?"

"I think so." She eased it out until she could see the corner of a towel in the drain. With one long tug, she yanked it out and dropped it on the floor.

"There. One clogged toilet, fixed," Lauren said as the toilet drained. She wiped the back of her hand across her forehead. "That'll save a hundred dollar plumbing visit."

"I don't understand why anyone would flush a towel down the toilet."

"My guess is they dropped it in the toilet and didn't want to fish it out, so they flushed it, hoping to hide the evidence." Lauren washed her hands in the sink and used the last hand towel on the rack to dry them. "Can you finish here?"

"Yep. I'll need to disinfect this floor. You go ahead."

Lauren went back to her office and opened her e-mail.

Hi, sis. Sorry I couldn't make it for Thanksgiving. I'm sure it was wonderful but Syd invited the whole cast over at the last minute. I couldn't say no, not if I want that new song in the finale. You know how it is. You've got to stroke his ego if you want the goodies. But count on me for Christmas. In fact, I need to talk with you about that. Got to go. Costume fitting. They're finally taking my advice and changing that dress I told you about. God, it was bad. I looked like one of those foo-foo cake toppers. Later. Love ya. Kelly.

Lauren pushed the speed dial button next to Kelly's name. Since it immediately went to her voice mail, she left a message.

"I got your e-mail, honey. I wish you could have made it for turkey day but I understand. Give me a call when you can so we can talk about Christmas. I look forward to seeing you. I hope you can be here both Christmas Eve and Christmas Day. Talk with you soon."

Lauren hoped Kelly wasn't going to blow off Christmas like she did Thanksgiving. Last year wasn't much better. She dropped in Christmas morning just after breakfast and was gone by dinner time, barely enough time to exchange gifts and get caught up on news. It didn't matter they had sibling squabbles from time to time. Who didn't? But they were sisters, family. They belonged together at Christmas. It was the one time of year jealousies and differences should be put aside. Maybe this year would be different.

She had just finished printing tomorrow morning's recipe cards when Kelly returned her call.

"Hi, Kelly. How was Thanksgiving at Syd's?"

"It was WONDERFUL!" She groaned dramatically. "He had it catered. You would have loved it. We had shrimp and chicken cordon bleu. There were three kinds of wine. Crab stuffed mushroom caps. God, sis. I've never eaten so much food in my

16

life. I stuffed myself."

Lauren knew that wasn't true. Kelly was extremely conscious of her weight. She was a performer and was well aware her image had everything to do with her success. Lauren's weight had never been an issue for her. She worked hard and ate sensibly. Kelly often felt she had to struggle to keep her figure under control. She had never been overweight. For most people, five extra pounds was just a cute love handle. But for Kelly it was a tragedy.

"I miss you. How's the show going?"

"Oh, fine. I've only got a minute to talk. We're doing a quick run-through for an understudy. Nanette has the flu. I just wanted to see if you had room for me at Christmas."

"Of course. I was just waiting to hear from you. And by the way, I'm supposed to tell you be sure and give Dee and Trina a call. They're anxious to see you."

"God, I haven't heard from them in forever. Do they still live in that ugly blue house on Crowder Hill?"

"No. Their landlord painted it. It's now green."

"Ugly green?"

"You didn't hear that from me."

They both laughed.

"Remind me again to call them when I get into town. I've got so much on my mind right now I can't remember shit."

"I'm doing a big Christmas buffet again this year. I hope you will be here for that."

"Are you open at Christmas?"

"Sure. You wouldn't believe how many people come for the Christmas flavor and the big meal. I'm expecting a full house for the buffet. At least thirty, maybe more."

"I thought you stopped doing those extra meals. Don't you have enough work with just the overnight guests?"

"It's just for special occasions. I don't serve dinners all the time."

"It's supposed to be a holiday, sis. Why are you taking on so much extra work?"

"It's called income, Kel. Income. I have to make hay while

the sun shines."

"Is that your way of saying we won't have a quiet peaceful Christmas?"

"No. That's my way of saying we'll have a house full of Christmas joy. And I'm only doing the Christmas meal. Christmas Eve is just for us."

"Whatever." There was something in Kelly's voice. Something unsaid. "I've got to go. Thanks, sis."

"Kelly, why do I sense there's something you're not telling me? What else should I know about you and Christmas?" she asked suspiciously. She was a veteran of Kelly's surprises. "Is everything okay?"

"It's really nothing."

"Kelly?"

"Really. There's nothing else. The show closes on the twelfth. Our last performance is at eight o'clock. Do you want tickets? I can get you center stage, row eight. Best seats in the house. The last few days of the Christmas show are never a sellout."

"Thank you but I can't. I've got guests checking in that day."

"I'll be dead tired after the show so I won't leave until the next morning. I should be in Eureka Springs by one, maybe two o'clock. I've got to stop by the storage building and leave a couple of things."

"That's the thirteenth. Why are you coming on the thirteenth and why do you have a storage building? Your apartment has a slew of closets."

"No, it didn't. That's why I'm moving. I can't wait for you to see my new place."

"New place?"

"You'll love it. It's brand new. Two bedrooms, two full baths, granite countertops, fireplace, balcony. And they have a fitness center with a private trainer. It's to die for. Really!"

"Sounds nice. But I didn't know you were moving."

"They were raising my rent in that crappy little apartment and for seventy bucks more a month I can have a brand-new

18

place. I even get to pick out the carpeting. I only have four choices to pick from, but at least I won't have gold. I hate gold carpeting. It draws your eyes right down."

"Is the carpeting in yet?"

"The one I picked was the most popular color. They were a little short so they had to wait for the next shipment. It should be in the carpet layer's warehouse by the twentieth."

"So, it won't be installed until when?"

"They said probably the twenty-third. Instead of installing part of it then finding the new rolls don't exactly match, they're waiting until they have all of it, just to be on the safe side. I'd hate to have a seam right down the middle of the living room with two different colors. God!"

"When do you expect to move in?"

"At least by the eighth. Maybe the seventh if the painters get the touch-up done."

"The seventh or eighth of January?"

"Sure."

"But you aren't really moving out of your present apartment until they have it ready, right?"

"That's the great part. Because of when I moved in to my present apartment, I can save a whole month's rent if I give it up on the thirteenth. That works out perfectly with our last show."

"Where are you going to stay?" Lauren tried not to focus on the sinking feeling in her stomach.

"Well, with you, sis. What do you think I've been telling you? Isn't it great? I can save a month's rent and we can have some real time together. Of course, we haven't been able to share a room since we were kids. We'd kill each other. But at least I'll be in the house. We'll have a great time together."

"Four weeks?" Lauren exclaimed.

"Great, huh?"

"Yeah, great." Lauren instantly thought back to their childhood when they had shared a room. The result? Kelly's makeup all over Lauren's clean bedspread.

"I didn't have a choice, Lauren. Really, I didn't."

She did have a choice but Lauren saw no use in saying so. After all, it was Christmas. There was something about having family together for Christmas that put a soft and vulnerable spot in Lauren's heart. That soft spot was going to be tested one more time.

"That's fine, Kelly. I'm looking forward to it. You can help with the tree trimming. We'll have a great time."

"You still do the real tree?"

"You bet. I can't imagine Christmas without a live tree in the living room."

"Do you still have the tree party?" Kelly sounded interested, something that surprised Lauren.

"Yes. One week before Christmas. I'd be too worried the tree would dry out and be a fire hazard to put it up any earlier. I still make hot cocoa and mother's cinnamon crisps."

"Sounds like fun. I've got to run. They're calling me. See you on the thirteenth." She hung up.

Lauren pushed the button to end the call and tapped the receiver against her forehead.

"When am I going to learn to say no to her?"

"Say no to who?" Tallie drew the dust mop around the door jamb.

"My gullible self."

"Is everything all right?" Tallie swept a ball of cat fur from under Lauren's desk.

"Kelly will be here for Christmas."

"Oh, good."

"She'll be here for four weeks."

"Four weeks?" She stopped mopping and glared over at Lauren. "Why?"

"Because she's my sister." Lauren ceremoniously dropped the receiver into the cradle. "And it's Christmas."

"Will you want the rollaway put in your bedroom for her?" Tallie went back to mopping.

"I have no idea. I'll worry about that tomorrow. Or next week." Lauren brought up the schedule on her computer screen.

"Maybe I'll have a room available for her."

Tallie rolled her eyes.

"I thought we were completely booked through Christmas."

"God, I hope not," Lauren muttered, studying the calendar. "Maybe I'll just sleep in the car."

Homemade Granola

We packaged this in holiday baggies or decorated jars, this recipe makes a great Christmas gift. Perfect for the jogger, hiker, or health food nut on your list.

2 ½ cups old-fashioned rolled oats (regular oatmeal)
1 cup shredded coconut
½ cup coarsely chopped almonds
½ cup shelled sunflower seeds
½ cup unsweetened wheat germ
½ cup honey
¼ cup cooking oil
½ cup dried apricots, chopped
½ cup raisins
½ cup dried cranberries, halved or chopped

In large bowl, combine oats, coconut, almonds, sunflower seeds and wheat germ. Combine honey and oil. Stir into oat mixture. Spread out on 9 x 13 baking pan. Bake at 300 degrees until light golden brown, 45 to 50 minutes. Stir every 15 minutes. Remove from oven. Stir in apricots, raisins, and cranberries. Remove to another pan to cool, stirring occasionally to prevent lumping. Store in jars or baggies. May be frozen.

Chapter 3

This was the weekend Lauren traditionally brought out the Christmas decorations. It would take Tallie and Lauren all weekend to get the house just so. Tallie helped sort through the boxes, substituting vases and baskets for an Italian crèche with hand-painted figurines and live Poinsettias. Every window in the house was adorned with a small wreath. Angels, ornate arrangements and Christmas garlands changed Gypsy Hill into a holiday fantasyland. Lauren's best ornaments, many of them family heirlooms handed down from her mother and grandmother, would eventually adorn a ten-foot Scotch pine set in front of the living room windows. By the end of the weekend after Thanksgiving Gypsy Hill would be gleaming with Christmas spirit, regardless of the weather. Lauren loved Christmas. She loved the lights, the decorations, the carols, even the cooking that kept her in the kitchen for hours on end. It was the one time of year she could be a kid at heart.

"There's a woman out front," Tallie said, coming into the kitchen. She was carrying an armload of sheets toward the laundry room.

"What woman?" Lauren was leaning over the kitchen counter, sipping peach tea and clipping grocery coupons.

"I have no idea. Good-looking woman though. She parked awfully close to the fence. I hope she didn't hit it."

"No, not again!" Lauren rushed down the hall. Sure enough, there was a silver SUV parked mere inches from the white picket fence. "I know that car. But I don't recognize the woman."

"Do you want me to go yell at her?"

"No, I don't want you to go yell at her. I'll take care of it. You can go start on the cottage. The Wilsons checked out." Lauren opened the screen door and stepped out onto the porch. "Hello," she called as she descended the steps. "Can I help you?"

The woman was unloading something from the back of the SUV. She was dressed in well-fitting jeans and a long-sleeved blue chambray shirt. Her hair was shoulder length and silky brown.

"Good morning." The woman smiled. It wasn't until she looked up and revealed her emerald green eyes that Lauren knew who she was.

"It's you. You're the one who knocked over my mailbox."

"I'm sorry I'm so late. I had to go to three places to find a post like yours. I guess I should have asked where you got it."

"What are you doing?" Lauren came through the gate and stared down at the pile of tools the woman had unloaded.

"Replacing your post and mailbox, of course. I said I'd fix it. I'm sorry the mailbox won't be as nice as the one I smashed. I'll pay you for that one. Maybe I can find someone to paint the flowers and little fence on it to match what you had. We should save the old one as a pattern."

Lauren hadn't expected to ever see the woman again. She was surprised at her integrity.

"If you can fix the post, I'll take care of the mailbox."

"Nope." The woman shook her head adamantly. "I killed it.

I'll replace it. Unless you painted it yourself. Did you?"

"No. I didn't paint it. I had it done."

"Then I'll have it repainted." She wiped her hand on her jeans and offered it to Lauren. "I'm Gaylin Hart. We didn't officially meet yesterday. I'm sorry about that but I was in a hurry."

Nice manners, polite, and what a cute dimple, thought Lauren. *Very cute.*

"I'm Lauren Roberts. You don't have to do this yourself. I was going to hire my maintenance man to fix it."

"Not a problem. It was my mistake." She unloaded a bag of gravel, heaving it over her shoulder. When she did, it raised her shirt. Lauren noticed a small teddy bear tattoo on her right hip, peeking out from under the waistband of her jeans. It was no bigger than a thumbprint, but it was cute.

"Lauren," Tallie called from the porch. "Eloise Corsini is on the phone. She needs to change her reservation."

"Be right there, Tallie. Will you excuse me, Gaylin? Let me know if you need anything. I'll understand if you change your mind. My maintenance man is just a call away."

"I'll let you know." Gaylin removed her shirt, exposing a well-fitting tank top. Lauren spent a moment enjoying her impressively fit body before going inside to answer the call. As she sat down at her desk, she took another look out the window. Gaylin was stomping the shovel into the hole and scooping out the rocks.

"Hello, Ms. Corsini," she said but her attention was on Gaylin's ass as she shoveled. *That's definitely an ass I wouldn't kick out of bed*, she thought.

One telephone call led to another. Before she knew it, an hour had passed. Gaylin's top was stained with sweat and her jeans were smeared with dirt when Lauren finally stepped outside, carrying a glass of ice water.

"How's it coming?" Lauren said, handing her the glass.

Gaylin looked up, her face wet with perspiration.

"It's coming," she gasped, leaning on the shovel to catch her breath. "You read my mind." She took the glass and drank it in one

25

long swallow. She wiped one of the ice cubes across her forehead. The droplets ran into her shirt, making a wet spot between her breasts. "I thought this was November. What happened to the cooler temperatures?" She handed Lauren the glass.

"Good question. I never look a gift horse in the mouth. Any time the weather is nice enough so I don't need the air conditioning or the furnace, I'm happy."

"Thanks for the water."

"You're welcome." Lauren eyed the pile of rocky soil next to the hole. "The hole sure has gotten bigger."

"I had to get the big rocks out so I'll have a clear spot to set the post."

"Do you need help with anything?" Lauren felt like she should at least ask. She wasn't sure what she could do but it was her property and her mailbox.

"As a matter of fact, yes. I could use a hand, if you've got a minute. Could you hold the post while I pour the gravel in the hole?" She set the post in the hole. "Like this."

Lauren put a hand on the post, standing well back from the hole.

"Move up a little." Gaylin placed her hands on the small of Lauren's back and guided her closer. "You'll probably need to use both hands."

"Okay, I got it."

"Slide your hands up a little." She placed her hands over Lauren's to move them. "I don't want to whack them with the shovel."

"Here?"

"That's perfect. I'll try to be as quick as I can." Gaylin began filling the hole, poking at the rocks with the shovel to settle them. "Doing okay?"

"Yes. But I feel like I'm not helping very much."

"You are. I couldn't hold it straight and fill the hole all by myself. I'd probably end up with it tilted and have to start over. I had to set my mailbox three times. I thought I never would get it set. It still leans a little." Gaylin stomped around the post, compressing the rocks. Lauren kept a firm grip as she moved in a circle to keep out of Gaylin's way. She gave one more stomp. "Let's try that. You can let go."

Lauren stepped back to admire the results.

"Looks good to me," she said, opening and closing the door to the mailbox. "That's pretty smart of you to attach the crosspiece and the mailbox before you set the post in the ground. I probably would have done it the other way around."

"Then you would have knocked the post over hammering on it." Gaylin fitted the last few small rocks around the base of the post, pressing them down securely.

"That's why I have a maintenance man. I leave that stuff to him."

"I learned that trick the hard way. I set my post and then tried to attach the mailbox." Gaylin rolled her eyes. "Another reason mine leans to the south like a barrel cactus."

"Maybe I should come hold it for you so you can straighten it up," Lauren chuckled.

"Not a bad idea. But I really don't want to dig it up again. It will have to remain a monument of my stupidity." Gaylin had begun reloading the tools into the back of her SUV. "Do you want the broken post or do you just want me to haul it away?"

"I don't need it."

"I didn't think so. Shall we put the mailbox someplace so it can be a pattern for repainting the new one?"

"I'll take care of it. Maybe I'll keep it as a reminder of the crash."

"I'm really sorry about all this trouble. I never thought the pavement was that slick."

"It's fixed. I can get my mail. That was my main concern."

Gaylin pulled a money clip from her pocket.

"I want to pay you for the mailbox. I know it wasn't cheap to have it painted like that. It was gorgeous. And it matched the house perfectly. How much do I owe you for that?"

"That's okay. I don't even remember. It was a friend of a friend who did tole painting."

27

"No, I want to pay you. Thirty? Forty? How much?" Lauren took the money clip and slipped it down into Gaylin's pocket.

"Don't worry about it. It wasn't that much."

"Are you sure? I don't want to take advantage of you."

"I'd be taking advantage of you if I took your money. I really didn't pay that much for it."

"So long as you're happy."

Lauren gave the mailbox a critical look.

"It's just like my old one. I'm happy. And thank you for your honesty. I really didn't think you'd come back and fix it."

"That's not the way I do business, Miss Roberts," Gaylin said, extending her hand to Lauren. "I'm always good for my word." She held Lauren's hand warmly. "You'll be hearing from me." She climbed in, started the engine, and slowly pulled away.

Lauren watched as she turned the corner at the end of the block and disappeared.

"I'll be waiting," she said. She stared down the street as if watching for the SUV to reappear. "By all means, I'll be waiting." She grinned, turned on her heels and headed inside.

"How did it go?" Tallie asked, coming into her office. "Did she get it fixed?"

"Uh-huh." Lauren was daydreaming about what Gaylin would look like naked.

"Who is she? Did you get her name?"

"Gaylin Hart."

Tallie studied Lauren's face and grinned.

"So, when is your first date?"

"What date?"

"You can't fool me, Lauren Roberts. I saw that gleam in your eye."

"There is *no* gleam in my eye."

"Yeah, right. And you don't secretly wish she'd drive right back here, throw you on the ground and have her way with you. Twice."

"I do not," Lauren scowled.

"Hey, I wouldn't blame you. If it wasn't for Sasha, I wouldn't mind a tumble with her myself." Tallie laughed then went back to work.

"She's probably not even gay," Lauren called after her.

"If you say so."

Tallie was so right, Lauren thought. Even dirty, Gaylin Hart was about the sexiest woman she had ever seen. Tallie had hit the nail on the head. Gaylin's arms and legs wrapped around her would be the perfect way to spend an afternoon. Lauren sighed softly as she turned her attention to work. Or at least as best she could with the location of Gaylin's tiny tattoo embedded in her psyche.

Blueberry Muffins with Cinnamon Crumb Topping

Mother's recipe

Makes 6-8

Sift together:
2 cups flour
3 teaspoons baking powder
1/2 cup sugar
1/2 teaspoon salt

Stir with fork until well blended:
1 egg – beaten
1/4 cup oil
1 cup milk

Add wet ingredients to dry. Fold in 11/4 cup blueberries Spoon into paper lined muffin cups. Fill only 1/2 to 2/3 full.

Topping

Blend until crumbly
1/4 cup butter
1/3 cup brown sugar
1/4 teaspoon cinnamon
1/2 cup flour

Sprinkle topping over top of muffins. Bake at 375 degrees for 30 minutes Serve and enjoy.

Chapter 4

"Hi, Tallie. What's up?" Lauren balanced her cell phone under her chin while she loaded sacks of groceries into the backseat of the car.

"I thought you said the mortgage company was sending the appraiser next week."

"No, this week. They called and changed it. They are supposed to be there tomorrow between one and five."

"Well, guess what? The appraiser is here."

"Today?"

"Yes."

"Today!" she shouted. "I wanted to be there."

"I told her you'd be right back. Should I tell her not to do anything until you get here?"

"No, no. I'm on my way."

"She's got her head in the flue of the living room fireplace.

31

What should I do?"

"Well, don't light it. Just visit with her, Tallie. I'll be right there." She hurriedly tossed the rest of the groceries in the car and climbed in.

"There's something else you should know," Tallie whispered into the receiver.

"Tell me later, Tallie. I'm on my way." She closed her phone and roared out of the parking lot.

Lauren sped home and rushed up the back steps, hoping Tallie hadn't driven the appraiser away with her suspicions.

"Hello. I'm here," she announced, striding into the living room, expecting to see a matronly looking woman with a clipboard and a tape measure, tapping her foot disgustedly at being kept waiting. However, as Lauren rounded the corner and entered the living room, Gaylin stood leaning against the fireplace, holding a small laptop computer in one hand and typing with the other. She was dressed in gray pinstripe slacks and a matching jacket.

"Hello," Gaylin said with a smile. "I'm here to conduct an appraisal of your property."

All Lauren could do was stare.

"That's the other thing I was going to tell you," Tallie said, patting Lauren's arm as she passed on her way to the kitchen.

"You? You're the appraiser? Why didn't you say something the other day?"

"Why? Weren't you satisfied with the repairs to your mailbox?"

"Yes, but you should have told me you were doing my appraisal." Lauren was still dumbfounded that the woman who ran over her mailbox was also the appraiser who held the future of her mortgage interest rate in her hands.

"I try to keep my personal life separate from my professional life." She handed Lauren a business card.

"Why? Were you afraid I'd try to take advantage of you?"

"I just saw no reason to mention it."

"But you knew you were going to be doing the appraisal on my property when you were here. It would have been polite to introduce yourself, don't you think?" Lauren couldn't help think Gaylin Hart had something to hide.

"I apologize, Miss Roberts. Do you think we can get past this and get to work?"

"I guess." Lauren was still apprehensive but she knew she had to put it behind her. She needed Gaylin on her side if she had any chance at refinancing her high-interest mortgage.

"First, maybe you could tell me a little of your history with Gypsy Hill. How long have you owned it? Any improvements you've made? Anything you think I need to know to make an informed appraisal of its value?" Gaylin sat down on the sofa and opened a file on her laptop.

"I bought Gypsy Hill five years ago. I printed off some information the mortgage company said you'd need. Let me get it."

Lauren went to her office and returned with a manila folder of paperwork.

"My insurance policy and my license are in there. The most recent improvement would be the commercial heat pump. I had additional insulation put in the attic and I had the cottage insulated as well."

"Where's the cottage?"

"It's on top of the hill beyond the garden." Lauren nodded toward the back window. "It's the original dwelling. Orlando Tate built the cottage for his daughter in nineteen o-four as a present for her eighteenth birthday. A few years later the main house, the one that sat here, burned to the ground. The cottage survived and the Tates lived up there on the hill in just two rooms while this house was built. They say Mrs. Tate was so upset at being cramped in that tiny house that this house was built in less time than any other house in Arkansas history. It went up in just four months. Considering the size of the house, the hilly terrain, and the era, four months is almost unheard of. I understand Mrs. Tate pretty much got whatever she wanted. They had three married sons with children. That's why there are so many bedrooms and bathrooms."

"Do you know who owned the property before you bought it?"

"My father's aunt. I always called her Aunt Edna. She bought it in nineteen fifty-one from the Tates' granddaughter, Felicia. Aunt Edna ran it as a guest house for forty years. I bought it from her. She wanted it to stay in the family."

"Why did she want to keep it in the family if you weren't the original owners?"

"Aunt Edna and Felicia Tate were more than just casual acquaintances." Lauren smiled coyly. "The sale of the property had something to do with estates and trusts. I never really understood exactly what. Aunt Edna considered herself *in* the family."

Gaylin looked up and studied Lauren for a long moment.

"Oh. You mean they were lesbian partners," she said, raising her eyebrows.

"Do you have a problem with that?"

"Nope. I don't have a problem with it."

"Then what's that look?"

"I'm sorry. I was just thinking about the reason for the sale. Sounds like I'll have a little digging to do to trace the property if there's a trust involved. Those things can get pretty technical."

"But they did a title search when I bought Gypsy Hill. Won't that take care of any questions of ownership?"

"We'll hope so."

"Well, some of the windows are new. And so are the kitchen cabinets. Aunt Edna had started to remodel the kitchen. Felicia had a heart attack and they had to hire someone to help with the housework. That left them a little strapped for cash. That's when I stepped in and made an offer on the house. I expected them to say no, but to my surprise, they accepted it. So, here I am." Lauren spread her arms and smiled. "Owner and custodian to Gypsy Hill." Just then Cleo sauntered through the living room. She rubbed up against Gaylin's leg as if christening her and welcoming her to the house. "I'm also custodian to Cleo the cat."

34

"Hello, Cleo," Gaylin said, rubbing a finger behind the cat's ear. Cleo immediately flopped down on her side and waited for more.

"She's spoiled. Don't pay any attention to her. She'll leave eventually."

"I don't mind." Gaylin scratched the cat's tummy, instantly turning on her purr motor. "Cats are okay. At least they don't bark."

"I bet you run into a lot of that."

"A lot. People want my services but don't bother to put their dog on a leash so I can do my job. That's why I carry this." Gaylin exposed the small can of pepper spray hung on her belt.

"You better watch out, Cleo. Gaylin is armed and ready. Don't be clawing up her pant leg."

"She does that?"

"She does lots of naughty things. Well, not naughty as much as strange. I found her sitting on the blade of the ceiling fan in the sunroom. She was watching a bird at the feeder outside the window."

"Ceiling fan? How did she get up there?" Gaylin continued to pet the cat with one hand while scanning a file on her laptop with the other.

"Good question. It's a wonder she didn't break it."

"You said some of the windows are new. Not all of them?"

"No. I couldn't afford to replace them all. The rest are on my list of future projects. Eventually, I want them all to be the triple pane kind. That's what I have in the kitchen, dining room, living room, sunroom and my living quarters off the kitchen. Upstairs are single-paned with storm windows."

"Heat rises. Your heating bill might be lower if you had replaced the upstairs windows first."

"But I live downstairs. There are times when I'm the only person in the house. That's why I did the downstairs first. And I didn't know the economy was going to take a nosedive. I expected to be able to replace the rest of the windows by now."

"Is the crown molding new or original?"

"Original. It's walnut. I'm sorry Aunt Edna had it painted. But I don't intend on having it stripped and refinished. That would cost a fortune. The house has hardwood floors, four fully functional fireplaces, and a full basement with a cement floor."

"Do you have any guests in the rooms upstairs right now?"

"Yes. Two of the rooms are occupied. The guests are out right now but they said they would be back around three. I'm expecting a couple to check in later this afternoon, too."

"So you expect three rooms to be occupied tonight."

"Yes. Unless I receive any other reservations."

"Does that happen very often? Last-minute reservations?"

"Sometimes. Most of my rooms are reserved at least a week, if not a month, in advance. For special events in and around town, it could be as much as six months in advance."

"I'll need to see your books. How many rooms you average per night or per week. Expenses. Gross and net income. Anything that would tell me the income potential of the property."

"I thought you were just going to look at the house and tell the mortgage company how much it is worth."

"I am, but appraising a residential property is not the same as appraising a commercial property. It's not just a house with windows, floors and walls. I'll need to do some research to establish comparative property values and income production potential."

The telephone in Lauren's office rang.

"Excuse me, please," she said, going to answer it.

"Do you mind if I take a look around and make some notes?"

"Help yourself. Tallie is upstairs. She can show you the rooms."

Lauren handled two telephone calls and an e-mail reservation before heading upstairs to check on Gaylin's progress.

"Where is she?" she asked Tallie, who was changing the sheets in the Harvest Room, named for the rich jewel-tone color scheme of gold, burgundy and brown.

"She wanted to see the attic." Tallie pointed up.

36

"Did you show her the rooms on this floor?"

"She didn't ask to see them. She said she wanted to start at the top and work down."

"I'm sure she'll want to see them eventually. How many haven't been cleaned yet?"

"This is the last one. By the way, that elderly couple who stayed in the Rose Room last night?"

"The Finches?"

"Yeah. They stole the towels."

"How many?" Lauren was disappointed but it was nothing new.

"Two towels and the bath mat."

"How did they get them in their luggage? They only had one suitcase."

"That's the second towel theft this week! That newlywed couple swiped a set of towels and the candy dish last Saturday."

"I told them they could have them as a souvenir of their honeymoon."

"You gave them towels and a candy dish?"

"Yes. I did. She's being deployed to Afghanistan next week. She is regular army and this will be her second tour of duty. It was the least I could do." Lauren headed up the stairs to the third floor. "Are you up here, Miss Hart?" No one answered. "Hello?"

The door to the storeroom opened and Gaylin stepped out. "In here."

"That's just storage."

"I see that. But it's also where I can get a good look at the bones."

"Bones? You mean the basic structure of the house?"

"Yes. It's to your advantage that I can see the wall and roof studs. Mr. Tate had the house framed in full dimensional lumber. Not the stock used nowadays. The two by fours are full two inches by four inches, not just one and a half by three and a half. So are the two by six and two by eight rafters and ties."

"That's good?"

"Much sturdier. A little more expensive to replace but this

house was built to last." Gaylin knocked on the wall. "He even had hardwood floors installed in the storeroom."

"I'm afraid I did that. I was going to have that room converted into a guest room, but then I realized I needed a storeroom for all the junk I save."

"Do you have hardwood floors throughout the house?"

"Yes. I understand there is even hardwood under the tiled kitchen floor."

"And the molding. Is it original?"

"Yes." Lauren took a key from her pocket and opened the door next to the storeroom. "Would you like to see the Sunflower Room?"

"Sure." Gaylin followed her inside.

Lauren systematically showed Gaylin each and every room in the house, pointing out the carpeting, trim, bathroom fixtures and tile work. They toured the six guest rooms on the upper two floors before moving to the first floor.

"This was originally Mr. Tate's office and the maid's quarters," Lauren said, opening the door marked *Private*. "Aunt Edna and Felicia had it turned into the owner's apartment to keep themselves separated from the guests. It has a bedroom with a walk-in closet, full bath and a sitting room. Another nice feature is the private back entrance." She opened a door that led out into the garden. "I don't have to enter through the rest of the house."

"That's handy." Gaylin made note of it in her laptop. "I think it was Mr. Tate's way of escaping without being noticed." Lauren's room looked the least like a Victorian home. Instead of period furniture, antiques and ruffles, it was decorated conservatively. The queen-size bed was covered with a sage green satin comforter, matching sheets and a lush pile of throw pillows. The focal point of the room was a large painting hung over the bed. It depicted an iron gate opening into a garden full of blooming flowers, overgrowing a stone path.

"I like the painting," Gaylin said, staring up at it. "Did it come with the house?"

"No. I found it at a flea market. The first moment I saw it I knew I had to have it. It was the strangest thing. I can't explain it but it was as if the painting was intended to hang right there. Have you ever felt something like that? Seen something you knew you couldn't live without?" Lauren reached over and straightened the edge of the painting.

Gaylin's eyes drifted down over the bed and back up to the painting.

"Yes. I know exactly what you're talking about." She gave it a last look and moved on with the appraisal.

"Would you like to see the cottage?"

"Yes, I would."

Lauren led the way through the mudroom and out the back door. She followed the stone path that wound through the garden and up the side of the hill.

"I like the little ceramic animals along the path. Did you do that?"

"Aunt Edna started the collection. She made a few of them herself, like the family of squirrels." Lauren pointed to a cluster of life-size squirrels grouped around the base of a tree. "The guests seem to like them. Watch your step." She noticed one of the stones teetered when she stepped on it. "I need to fix this one."

Gaylin looked down at it, pressing the edge of it with her toe.

"Hold this," she said, handing Lauren her laptop. She squatted over the stone, working her fingers under the edge.

"I'll fix it. I'll probably need to dig out underneath it so it will sit flat."

"It might be roots pushing it up." Gaylin slipped her fingers under the corner of the stone and lifted it, exposing a crop of bugs, worms and a tiny lizard. Lauren gasped and stepped back. The mature side of her brain told her they were harmless. The other side wanted to shriek and run for the house. Gaylin removed a few pebbles then repositioned the stone. She stomped down on it to test it. "There. All fixed."

"Thank you. But you didn't have to do that."

"I know." She brushed off her hands and reclaimed her laptop. "Okay. Let's see the cottage."

Lauren climbed the two steps onto the porch. The cottage was yellow with white shutters and trim, just like the big house. It had a steep pitched roof and a row of gingerbread trim across the front.

"I like the dormers."

"They aren't real dormers. You can't see out of them. I thought about having them cut through to be skylights in the ceiling but that would ruin the original flavor of the cottage." She unlocked the door and swung it open.

"This is nice." She stepped inside. "Very nice."

"The house is original but the décor is reproduced. The wallpaper is as close to early nineteen hundreds style as I could find. So are the curtains, rugs and linens. The bathroom was updated because it was too old to find replacement parts."

"It's adorable. It looks like a Victorian dollhouse. Everything is pink and cute." Gaylin walked around, smiling like a child in a toy store. "And you say three people lived here while the big house was being built?"

"Yes. Can you believe it? They cooked on a tiny stove that they also used for heat. The bathroom sink was the running water."

"Where did they all sleep?" Gaylin looked over at the queen-size bed that filled half the room. "I bet they didn't have a bed that big."

"My guess is they had some kind of trundle bed. The parents slept in a three-quarter size bed. Their daughter slept in the pull-out."

"That would certainly cut down on nighttime activities." Gaylin smiled at Lauren.

"I thought of that. It's no wonder they wanted the big house finished in a hurry."

"Anything else I should see?" Gaylin took a last look around the cottage.

"That's pretty much it. You've seen all the guest rooms,

the living room, dining room, sunroom, kitchen, basement, my apartment and the cottage."

Gaylin followed Lauren back to the house.

"If you think of anything else I should know about Gypsy Hill, give me a call. Like I said, I need to establish the income potential. That's how I'll appraise the property value."

"Do you think we could get this taken care of before the holidays?" Lauren asked hopefully.

"That's not much time. I still have to research the history of the inn. I'll need to compare income stream with similar properties, study demographics and check with the county. My report could be dozens of pages long and could take weeks to prepare. It all depends on how readily available the information is."

"Weeks?" Lauren gasped.

"Not always, but you never know what complications are going to pop up. And the older the property and the more convoluted the previous ownership, the more possible problems. I conducted an appraisal on a B and B last year that I thought would sail right through, but when I did my research on the plot map, I found the house wasn't built on the lot where it presently sat. It had been moved three blocks from its original location."

"That can't be good."

"It killed the value of the house because it hadn't been disclosed."

"Gypsy Hill hasn't been moved. That much I do know. I even have pictures taken of the house during construction. It shows the little cottage in the background."

"I didn't mean there was anything like that here. I wanted you to know there are certain pieces of information I have to find. Some of it takes digging. The housing market has enough trouble without misrepresenting property values."

"I'm not suggesting you do anything unscrupulous. But weeks?" Lauren couldn't hide her disappointment. She hoped finalizing her refinancing would only take a matter of days, not weeks.

41

"Maybe it won't. Cross your fingers." She tucked the laptop under her arm and picked up the folder of papers. "Do you mind if I take this with me? I'll need some of the information."

"Help yourself. Those are all copies. You can keep them as long as you need them." She followed Gaylin out the front door. "Thank you, Miss Hart," she said, extending her hand. She wanted to feel Gaylin's hand in hers one more time.

"You're welcome." Gaylin shook her hand, holding it warmly. "And again, I'm very sorry about the mailbox and the confusion."

"I'm sorry you had to do all that shoveling." Lauren didn't want to let go of her hand. "Let me know if there is anything else I can do."

"Sometimes it requires a second look at the property before I can finish my report. It depends on what my research turns up. By the way, I like what you've done with the house. It's truly charming."

"Thank you. Come by anytime." She finally released Gaylin's hand.

"I'll remember that." Gaylin smiled.

Lauren stood on the porch and watched as Gaylin strode out to her car and pulled away. She smiled to herself. Gaylin was more than just the woman who ran over her mailbox. She was her appraiser. Surely there was something Lauren could find to lure her back. Some tidbit of information she just had to share.

Raisin Scones
Kenna's family recipe

Makes 6-10 scones

2 1/2 cups flour
2 tablespoons baking powder
1/3 cup sugar
1/4 teaspoon salt
6 tablespoons butter at room temperature
1 egg beaten
1 teaspoon vanilla
3/4 cup milk
1/2 cup raisins
1 egg yolk – beaten – for wash

Combine flour, sugar, baking powder and salt. Add in butter until mixture resembles coarse crumbs and then add milk, egg and vanilla. Stir until dry ingredients are moistened. Add in raisins.

Roll out dough on floured surface to ¾ to 1 inch thick. Traditional scones are cut into triangles but you may use round biscuit cutter to cut scones if you prefer. Place scones on prepared baking sheets (baking parchment or buttered), spacing apart. Brush tops with beaten egg yolk and sprinkle with sugar. Bake scones until golden brown, about 15-20 minutes at 400 degrees. Serve warm with clotted cream or favorite jam.

Chapter 5

Lauren hurried through breakfast cleanup then slipped away to her office. Ever since she remembered the online reviews and the magazine articles about Gypsy Hill, she couldn't wait to call Gaylin to see if she could use any of it. The chance to meet with Gaylin again had her heart racing. She could hardly wait to schedule a meeting with her.

"Hello, Lauren," Gaylin said cheerfully. "What can I do for you? The mailbox hasn't fallen over, has it?"

"No. It's fine. I was remembering what you said about any additional information that might help with the appraisal."

"Have you got something for me?"

"I think so. I copied them off and I thought maybe I'd bring them to you, if that's okay."

"I can come by and pick them up."

"I have a few errands to run. I could bring them to your office."

"I'm not at my office right now. The exterminators are spraying the entire building so I'm on my way to have coffee. Would you like to meet me?"

"That sounds good. Where?"

Wow, my first date with Gaylin Hart. Okay, it isn't really a date, but I can always dream.

"The balcony café at Basin Park Hotel. How's that?"

"Great. I love the view."

"Twenty minutes?" Gaylin asked.

"I'll be there." Lauren collected the papers for Gaylin and slipped them into a brown envelope then went to change her clothes.

Eureka Springs, a quaint town of just over 2,300 people nestled in the Ozark Hills of northern Arkansas, clung to its Victorian flavor as a tourist attraction. The historic Basin Park Hotel was a seven-story granite and brick building built in the height of Eureka Springs's Victorian tourist boom when city dwellers flocked to the hot springs thought to heal everything from arthritis to the common cold. The hotel was a carefully preserved piece of local history from the marble floors to the brass beds. The second-floor balcony housed an open-air restaurant that overlooked the bustling downtown shopping district. Next to her own kitchen or garden, the Basin Park balcony restaurant was Lauren's favorite place to sit and enjoy a quiet cup of coffee or a leisurely lunch. She was glad it seemed to be one of Gaylin's favorite places as well. She pulled into a parking spot across the street from the hotel, checked her looks in the mirror, and headed for the balcony.

Gaylin was already seated at a table by the railing. Plastic screens covered the open railings and a pair of patio torch heaters hummed quietly to warm the chilly December air. Gaylin was reading from a folder and hadn't noticed Lauren.

"Am I interrupting?" she said, after waiting a moment for her to look up.

"Oh, hi. No. I was just looking over the results of the title search on Gypsy Hill. Please, sit down." Gaylin stood up and helped Lauren off with her coat. "Coffee?"

"Yes. That sounds good." She set the brown envelope on the table in front of Gaylin. "I made copies so you can keep these."

Gaylin ordered coffee for them then pulled the papers from the envelope.

"Let's see what we have." She began reading.

"I've had two different articles written about Gypsy Hill. That first one was in an Ozarks travel magazine two years ago. It recommends the inn as having 'the true flavor of turn of the century Eureka Springs.' The other article from last year lists the five best romantic getaways in Arkansas. Gypsy Hill is number two. We lost out to the Crescent Hotel just because they claim the hotel is haunted. That seems to make it romantic. But our breakfasts are better and they are included. Breakfast isn't included at the Crescent."

"Anytime you make a short list in a periodical it will certainly help the value. This is good. What else?"

"I printed the Web Site that shows Gypsy Hill's five-star rating and the nine reviews. All of them rated Gypsy Hill ten out of ten. No, I take that back. One was eight out of ten because I didn't serve a vegan alternative menu."

"What? No soymilk and bird seed?" Gaylin chuckled.

"My menu is pretty simple, much to my mother's chagrin."

"So your mother is a good cook?"

"She's not just a good cook. She's an excellent chef. She's French." Lauren raised her eyebrows. "She owns a restaurant in New Orleans in the French Quarter. Le Vin Rouge. Her crème brulee and brioche are to die for."

"What is brioche?"

"French bread, usually made into fancy rolls. It is very sweet, very flaky and very delicious."

"Are your parents the chefs?"

"My mother is divorced. My father was an absentee parent even when they were married. He passed away several years ago." Lauren shrugged and looked away as she remembered him. "Mother is the driving force behind Le Vin Rouge. It's her passion."

"You're probably looking forward to seeing her at Christmas, then."

"I wish I could but we each have a business to run. Christmas is a big season for both of us. We talk on the phone a lot but it has been months and months since I've seen her."

"How many generations removed is your mother from her French roots?" Gaylin asked. She seemed amazingly attentive.

"None. She was born near a little village in northwest France nine months after the Americans stormed ashore on D-day."

"An American GI?"

"Yes. Grandpa was just nineteen. He was wounded and cut off from his unit. My great-grandfather, a French farmer who had a teenage daughter, took him in." Lauren gave a little grin. "He said they fell in love instantly even though they couldn't speak a word in each other's language. They used sign language. When he recovered enough to leave, he told her he would come back for her. After the war he walked back up that road and asked her to marry him. He didn't know he had a baby daughter."

"Can you speak French?"

"A little. I picked up a few words from grandmother here and there."

"Have you ever been to France to visit your mother's homeland?"

"Once when I was a teenager. I'd love to go again but I never have enough time. Gypsy Hill keeps me hopping most of the year."

"Some of the B and Bs in town close during the winter. Have you ever thought of doing that?"

"Not really."

"Why not? Aren't you asking an awful lot of yourself?"

"Those who close during the winter are people who use their homes as a bed-and-breakfast. I run a bed-and-breakfast that happens to be my home. I'm open year round because it's my full-time business. That's the only way I know to be a successful innkeeper in this economy. I provide a very specialized form of lodging. It's more expensive than Best Western or Holiday Inn for a reason. I know all my guests by name and they know me. I give them a friendly and comfortable home-like environment where they can relax and enjoy being spoiled. And you can't do that haphazardly or only part of the time. Not if you want to earn those kind of ratings," she said, pointing to the papers.

"Oh, would you like something to eat? I'm sorry. I should have asked. A sandwich? Piece of pie? They have great pie here," Gaylin said, looking for the waitress.

"No, thank you. Just coffee. We'll do that another time."

"I'll look forward to it." Gaylin checked her watch.

"Do you have another meeting? Am I keeping you from something important?"

"I have to return some papers to the courthouse but their office isn't open yet. How about you? Are you finished for the day? Have all your guests checked out?"

"Me?" Lauren laughed. She hadn't had a free afternoon in months. "I've got three reservations coming in by four o'clock. I still have grocery shopping to do. I have to run by the post office, pick up dry cleaning and buy bird seed. I have an electric bill to pay because their online payment system isn't working. And I need a new mop head. My cat did a no-no on my old one."

"Cleo?" Gaylin laughed.

"Yes. Do you want a cat?"

"She's cute but no, thank you."

"The mop thing was her retribution for me forgetting to empty her litter box. We have this understanding. She has demands. I respect them."

"Have you always been this busy?"

"Pretty much. It's a little more than a nine-to-five job but I like it that way."

"I'd say that's why you've got five-star ratings." Gaylin patted the stack of papers.

"Oh, gosh," Lauren gasped. "I just remembered the photographs. I should have brought those for you to see."

"Photographs of what? Gypsy Hill?"

"Photographs taken from Gypsy Hill from the upstairs windows. During the fall, when all the trees are in full color, the view from the guest rooms is magnificent. One of my guests sent me some shots she took. They are really good. She has some kind of high resolution camera and these shots look like something out of a magazine. Would you like to see them? Couldn't the view be considered an intrinsic value?"

"Absolutely, it is."

"If you'll look at my spreadsheet, you'll see that autumn is a very lucrative time of year."

"I noticed that. You also have peak seasons that coincide with some of Eureka Springs's local events."

"You mean diversity weekends?"

"Yes."

"I'm proud to say a large percentage of my clientele, especially repeat customers, are derived from LGBT Web Site references. Several lesbian couples have reserved rooms for upcoming events through next year. I have a couple who have been with me every fall since I took over ownership of Gypsy Hill. One is a doctor and her partner is a rustic furniture maker. They reserve the cottage and go to every one of the lesbian events. Dr. DeMont said they wouldn't stay anyplace else. She has referred at least a dozen people to us."

"Word of mouth is the best form of advertising." Gaylin scanned the list of reviews. "Wow. Is this who I think it is? That's quite a glowing review."

Lauren leaned over to see where her finger was pointing.

"Yes. I'm very proud of that one. Her agent made the reservation so I didn't know she was coming until she walked in the door. She is the sweetest lady. She even offered to carry her own luggage upstairs. You'd never guess she earned millions performing in Vegas last year."

"She carried her own luggage?"

"No. She offered but that's something we do."

"Okay. I have to ask." Gaylin folded her hands and stared over at Lauren. "You keep referring to us and we. Who is this we?"

49

Lauren laughed.

"The we is really only me. Of course, Cleo thinks she is part owner. And there's Tallie, my housekeeper. But no, there isn't anyone else. I'm singular, not plural."

"I couldn't find a reference to anyone else in the county records for the deed or taxes. I assumed there was no one else bringing you roses."

"Nope. It's just me. Gypsy Hill has always been solely owned and operated by *moi*." Lauren placed her hand on her chest humbly. "The blame and the success are both all mine."

"Am I being nosy if I ask if there has ever been anyone else?"

"A few times, but never for long. How about you? Are you single or plural?"

"Single. At least at the moment."

"That sounds suspiciously like a failed relationship."

"Not failed as much as just another in a long line of casual relationships."

"Casual is good." Lauren wanted to admit she would rather have a long-term committed relationship than a string of one-night stands but she didn't. She didn't want to scare Gaylin off.

"I'm not saying long-term relationships are bad. Someday I may find someone I can go to bed with and be glad they're still there the next morning."

My, God. She can read my mind.

"The problem with that is finding time for a full-time lover when you have a full-time business to run." Lauren chuckled.

"From what I see, you've been very successful with the inn. By the way, I hear you're a pretty good cook."

"Thank you. You should come by sometime and judge for yourself."

"I should do that. We could call it research."

"Do you think any of this information will help bolster the appraisal value? With the housing problems, I know property values have dropped. Gypsy Hill may not be worth what it was a few years ago. I just need it to cover the mortgage valuation. I'm sure I haven't established much equity yet."

"I don't think you're underwater. I'll take a look and see."

"Underwater? You mean my mortgage is higher than the value of the property?"

Gaylin nodded her head.

"What happens if it is?" Lauren was almost afraid to ask.

Gaylin slipped the papers into the envelope, obviously planning her answer.

"It's hard to say. I don't know the specific terms of your mortgage." Gaylin seemed to be avoiding the question.

"If the value is less than my mortgage, could that mean I won't be approved for the refinancing?" she asked, trying to read something into her nonanswer.

"Let's just hope for the best."

Lauren was ready to press the subject when Gaylin's cell phone chimed.

"Hello," she said, flipping it open with her thumb. "Sure. I can be there in twenty minutes if that works for you. Thanks." She hung up.

"Sounds like an appraiser's work is never done," Lauren finished her coffee and pushed the cup back.

"That was my plumber. I'm having sewer problems."

"Again?"

"Still. Between the rocks and the tree roots, my sewer line is in bad shape. My plumber is busier than I am. You'd think he was a doctor. It took me a week to find someone to come take a look at it. I'm sorry to cut this short, but if I don't keep this appointment it could be weeks before he can work me in again."

"I understand completely." Lauren stood up and fished in her pocket for some money.

"I've got it, Lauren. You're my client."

"Technically, I don't think I am." She pulled out three ones and set them on the table for her coffee and tip. "Aren't you really working for the mortgage company?"

"Wow. Efficient businesswoman and smart, too. Yes, technically I work for them. But I can still pay for your coffee."

51

She folded Lauren's money and tucked it back in her pocket, poking it down deep. "You wouldn't let me pay for the mailbox, remember?"

"Thank you." For a moment Lauren imagined Gaylin's fingers somewhere farther down in her pants.

God, it has been a long time since anyone touched me anywhere near a pocket.

"If you find those photos, I'd like to see them. I can certainly guess how beautiful the fall foliage is from Gypsy Hill but pictures might be even better than my imagination."

"I'm sure I can find them. I'll give you a call and we can get together so I can show them to you."

"Great." Gaylin followed her down the stairs to the lobby. "I hate to coffee and run," she said, stepping out onto the sidewalk. "But my plumber awaits. Thanks for the information though. I'm sure I can use some of it." She offered Lauren her hand.

"Thank you for the coffee."

Gaylin's fingers wrapped around Lauren's and held them.

"You are most welcome. I'll do what I can to hurry things along but appraisals take time. I will try though."

"I appreciate that." She reached up and pushed a lock of hair the breeze had blown over Gaylin's forehead. She stood motionless as Lauren's fingertip carefully guided the lock to the side.

"Am I all set? Ready to impress my plumber?" She grinned shyly.

"Absolutely you are." Lauren looked her up and down. "Perfect."

"I wish I had more time to discuss the appraisal." Gaylin's voice was soft.

"You better go. You've already used fifteen of your twenty minutes."

"Yeah, I better."

Lauren watched and waved as Gaylin climbed in her SUV and pulled away. That little devil in her couldn't decide if she should give Gaylin all the photographs at once or space them out. Perhaps one at a time, she thought, smiling to herself. She looked down the street where Gaylin's car had gone. Practicality said give her all the photographs at once. That would be the businesslike thing to do. But she wasn't sure she wanted to be practical when it came to Gaylin Hart.

Italian Sprinkle Christmas Cookies

Kenna's partner's mama's cookies
These were Ann's favorite cookies at Christmas. She just couldn't wait
until mama started making them.
Makes 2-3 dozen
6 eggs
5 cups all purpose flour
2 cups confectioners' (powdered) sugar
2 tablespoons plus 1 1/2 teaspoon baking powder
1 cup shortening
3 teaspoons almond extract
1 1/2 teaspoon lemon extract

Glaze
3 3/4 cups confectioner's sugar
1/2 cup warm milk
1 teaspoon almond extract
1 teaspoon vanilla extract
colored sprinkles

Using a heavy-duty mixer, beat eggs on high speed until light and foamy, about 5 minutes; set aside. In a large mixing bowl, combine the flour, confectioners' sugar and baking powder; on low speed, gradually beat in shortening and extracts until mixture resembles fine crumbs. Gradually add beaten eggs (dough will be stiff).

Roll dough into 1-inch balls. Place 2 inches apart on ungreased baking sheets. Bake at 350 for 12-14 minutes (tops of the cookies will not brown, but bottoms should brown slightly).

Meanwhile prepare glaze in a small bowl. Combine the confectioners' sugar, milk and extracts until smooth. As soon as cookies are removed from the oven, quickly dip two or three at a time into glaze.

Remove with a slotted spoon or tongs. Place on wire racks to drain. Immediately top with sprinkles. Let dry for 24 hours before storing in airtight containers.

Chapter 6

Lauren had just answered the telephone in her office when the doorbell rang. She had been busy with reservations and a constant stream of guests since her meeting with Gaylin over a week ago. So busy she hadn't had time to deliver the photographs to her.

"Let me check and see if the Rose Room is available. How many nights will you be with us?" She tucked the cordless under her chin and began entering information into the computer, ignoring the doorbell. Tallie's dusting the living room. Maybe she'll answer it, she thought.

The doorbell rang again followed by a loud knock.

"Can you get that, Tallie?" she said, covering the receiver with her hand. "Yes, the Rose Room is available for both of those nights. I'll put you down for the twentieth and twenty-first."

The knocking became louder and more persistent.

"Tallie?" Lauren rolled her chair to the doorway. "Tallie, can you get the door? I'm on the phone." There was no answer. The doorbell rang twice more.

"I'm sorry about that, Miss Perry. Yes, we are completely nonsmoking. No, pets are not allowed. I have one cat and she prefers it that way." She covered the receiver and called again. "Tallie, the door."

The sound of the vacuum could be heard from the top of the stairs.

"The twenty-second, too? Let me check and see."

Whoever was at the door wasn't giving up. The doorbell rang several more times.

"The twenty-second is still available. Shall I reserve that night as well?" Lauren stood up, waiting for the woman's reply. There was another loud knock. Lauren went to the door while she explained the rules of reservation cancellations to the caller. She opened the door expecting to see FedEx delivering her new printer or some religious zealot offering a free Bible. It was neither. It was someone Lauren hadn't seen in several years and had thought she might never see again. She stood staring at the woman, her attention no longer on the caller.

"Hi Lauren." The woman gave an apologetic smile.

"Carly." Lauren still had the telephone up to her ear and knew she looked dumbfounded.

"Did I come at a bad time?"

Lauren could only stare.

"Should I come back another time?"

"No. Come in." Lauren opened the screen, waved her in, and held up a finger as she went back to her call. "Yes, Miss Perry. I'll be expecting you. Thank you." She ended the call before turning her attention to Carly.

"Reservation?" Carly said, standing just inside the door.

"Yes. Three days for the Rose Room." Lauren was still adjusting to Carly's presence.

"Three days? That's good."

"I thought you moved somewhere up north. Chicago or Detroit."

"Indianapolis. Yeah. I moved back to town a couple months ago. The job didn't work out." She shrugged indifferently.

"I'm sorry."

"Sorry the job didn't work out or sorry I moved back to Arkansas?" She sounded sarcastic.

Lauren had absolutely no idea why Carly Benson was standing in her hallway, fishing for a conversation. Their past was a closed chapter in Lauren's life. The pain had subsided. The wound had healed. There was nothing more to say, but here she was, trying to be amicable. Lauren had no feelings for Carly one way or the other. Even the animosity she once held for her had dissolved. In spite of the three years since she last saw her, Carly was still attractive. She still had that one stray curl over her temple that gave her a dashing, provocative look. Her eyes were still the softest shade of blue Lauren had ever seen. *She's just someone I once knew. That's the way I want to leave it.*

"If the job was something you really wanted, I'm sorry it didn't work out for you. That's all I meant."

"I know I'm the last person you want knocking on your door. I thought about calling but I figured you'd see my name on the caller ID and not pick up. I couldn't help it, Lauren. I had to come by and find out for myself if the rumor I heard was true."

"Find out what?"

"Is Kelly back?"

"She arrives this afternoon."

"Really? I thought she was in LA" Carly's interest in Kelly was unmistakable.

"She's been in Branson for two years. She's with one of the shows down there."

"How is she, Lauren? Is she okay?"

"Yes. I think so." Lauren saw no reason not to tell her about Kelly. After all, they had been together longer than Carly and Lauren.

"Is it terrible of me to ask about her? Do you hate me, Lauren?"

"I don't hate you."

"Then would it be all right if I come by to talk with her? I mean, if she'll see me."

"Sure. I guess so."

"Do you know if she is seeing anyone? You know, anyone seriously."

"Seriously?" Lauren wanted to laugh. If anyone should know about Kelly's relationship habits, it was Carly. Kelly never dated anyone seriously. At least that's what the victims would say who lay strewn in her wake.

"I know. You don't have to say it, but I can't help myself. I still love her, Lauren. I've tried to forget her, but I can't. Whoever I meet, I always end up comparing them to Kelly."

Lauren wanted to tell her Kelly probably hadn't changed. If she expected a reconciliation, she was only headed for more heartache. But that was Carly's decision.

"I'll tell Kelly you stopped by."

"No. Don't tell her. Please!"

Carly was probably right. That might give Kelly an unfair advantage to know one of her ex-girlfriends was still interested, not to mention it would undoubtedly inflate her ego.

"Okay. I won't mention it. Carly?"

"Yes?"

Lauren couldn't do it. The enthusiasm in Carly's eyes and the anticipation in her voice told Lauren she wasn't going to listen to any warnings.

"What?"

"Nothing. Nothing at all."

"I know what you're going to say. But it doesn't matter. Kelly is like kryptonite. I can't help myself. I have to see her again." She gave a weak smile and closed the door behind her.

At least she knows what she is getting herself into, Lauren thought as she returned to her office.

Kelly said she would arrive by one o'clock, no later than two. However, it was four fifteen when her convertible roared into the driveway, her horn honking her arrival. Lauren pushed the save key on her computer and rushed outside to greet her.

"Hey, sis," she shouted.

"Hi." Kelly waved and shot Lauren one of her ravishingly gorgeous smiles. Lauren grabbed her and hugged her warmly.

"My God, you look good, Kel. I love the hair color."

"Thank you. It cost me eighty-five bucks but you only live once, right?" She hugged Lauren again. "You're looking good, too. I like the sweater. Good color on you."

"Sorry I didn't get to see the Christmas show before it closed, but I've been snowed under with work."

"Don't worry about it. Between you and me, last year's show was much better. The blue-haired people want to hear Christmas songs they know. We had twelve songs no one outside of Nashville ever heard of. Syd said he wasn't going to make that mistake again. Next year will be better."

"I can't wait. Come on. Let's get your stuff in the house. How many suitcases did you bring?"

"You don't want to know."

"Just the bare essentials, right?" Lauren teased.

"You got it." She flipped her hair and went to open the trunk.

"Kelly, what is that?" Lauren peered through the window at the pet carrier on the backseat.

"What?" She kept her attention in the trunk, ignoring Lauren's question.

"That!" Lauren pointed.

"Oh, that's Roxie."

"Roxie?"

"She's so cute. Wait until you see her. She's a long-haired miniature Dachshund. You've never seen anything so adorable in your life."

"But Kelly, you know I have a no-pet policy."

"Don't worry about it, sis." Kelly smiled confidently. "She'll be fine. She's trained to go potty on those blue puppy pads. She's never had an accident on the floor. I couldn't very well leave her in the storage building with my furniture, now could I?"

"Of course not, but she's a pet. How do I explain to my

other guests that they can't bring a pet if I let you have one? I get requests all the time. You know my policy." Lauren didn't want to start Kelly's visit off with an argument, but she knew the house rules. How could Lauren allow Kelly to have a pet on the premises and deny that privilege to her other guests?

"I couldn't leave her with a stranger. Her puppies are worth eight hundred dollars apiece. Roxie is AKC registered and worth a lot of money. I certainly wasn't going to leave her with some inane pet sitter."

"Puppies?!!" Lauren gasped. "She has puppies, too?"

"She will. She's due anytime now. It'll be her first litter and I'm not going to let her go through that alone."

"It's not as if she's going through Lamaze and needs a breathing coach. Dogs have puppies all the time and do it without help."

"I don't care. If she has trouble, I want to be there. She's very delicate."

"You want to be there?" Lauren laughed out loud. "You're going to help a dog give birth? Kelly, you faint at the sight of a Band-Aid. How are you going to help a dog have a litter of puppies?"

"I don't know. I just know I couldn't leave her. I thought she'd have them by now. I already have homes for three of them. If they look anything like her, they'll be adorable. Little reddish-brown fuzz balls."

"Not only did you bring a dog without asking, you brought a pregnant dog? I run a bed-and-breakfast. Not an animal hospital. I don't even want to know what the health department would say about this."

"All she'll need are a few clean towels and a blanket. I'll take care of everything. I thought I could just stay in the cottage. No one would even know Roxie and her puppies are here and I'd have a little privacy. Things get a little chaotic when you've got a bunch of noisy guests running around. I don't know how you stand it. I don't want Roxie to be upset, and besides, with me out there in the cottage, you'll hardly know I was here."

Lauren, puzzled, watched her sister carefully before chuckling sarcastically.

"You *are* kidding, aren't you? The cottage?"

"I know it's rustic and a little remote up there on the hill, but at least it has a decent view. Plus, there's enough room so I won't feel claustrophobic. I can adapt. I'm good at that."

"Then you're going to have to adapt to the Sunflower Room. The cottage is booked right through New Year's. So are the Rose Room and the Lavender Room. Kelly, this is one of my big seasons. I have a wedding and an anniversary couple coming this week. I can't give you the cottage. I need that income."

"The Sunflower Room?" Kelly rolled her lip. "That's the butt-ugly attic room."

"It is not butt-ugly. And I can't help it if it's on the third floor. That's all I have available. And it isn't an attic room. You make it sound like you're Pollyanna and I'm banishing you to the tiniest room in the house. The Sunflower Room has a lovely view on both sides of the house. It has a whirlpool tub *and* a king-size bed. By the way, *I do not* want that dog giving birth to a litter of puppies on the bed. It would ruin the mattress and that bed is new. And I don't want her on the velveteen settee either."

"It's on the freaking third floor, Lauren," Kelly whined.

"And I'm not charging you to use it for four weeks. You said you wanted privacy. Well, you'll have the entire top floor all to yourself. I'll put an old blanket in the storeroom for Roxie and she can have a private room all to herself, too."

"Roxie is *not* staying in a storeroom. My God, Lauren. It's winter. Do you really want her to freeze to death? Her puppies, too? How callous can you get?"

"The entire house is heated, Kelly. Even the storeroom. She won't freeze to death. I don't want her running all over the place. I just had the carpets cleaned."

"Like your guests don't track in mud," she replied caustically.

"I don't want that dog tormenting Cleo, either."

"Do you still have that moth-eaten cat? She's a disgrace to the entire animal kingdom."

61

"Cleo is not moth-eaten. You just happened to see her when she was shedding. Now, are we going to carry your stuff upstairs or leave it in the car?" Lauren picked up one of the suitcases, groaning at the weight of it. "What did you pack? Bricks?"

"That one has my music in it. Don't drop it." Kelly picked up the pet carrier and a small tote bag.

"How could I possibly hurt it?" she said with a groan, using two hands to carry it to the back door.

"Did I tell you? I'm going to have another solo right before the finale in next season's show. Something upbeat I hope. Lots of lights and a costume that moves with me." Kelly looked back at Lauren, grinning proudly. "I get to have a say in what I sing for a change."

"Good." Lauren heaved the heavy case up the back steps, taking them one at a time.

"Come on, Roxie baby. Let's get you up to your new home." Roxie yipped. "Yes, sweetheart. You're going to be all right. Mama is going to let you out as soon as we are in our room."

Lauren used her last ounce of self-control not to say anything. Kelly was home for Christmas. She would concentrate on that.

Grandma Leona's Waffles

My grandmother had an old round waffle iron from the early 1950s, the kind that had to be brushed with oil or everything would stick. She told me a good waffle wasn't about the waffle iron you used. It was the recipe that made the difference. And her secret? Folding in stiffened egg whites. It takes a little longer to make than the all-in-one mixes but it is definitely worth it. She lived to be 100 years old, kept her own home and made these for us on Christmas morning. We had to eat breakfast and wait for the kitchen to be cleaned before opening our presents. As wide-eyed children, eager to see what Santa brought us, my brother and I probably would have preferred a Pop-Tart. Those waffles were wonderful.

Serves 6

2 cups flour
4 teaspoons baking powder
2 eggs – separated
2 cups milk
1/4 teaspoon salt
8 tablespoons melted butter
1 1/2 tablespoon sugar (optional)

Mix flour, salt, baking powder and sugar (if used).Add milk and beat until smooth. Add beaten egg yolks and stir in butter (or margarine). Fold in beaten eggs whites gently.
Bake in your favorite waffle iron until golden brown. Serve with butter, syrup, jam or fruit topping and enjoy!

Chapter 7

After breakfast the next morning, Lauren finally found time to give Gaylin a call and make plans to show her the photographs. The kitchen was clean and the leftovers put away. She could hardly wait.

"Tallie, did you see a stack of photographs on my desk?" she asked, sifting through her papers.

"No." Tallie hummed to herself while she dusted the picture frames in the hall. "Are you sure that's where you left them?"

"Yes. I'm sure. I put them right here. I wanted to show them to Gaylin."

"Were they pictures of trees?"

"Yes. Did you see them?"

"I think Kelly was looking at them. I thought she put them back."

"Well, they aren't anywhere on the desk. Did she go back upstairs?"

"I think so."

Lauren gave one last look around the office before she pulled out her cell phone and dialed Kelly's number. It was quicker and easier to call her than run up two flights of stairs.

"What?" Kelly said, picking up after several rings.

"Kelly, do you remember where you put the photographs that were on my desk?"

"Huh?"

"Tallie said you were looking at them. I need to take them downtown."

"What photographs?"

"The pictures of fall foliage you took off my desk. Where did you put them?"

"The pictures of trees?"

"Yes."

"I put them back, didn't I?"

"No, you didn't. I've combed my office and they aren't here. Please try to remember where you put them. It's important."

"I thought I put them back where I got them."

"Well, you didn't."

"Can't you just print them off again?"

"I didn't print them. I don't have them scanned into my computer."

"Why not? I've got all mine in my computer. With a digital camera, there's no excuse not to zap them right onto the hard drive."

"Maybe I'll do that if you'd just tell me where you put them."

"What software do you use? Picasa? Paint Shop Pro?"

"Kelly, I don't have time for this."

"All right, all right. I'll be down in a little while and find them."

"It's after ten thirty. I told the appraiser I'd bring those photographs to her *before* eleven."

"So call her and tell her you'll come this afternoon."

"She is going out of town on business this afternoon. I've

been trying to catch her for a week. I told her I'd be there this morning."

"There's always tomorrow."

"Will you please stop offering excuses and come help me find them?" Lauren's patience was running thin.

"Geez." Kelly groaned. "All right. I'll be down in three minutes." She hung up.

It was more like ten minutes before Kelly came strolling down the stairs. Lauren had turned the office upside down.

"Did you look under the papers?" Kelly asked.

"Yes. And behind the computer and on the floor and even in the trash. What were you doing when you were looking at them?"

"I was standing right here by the desk." Kelly put her feet on the spot. "I came down to get a magic marker to mark my pillowcases so I wouldn't get them mixed up with yours. I have to have cotton sateen or I can't sleep."

Lauren opened the desk drawer where she kept the pens and markers even though she had already checked it twice.

"I marked the tag on the pillowcases and put it back."

"Of course!" Lauren gasped and rushed down the hall toward the laundry room. She returned a minute later with the photographs.

"Where were they?"

"On the shelf over the washer. You washed your pillowcases, right?"

"Oh, yeah. I did," she giggled. "What do you know?"

Lauren checked her watch. She had fifteen minutes to meet Gaylin before she was scheduled to go out of town. She dropped the photographs in an envelope and grabbed her keys.

"Where are you taking them?"

"Downtown to my appraiser's office." She pulled on her coat and headed down the hall.

"Will you be anywhere near Pet Paws?" Kelly followed her through the kitchen.

"Where is that?"

"Across from the post office and down about two blocks. It's the only place in town that carries Roxie's vitamins."

"I wasn't going that far." Lauren knew from experience if she offered to pick up the vitamins, she would be roped in to several more errands and she wouldn't be back until three.

"And right next to the pet store or maybe a door or two down, is Shantell's Hair Salon. She carries my shampoo. She may even have the conditioner so you might get both of them while you're there. It's the one in the blue bottle. She'll know which one if you tell her it's for me."

"Shantell's is four blocks down."

"Oh, that's right. She's next to Wheeler's. You know, since you're going to be right there, could you run in and see if they have those protein bars I like? The ones in the green striped package?"

Lauren turned back and frowned at Kelly.

"I don't have time for all that. I've got three couples checking in this afternoon. If you want to go with me and do your shopping while I'm meeting Gaylin, go get your jacket. Otherwise, you'll have to go on your own."

"Can you give me thirty minutes?"

"Nope. I don't have thirty minutes." Lauren went through the mud room and opened the back door. "Are you coming?" She expected her to say no.

Kelly grumbled and ran down the hall.

"Let me get my coat," she said, vaulting up the stairs.

"I'll be in the car. Hurry." Lauren knew if Kelly stayed true to form, she would change her clothes, her shoes, her lipstick, and come trotting toward the car with the fresh scent of cologne billowing in her wake. Lauren started the car and pulled up to the back walk.

"Come on, Kelly," she mumbled, drumming her fingers on the steering wheel. "It's almost eleven." Ten minutes passed and still no Kelly. Lauren leaned her forehead against the wheel to keep from screaming.

"Here I am," Kelly said, bouncing out the door as if she had all the time in the world. Sure enough, she had changed everything but her watch. "Let's go."

Lauren shook her head and rolled her eyes but didn't say anything. That would only delay them more. She roared out of the drive and down the street, hoping Gaylin was as slow as her sister and would still be in her office. She pulled into the first available parking space.

"Couldn't you find a place on down the street? Maybe there's a parking spot down by Shantell's," Kelly said.

"You'll have to walk. It's after eleven and I'm late." She climbed out and hurried into the small, storefront office marked Hart Appraisal. A long row of file cabinets lined one wall. A county plot map was taped up to the opposite wall. A desk sat unattended just inside the door. The light on the telephone was lit. Lauren could hear Gaylin talking in the back room.

"I can't use that figure. That's a foreclosure. Don't you show anything else? I need something better. Well, call me if you find it." The telephone light went out. "Be right with you," she called.

"Take your time," Lauren replied.

Gaylin appeared in the doorway.

"Lauren? Hello. I was starting to think you were going to stand me up." She shook Lauren's hand and offered a wide smile.

There's that adorable dimple. God, she's cute.

"I know. I'm terribly late and I'm really sorry about that." She handed Gaylin the envelope of photographs.

"Are these the pictures?"

"Yes. I hope you can use them."

"Let's see what we have."

While Gaylin looked at the photographs, Lauren nonchalantly looked at Gaylin. She couldn't help it. Gaylin exuded professionalism and a sexy confidence.

"Wow, these are incredible."

"This one is on my Web Site." Lauren stood close enough to catch the faint aroma of something wonderful. "Holly gave me permission to use it. You've probably seen her work. She does photography for the Arkansas Board of Tourism."

"They really capture the beauty of Arkansas's autumn foliage. To think they were taken from Gypsy Hill."

"I think they show why fall is one of my peak seasons. The view and the incredible color are the attraction."

"Would you mind if I copy these for the folder?"

"Help yourself. I guess I should have had that done."

"Are these your only copies?" Gaylin asked, stepping to the copy machine in the corner.

"Yes. I really should scan them into my computer."

"What's your e-mail address?" She opened the lid and typed in some information.

"L Roberts at Gypsy Hill dot com." Lauren watched over her shoulder. "What are you doing?"

"Copying and e-mailing you a set."

"Really? You can do that with that little copier?"

"Sure. You can adjust the resolution with your software if the files come through too large."

"Thank you. I didn't know you could do that."

"I'll print you off another set, too," Gaylin said, over the sound of the machine.

"There you are," Kelly said, coming through the door. "Did she leave already?"

"Not yet. Gaylin, this is my sister, Kelly Roberts. Kelly, this is my appraiser, Gaylin Hart."

"I could have guessed that. Strong family resemblance," Gaylin said, offering her hand. "Hello."

"Hi." Kelly's eyes flowed down Gaylin's body and back up again. "Appraiser? Wow. That sounds complicated."

"Kelly is a singer with the Gold Mountain Jubilee in Branson," Lauren offered.

"A singer? Really? I don't think I've ever met a performer before. Not a real one, anyway."

"Do you ever get over to Branson?" Kelly gave Gaylin one of her captivating smiles.

69

"Once in a while on business."

"You've got to come see the new spring show. You'll love it. Lots of music. Great costumes. We're adding more production songs and fewer dumb hillbilly jokes."

"What do you sing?"

"A little bit of everything. Soft country mostly. We're changing the whole feel of the show this year. I'll have a medley of country oldies in the second act. Anne Murray, Crystal Gayle, Patsy Cline. Patsy and I sing in the same key."

"I love her music. Especially 'She's Got You,'" Gaylin said.

"What was that one of Patsy's you did?" Lauren asked.

"Which one?"

"I can't remember the name of it. Something about dreaming."

"'Sweet Dreams?'" Gaylin suggested.

"Great song." She smiled. "Sweet dreams of you." Kelly sang, touching Gaylin's arm and leaning into her.

"Good, isn't she?" Lauren said proudly.

"Yes, she most certainly is. Wow!"

"Oh, stop." Kelly blushed.

"How long have you been a professional singer?" Gaylin retrieved the photographs from the printer and handed them to Lauren.

"Since I was sixteen. I won twenty-five dollars at the Fourth of July talent show in Little Rock."

"She sang 'I Only Want To Be With You' by Dusty Springfield and had the crowd eating out of her hand." Lauren elbowed Kelly. "Remember that judge with the cowboy hat?"

"Yes. After I finished the song, when everyone was applauding, he tossed his hat in the air. His toupee went with it. It landed at my feet and I thought it was a dead rat."

"You're kidding. What did you do?" Gaylin chuckled.

"What else? I stomped on it." They all laughed loudly.

"And your career took off from there?"

"Not exactly. My first contract job wasn't until I was twenty. I had a bit part in a community theater production of *Grease*.

70

Mostly I just roamed around the stage, wearing a poodle skirt and harmonizing with everyone."

"You were a Pink Lady?"

"I was more of a groupie. My one line was *He's so cute*. Then I had to squeal like a teenager." She demonstrated.

"Do you sing too, Lauren?" Gaylin asked, splitting her attention between the two women.

"No. Kelly inherited mother's creativity. I only inherited her practicality."

"You don't want to hear Lauren sing. It's not a pretty thing," Kelly teased. Lauren nodded in agreement. "How about you, Gaylin? Do you sing?"

"Only in my dreams and in the shower. But you have a lovely voice. I will definitely have to come hear you in Branson."

"I'll send you some tickets."

"You don't have to do that."

"But I want to. I can get all I want. And not way in the back either. I'll get you good seats. Just tell me when you want to go and I'll send them to you. Are you married or dating anyone?" There was nothing subtle in Kelly's curiosity.

"No, I'm not married."

"Dating?" she asked coyly. "You know. So I'll know how many tickets to send."

"Nope. Not dating anyone right now."

Lauren was surprised how calmly Gaylin replied to Kelly's questions.

"So there isn't anyone you'll need an extra ticket for?" Kelly asked, giving Gaylin another look up and down.

"As of August, no. There isn't."

"Oh, I'm sorry. Was it a terrible breakup?"

"Kelly," Lauren said, bumping her. "Don't be so nosy."

"I'm not being nosy, am I Gaylin? I'm just being sympathetic."

"No, it wasn't that terrible. In fact, I don't think we ever really got going. Terry and I never got on the same page, so to speak."

"Terry as in Terrance or Terry as in Teresa?" Kelly wasn't

going to stop until she knew everything she wanted to know about Gaylin Hart. Lauren was embarrassed at Kelly's brashness but she was curious herself.

Gaylin blushed and grinned at the floor.

"Terry as in Terry Louise."

Kelly's eyes lit up. But before she could ask anything else, the telephone in the back office rang.

"Excuse me one minute." Gaylin went to answer it. Lauren waited until she disappeared through the door then turned to Kelly.

"Will you stop it?" she said through gritted teeth.

"Stop what?"

"You barely know Gaylin and you're asking her about her lifestyle. What's the matter with you?"

"What's the matter with me? What's the matter with you? She's cute." She looked toward the partially closed door. "You may be an old stick-in-the-mud but I certainly am not. And what's the big deal with exchanging polite conversation? What do you talk about with her? Appraisals?"

"Yes. I told you. She is doing the appraisal so I can refinance."

"Yeah, well if that's all you talk about, you're an idiot."

"Shh," Lauren whispered. She had no intention of admitting to Kelly she found Gaylin interesting and extremely attractive. Lord only knows what she would say to Gaylin if she knew.

"I'm sorry about that," Gaylin said, coming back through the door.

"That's okay." Kelly grinned. "We forgive you for conducting business during business hours."

"It's my fault," Lauren said, checking her watch. "I was late and now I've made you late for your next appointment." She grabbed Kelly's arm. "Come on, sis. Let's leave Gaylin alone. She has work to do."

"Actually, I do need to run." Gaylin walked them to the door and held it for them. "I wish I didn't have to go. It was great seeing you again, Lauren. And meeting your sister. I hope I'll get to see you again sometime."

"I'm looking forward to it," Kelly said, flipping her hair. "I'll be around through New Year's. Eureka Springs isn't that big. I'm sure we'll run into one another now and then." Kelly was flirting her little heart out.

"Come on, Kel." She gave her arm a tug then smiled back at Gaylin. "Let me know if you need anything else for the appraisal."

"I will." She stood on the sidewalk and watched as they walked toward the car. Kelly smiled and waved as she opened the passenger door and climbed in. Lauren pulled away, a smile on her face to hide her anger at Kelly being such a flirt.

Orange Cake

Kenna's sister-in-law Irene's recipe

1/2 cup butter (soft)
1/2 cup sugar
2 eggs
1 1/2 cup flour
1 1/2 teaspoon baking powder
1/2 teaspoon baking soda
1/4 teaspoon salt
1/2 cup orange juice (can use more concentrated juice made
from the frozen stuff)
A fistfull of chocolate chips (Optional and very good)

Cream butter and sugar together until smooth. Then stir in one
egg at a time. Mix flour, baking powder and baking soda together
and add to the mix, alternating with the orange juice until creamy.
(Fold in the chocolate chips.) Bake at 350 degrees in a 9 x 13 pan
for 35 to 40 minutes (or until a toothpick comes out clean).

Glaze

Heat for five minutes
1/4 cup orange juice
1/4 cup sugar

While the cake is still warm, poke it with a fork and then pour
the glaze over it. This delicious cake keeps moist and yummy for
days!

Chapter 8

The grandfather clock in the hall struck ten o'clock and the house was quiet. If Lauren was lucky, she would have the rest of the silverware polished and tomorrow morning's breakfast tables set by eleven. It had been a long but rewarding day. For the fifth consecutive night, she was booked solid. In fact, if Kelly wasn't in the Sunflower Room, she could have booked that room as well. For Lauren, it was equivalent to hitting a home run or being on the New York Times best-seller list. It meant she had done her job and done it well. But she never rested on the laurels of her success. There were always tomorrow's customers. And tonight she wanted sparkling silverware.

The sound of a car and the glare of headlights circling the house brought her attention out the kitchen window. It was Kelly returning from an evening out with her friends.

"Hey, sis," she called, coming in the back door. "What are

you doing up this late?" She unwrapped the scarf from around her neck and opened her coat.

"Polishing silver. How was your evening with Dee and Trina?"

"Great. We went to Heston's. The food was good but the service was a disaster. They've got a couple swishers with real attitudes." Kelly took a bottle of water from the refrigerator.

"Really? I thought you liked Heston's."

"I like Heston's. I just hate their fag waiters. Ours was this skinny guy named Richard. He had a ridiculous looking spiky haircut with orange streaks. He was so gay he was practically our waitress. They sat us at one of the tables with two chairs on one side and a booth on the other. You know, that long padded bench that runs all the way down the wall. The dipshits had turned the tables so the corner was pointed into the bench. I don't know how the hell you're supposed to sit and eat with the table at an angle like that. Trina and Dee wanted to sit next to each other so we turned the table back straight." Kelly rolled her eyes dramatically. "My freakin' God! You'd think we robbed the place. Richard came out with our drinks and when he saw the table, he screamed over at the hostess that unless the table was turned back like it was, he was walking out. He wouldn't work under such conditions. He waved one of those stupid finger snaps and glared at us like we were criminals. I don't have a problem with gay guys. Some of them are the sweetest things. But this waiter, Richard." She said it vindictively. "He was nothing more than an arrogant, egotistical fag."

"What did you do? Leave?"

"I wanted to but Trina and Dee wanted to stay. They wanted me to sing karaoke."

"What did you sing?" Lauren thought it best if they moved on to a different subject.

Kelly groaned and covered her face with her hands.

"God, it was terrible. I sang that Celine Dion song, 'Where Does My Heart Beat Now.'" Kelly hummed a few bars.

"I like that song. Good range for you."

"The backup singers on the CD were terrible. Half of them were flat."

"Did you sing anything else?"

"Oops."

"Oops, what?" Lauren asked, looking over at her as she finished the last fork.

"That Britney Spears song. 'Oops, I Did It Again.' Somebody requested it."

"What all did you have to eat?" She carried the basket of silverware into the breakfast room and began setting the tables. Kelly stood in the doorway, watching from a safe distance.

"Steak. I had to send it back. I ordered it medium rare and it came medium well. I think Richard did it on purpose."

"Oh, by the way, there's an envelope for you taped to the refrigerator."

"What is it?" Kelly retrieved the envelope and slid her car key under the flap.

"She dropped it off this afternoon. She said she'd call you tomorrow." Lauren looked over to see Kelly's reaction.

Kelly stared at the letter. Her face slowly changed from curious to indifferent. She took a deep breath then closed the letter and tore it in half.

"I don't want to talk to her. Tell her I'm busy. Tell her I'm out. Tell her anything." She tossed the letter in the trash. "I do not want to talk to her."

"She's been by twice. She heard you were back in town."

"Carly Benson can go screw herself as far as I'm concerned."

"I think all she wants is to talk to you."

"Yeah, right." Kelly scoffed.

"If you don't want to see her, that's up to you. But I'm not going to be your go-between. If you're here, you are going to have to tell her yourself. You owe her that much."

"I don't owe her anything."

Lauren didn't like the arrogance in Kelly's tone. She had lured Carly into a relationship then tossed her aside for greener pastures. The least she could do was see her.

"She moved back to town a few months ago. I don't think she's involved with anyone right now."

"What am I supposed to do? Take pity on her?"

"No. But you could give her a few minutes of your time. She doesn't harbor any bad feelings about the way things ended with you. Maybe she just wants to clear the air. Couldn't you be benevolent enough to at least talk to her?"

Kelly was leaning against the counter, fiddling with her scarf.

"I don't know."

"At least think about it, Kel. She still likes you."

"Likes me? Did you read that letter?"

Lauren shook her head.

"Carly Benson loves me more than the stars love the sky," she said, chuckling at the sentiment.

"And you're surprised?"

"I never asked her to do that. I told her that it was over and I needed to move on. We just weren't right for each other. What do I have to do? Hit her over the head with it?"

"I think you already did that."

"I don't want to talk about it." Kelly tossed her scarf over her shoulder. A signal for a subject change, thought Lauren. "By the way, what's for breakfast tomorrow? Are you making pumpkin pancakes?"

"Quiche."

"No pumpkin pancakes?" She frowned.

"No. I've made those twice in the last week for you. I don't want to be known as the pumpkin house."

"But everybody loves them."

"Sorry, Kelly. No pumpkin pancakes."

"How about pumpkin muffins?"

"I've made pumpkin walnut muffins before. You'd probably like those."

"How about pumpkin blueberry or pumpkin cranberry?" Kelly suggested, showing a surprising interest in culinary creations.

"I don't know about blueberry. The color bleeds. Orange and blue might make a pretty nasty looking muffin. But the pumpkin cranberry is good."

"Pumpkin cranberry walnut?" Kelly encouraged.

"Yes. That would be good."

"Could you make those for tomorrow?"

"I'll have to see if I have everything I need." Lauren tucked the last napkin in place and turned out the light in the breakfast room.

"I'm sure you do. Think how much your guests would like to experience an original creation for the very first time. I really think you should make them for tomorrow morning." Kelly followed her to the pantry. "They'll be great."

"Admit it, Kel. You like pumpkin." Just like when we were kids, Lauren thought. She still hasn't learned to quit.

"Okay, I like pumpkin. But it's good for you, isn't it?"

"Yes. And yes, I have everything I'll need to make pumpkin cranberry walnut muffins."

"Great." Kelly finished the bottle of water and tossed it in the recycle bin then headed down the hall. "By the way sis, would it be okay if I invite someone to breakfast?"

"When?"

"Tomorrow for your pumpkin cranberry walnut muffins." She grinned.

"Then you already invited her, right?"

"Yeah. I told her you wouldn't mind. Are you sure you couldn't make pumpkin pancakes?" Kelly whined.

"Quiche, Kel. Quiche."

"Okay. Pumpkin muffins then."

"Since this is your guest, could you at least come down and help?" Lauren called as Kelly started up the stairs.

"Of course. Just call me if I oversleep. I'll be down." Kelly trotted upstairs.

"Uh-huh," Lauren muttered. "Like that's going to happen. Hey!" Lauren called after Kelly. "Who is it? Do I know her?"

No answer.

Lauren wondered if she had invited both Dee and Trina. With a full house, two guests would make things a little cramped in the breakfast room. Surely Kelly would have told her if she had invited two guests. Lauren shook her head. *I'm not going to worry about that tonight. I have to come up with a recipe for pumpkin cranberry walnut muffins before tomorrow morning.* She checked her files and did a little combining here and there to create an acceptable recipe.

Lauren snapped off the lights in the living room and hall and stood at the sink, tidying up before she officially closed the kitchen for the night. The guests were still welcome to come down and take a can of soda or some cookies, but as far as she could tell, all the guests had retired to their rooms. All except Michelle and Donna, the two young women from the Crimson Room who were strolling the garden outside the kitchen window. The soft glow from the path lights silhouetted them against the gazebo. They cuddled together, their arms around each other. It was like watching a romantic movie. The music would swell and the camera would zoom in for a close-up as they kissed. Lauren smiled and looked away as their kiss became long and passionate.

"Good for you," she whispered. "I hope it's always like that for you." An unexpected tear rolled down her cheek as her chin began to tremble. Romantic scenes like this didn't usually touch her so deeply. *I'm a big girl. I know what can happen when relationships fail and how easily hearts can be broken when love is taken for granted.* But tonight, the sight of two lovers lost in an embrace was enough to scratch those old memories into an open wound. Lauren turned away from the window. She didn't want to see the passion in their eyes or the softness in their touch. Not tonight when she had only an empty bed to run to. There were no warm arms waiting in the candlelight. No tender touch waiting to whisk her away to paradise. Just a lonely bed full of empty memories.

"Good night, Ms. Roberts," Donna said, coming into the kitchen from the back door.

"Good night, honey. See you in the morning."

"Good night," Michelle said. She linked her little finger with Donna's as they made their way down the hall.

"Sweet dreams, kids."

Lauren waited for them to get upstairs then turned off the kitchen lights and went to her room. She knew she wasn't going to sleep, at least not right away. Not with her heart yearning for that one special person she could lock fingers with.

Pumpkin Cranberry Walnut Muffins

Kenna's Recipe

Makes 6-8 muffins

4 oz. softened unsalted butter
1 cup sugar (may use part brown sugar)
2 eggs and 1/2 cup milk
2 cups flour
2 teaspoons baking powder
1/2 teaspoon salt
1/2 teaspoon ground cinnamon
3/8 teaspoon ground cloves
3/8 teaspoon allspice
3/4 cup packed pumpkin puree
1 cup chopped walnuts
1 cup halved cranberries

Preheat oven to 350° standard. Grease standard-sized muffin tin or use muffin papers. Combine flour, baking powder, salt and spices. Set aside. Cream butter and sugar until slightly lumpy. Beat in eggs and milk. Add flour mixture and fold gently. Add pumpkin and continue to fold. Add cranberries and walnut pieces and give one or two more folds. Fill muffin cups about ¾ full. Bake until set, approx. 35 minutes. Cool and enjoy!

Chapter 9

Lauren finished printing the recipe cards for her muffins and placed them in the holder on the buffet table. The muffins and the quiche were in the oven. Originally, she had planned on using the quiche recipe as her souvenir recipe card but since Kelly was so insistent on the pumpkin muffins, she thought she might appreciate the muffin recipe as her card of choice. Lauren couldn't take credit for the recipe card idea. Aunt Edna and Felicia had started the tradition years ago to set themselves apart from the rest of the guest houses in town.

The bacon was browned and in the warming tray. The coffee was brewed. The granola was in the canister. Breakfast was ready, but Kelly was nowhere in sight. Lauren checked the muffins then called Kelly's cell phone again. Once again, it went to her voice mail.

"Good morning, Kel. It's eight fifteen. I thought you were

coming down to help. Are you at least coming down to greet your guest when she gets here?" Lauren closed the cell phone and tossed it on the counter disgustedly. She started a second pot of coffee then took the muffins and quiche out of the oven to cool. Just as she was ready to run upstairs to wake Kelly, there was a knock at the front door.

"Oh, great. There's your date, Kelly. Where are you?" Lauren wiped her hands on the towel and went to answer it.

"Hello, Lauren," Gaylin said, leaning against the porch railing, a folder under her arm.

"Gaylin? Hello. If you need another look around for the appraisal, this really isn't a very good time for me. I'm serving breakfast to a full house."

"Already? She told me eight thirty." Gaylin looked at her watch.

"Kelly?" Lauren gasped. "You're the one she invited to breakfast?"

"Didn't she tell you?"

"She said she invited someone but she didn't say who."

"If this is a problem, I'll understand. It sounds like you already have your hands full."

"No, no. Come in," Lauren said, realizing she hadn't been hospitable. "You're right on time."

"Are you sure?"

"Absolutely." Lauren pulled her through the door. "I'm glad you could join us. Come in the kitchen and get a cup of coffee while you wait." She led the way down the hall. "I'm sorry to say Kelly isn't up yet."

"She called me a few minutes ago and said she was running late but she'd be down shortly."

Lauren pointed to the tray of cups and the coffeepot on the counter.

"Please, help yourself. I need to get the muffins in the basket." She could hear the first of her guests coming down the stairs.

"Can I help?" Gaylin asked, pouring herself a cup. "I'm not much of a cook but I can fetch and carry."

"Thanks, but I think I've got everything under control."

"Something smells really good. Kelly is very proud of your cooking."

"I hope you like mushroom quiche and pumpkin cranberry muffins," Lauren said, carrying the quiche to the buffet table.

"I like anything I don't have to cook."

One by one Lauren's guests filed through the dining room, filled their plates and found a place to sit in the breakfast room. In the temporary confusion of getting everyone seated, Lauren lost track of Gaylin. She finally found her in the hall checking over the papers in her folder, looking like she felt out of place.

"What are you doing out here in the hall?" Lauren hooked her arm through Gaylin's. She hated Kelly for making Gaylin wait like this. "Come on. Let's get you something to eat. You're probably starved. Besides, I want to hear how the appraisal is coming. Any chances it will be done before my January payment is due?" she asked, making polite conversation.

"Gaylin!" Kelly came rushing into the kitchen, fresh and full of energy. "I'm so glad you made it." She kissed Gaylin's cheek as if they were old friends.

Kelly's effervescent entrance and Gaylin's smiling, almost blushing acceptance of her kiss did not go unnoticed by Lauren. She couldn't help wonder if this was their first kiss. If not, she wondered how much more Kelly and Gaylin had shared. Lauren had only met Gaylin a few short weeks ago but had hoped something was there, something for them to build at least a friendship on. Now, Kelly had changed that. She had, in her unflappable way, laid claim to something Lauren had found alluring. Kelly didn't know that and Lauren certainly wasn't going to tell her, not now. She wasn't going to make that mistake twice.

"Come on, honey. Let's get some breakfast," Kelly said, locking her arm through Gaylin's and leading her into the dining room. "Let's see what good old sis has made for us today."

Lauren tried to concentrate on her guests but there was Kelly, leaning into Gaylin's side and Gaylin responding to it

85

with her hand in the small of Kelly's back. For a brief moment Lauren imagined that she was the one giggling at Gaylin's every word and tossing her hair enticingly. That's not your style, she reminded herself. If that's what Gaylin *is* looking for in a woman, I'm better off. I've never played the flirty helpless damsel. I'm certainly not going to start now.

Lauren kept the serving bowls refilled and made polite conversation, fulfilling her role as hostess and innkeeper. She answered questions about sightseeing destinations in the area, humbly accepted compliments on her cooking, and encouraged everyone to eat hearty. It also helped take her mind off of Kelly's giggles.

"Gaylin, help yourself to another muffin. I helped with the recipe." Kelly winked at her sister and took a bite of Gaylin's bacon, stealing it from her plate.

"They're wonderful, really, but I'm stuffed. This was an incredible breakfast, Lauren. Thank you."

Kelly and Gaylin remained in the breakfast room long after the other guests finished and left. They sat chatting across the table as Lauren made repeated trips to the kitchen, clearing away the dirty dishes.

"Shouldn't we help?" Lauren heard Gaylin say.

"No. Lauren's got it. Besides, she doesn't like anyone to touch her dishes. She'd rather do it herself than risk breaking anything," Kelly replied.

"Would you two like more coffee?" Lauren called from the kitchen. "I've made a fresh pot." She didn't know why she did that. She knew better than to interfere with a private conversation.

"No, thank you, Lauren," Gaylin said, coming through the doorway with her cup and saucer. "Breakfast was wonderful. I'm going to have to find a way to include it in the property value."

"I'm glad Kelly talked you into coming by."

"I'd love to stay and visit, but I better get to work," Gaylin said.

"I'll walk you to the door." Kelly latched onto her arm.

They stood by the front door, talking softly, too softly for

Lauren to hear. It was a straight shot from the kitchen down the hall to the front door, so when Lauren peeked around the kitchen door, she could clearly see Kelly's coy smile and the kiss she placed on Gaylin's lips. She also saw Gaylin's humble blush. Like always, Kelly wasted no time in staking her claim. She lingered at the door, smiling and waving as Gaylin walked out to her car.

"I hope she got enough to eat," Lauren said as Kelly returned to the kitchen, sporting a smug little grin.

"She liked the pumpkin muffins. I'm glad I suggested them." Kelly sat on the stool at the end of the counter and played with the napkin rings. "She's nice, isn't she?"

"Yes, Gaylin is very nice. She seems very honest and very dedicated."

"I think I'll ask her out again. I usually prefer someone to ask me out but I think Gaylin is a little shy about things like that. So I'll have to make the first move this time."

"Since when do you ever wait for someone else to make the first move?" Lauren chuckled. "That has never been your style."

"It was, but look where it got me. Remember Marsha Binkleman? I waited a whole year for her to ask me out. I did everything but make the reservation at the restaurant. She ended up with that stupid Lynn Hotsinger."

"Lynn Hotsinger, the one with the triple D cups?"

"Yes. If I had followed my instincts, I could be living in a three thousand square foot, lakefront house with maid service and a terraced swimming pool."

"No, you couldn't. You aren't *that* shallow, Kelly."

"Well, maybe. Besides, I think Gaylin Hart is definitely better than Marsha Binkleman." Kelly hopped down and leaned into Lauren. "And she has the sexiest ass I have ever seen. It's so round and cute you just want to grab it." She giggled. "Oh, by the way, I won't be home this afternoon. I have to run over to Branson for a costume fitting. I might be late."

"How about Roxie? I thought you said she could have her puppies any day now."

87

"If something happens you can call me. I'll come right back." She headed down the hall.

"Couldn't you take her with you in that pet carrier?"

"She wouldn't be comfortable in that thing all day. She'll be fine. I have to change and get going. Later, sis." She sprinted up the stairs.

Lauren continued to load the dishwasher, torn between daydreaming about Gaylin and worrying about Roxie giving birth.

Ice Box Toffee

Kenna's Mother's recipe
If my mother ever asked me what dessert I wanted, I usually said
this one. It has a rich chocolate pudding texture. It's easy to make and
you'll love it!

2 cups powdered sugar
1 1/2 tablespoons cocoa
1/2 teaspoon salt
1/2 cup butter (1 stick) creamed
1cup chopped nuts (usually pecans)
1 teaspoon vanilla
1 3/4 cups vanilla wafer crumbs
2 eggs (separated)

Cream butter, sift sugar and cocoa and salt together. Add sugar mixture to creamed butter – beat until light and fluffy. Add beaten egg yolks, nuts and vanilla extract. Fold in egg whites. Layer 8 x 8 pan with wafer crumbs, then batter, then crumbs on top. Chill 12 hours.

Chapter 10

It was after ten o'clock and the last guest had retired to their room by the time Lauren was able to check on Roxie, who, thank God, had not given birth. The house was quiet for the first time since early morning and Lauren was exhausted. She was so tired she knew she wouldn't be able to sleep. She would lay awake, arguing with herself about Kelly, Gaylin, Roxie and the impending puppies. And that she didn't want to do.

She decided she needed movement. After turning out the lights throughout the house, she went into her room and changed into her swimsuit. Wrapping her fluffy robe around her, she headed into the garden for a dip in the hot tub. She didn't use it very often but tonight she needed a little peace and quiet to smooth out the creases of the day. She pushed back the shutters on the gazebo, checked the water temperature, and climbed in. She kept the water hot enough to be soothing without sapping the last of her strength. She eased down in the seat, moaned, and closed her eyes as the warmth embraced her.

"Calgon, take me away," she sighed.

Cleo had followed her outside and was walking the rim of the hot tub, meowing plaintively.

"No, I'm not going to feed you right now," she said without opening her eyes. The cat rubbed her face against the back of Lauren's head, purring loudly. "Nope. You should have planned ahead and saved some of your dinner for a late night snack." Cleo gave a disgruntled meow, sat down, and began washing her face as if she was willing to wait out Lauren's decision.

One by one, the lights went out in the upstairs guest rooms until the house was dark.

"Good night, everyone," Lauren whispered and turned on the jets. She was so relaxed she was nearly asleep when the back door opened and Kelly came rushing out wearing a white bikini and carrying a towel.

"God, it's cold," she said, scurrying across the patio. She dropped the towel on a nearby chair and climbed in the hot tub. Her body, like Lauren's, was pale and evenly toned.

Lauren immediately noticed her sister's breasts. Or whoever's breasts they were because they certainly weren't the ones Kelly had in high school. She thought there was something different about Kelly's shape the first day she arrived but it wasn't until now she knew what it was. Her tiny nipples were clearly visible through the thin fabric of the bikini but they were the only things that were tiny. Her breasts were round, firm, perfectly symmetrical, and a healthy D cup.

"Wow. Where did those come from?" Lauren asked, remaining comfortably submerged to the neck.

"Where did what come from?" Kelly gasped as she settled into the hot water. "Can we turn this down? It's a little hot, don't you think?"

"It's not that hot."

"But I'll wrinkle."

"How could you possibly wrinkle? Overinflated balloons

don't wrinkle."

"Oh, these?" she giggled. "I did it on a lark when I was in LA. Do you like them?" Kelly leaned back and thrust her boobs above the surface of the water.

"Why did you do that to yourself? You had a nice figure."

"Yeah, but look what big knockers did for Dolly Parton."

"Are those Dolly's hand-me-downs?"

"You have to do whatever you can in this business. You have to be noticed. And believe me, these babies get me noticed." Kelly wobbled them back and forth.

"Wouldn't it be better to be noticed for your talent?"

"You can't show off your talent until you get them to notice you." Kelly reached behind her neck and untied her bikini top, exposing her bare breasts. "Doctor Graham did a great job, don't you think?" She cupped her hands around them fondly. "You can't even see the scars. Graham is one of the best in the country. He's so busy you have to have a referral just to get in to see him. I'm sure I could get you in. What do you say? How about adding a cup size to your midgies, sis?"

"No, thanks." Lauren closed her eyes and sunk a little deeper in the water. "I don't need a Barbie doll figure. And my boobs are not midgies. I'm very happy with them."

"Where's the temperature control? I'm dying over here." She stood up, using the chilly night air to cool herself from the waist up.

Lauren pushed the button to reduce the temperature, knowing Kelly wasn't going to give up until she got her way. It was easier to turn it down and retain the peace.

"How was your meeting with your costume designer?" Lauren asked.

"I canceled it. She has the flu. I told her I didn't want to get sick right before rehearsals start. Her assistant is going to set up a meeting with me in a couple days." Kelly stripped her bikini off and tossed both pieces on the ground.

"Are you naked?" Lauren chided.

"Sure. You're supposed to be naked in a hot tub. Take off

your suit."

"I've got a house full of strangers who could come through that door at any minute. I'm not taking off my bathing suit. And you shouldn't either."

"Are you jealous of my gorgeous hooters, sis?" She gave a witchy cackle.

"Not hardly."

"Haven't you ever sat in here naked?"

"Yes. But not with guests upstairs. What would you say if somebody decided to take a midnight stroll through the garden?"

"I'd say come on in," Kelly said, waving the imaginary person toward the hot tub. "Let them take this memory home with them." She grinned and let her breasts break the surface again.

"Kelly, please behave yourself while you're here."

"I always behave myself. You're the one who gets uptight about the least little thing. So what if someone sees your tits or ass. Everybody has them. Maybe your guests would be more likely to come back if they thought there was something special to see at Gypsy Hill." Kelly smiled and winked.

Lauren groaned and closed her eyes, trying to ignore her.

"So what did you do this evening? Meet Dee and Trina?" Lauren didn't want to talk about Kelly's boobs anymore.

"No. They were at Trina's mom's for dinner. So I went to Jolene's Java House."

"Alone?" Kelly seldom went anywhere alone. She never had to. She always had a date.

"No," she replied casually and smiled. "Gaylin went with me."

"Gaylin Hart?"

"And you'll never guess what I did." Kelly raised her eyebrows.

"Flirted with her unmercifully."

"No, I did not. What makes you think I did that?"

"Since when do you wait a discreet amount of time before pouncing?"

"I did no such thing." Kelly sank down in the water. "I just invited her over for the tree trimming party tomorrow night. She liked breakfast so I thought she'd like coming over for that. She has to go out of town on business tomorrow morning but she should be back around six or so. She's going to call."

"Good. I'm glad you did. What did you two talk about? Her work?" Lauren couldn't help herself. She wanted to hear about Gaylin.

"That and music. Inviting her over was the least I could do. I suppose you're going to say I should have asked before I invited her."

"No. She's welcome to come."

"Did you know Gaylin wears bikini underwear?" Kelly said coyly. "Black ones."

"How do you know that?" In spite of herself, Lauren slipped on the seat. "What did you do? Follow her into the ladies' room and peek under the door?"

"She told me. We were playing truth or dare."

"You were playing truth or dare with Gaylin and you asked her what kind of underwear she wore?" Lauren wanted to duck under the water and stay there.

"Yep. You can break the ice with someone when you discuss what kind of underwear they wear. I read that in one of those tabloids."

"What did she ask you?"

"She asked where was the most outrageous place I ever had sex."

"And you said?"

"In the window of McGinness's Department store."

"You did not," Lauren gasped.

"Oh, yes, I did. Remember Susie McGinness. The one with long braids?"

"In high school?"

"Yeah. She had the key to her grandpa's store. She got in trouble for skipping school. Her punishment was to sweep out the entire store. She told me if I'd help her she'd make it worth my while. And boy, did she ever."

"Is that the night you snuck out the window in the rain?"

"Uh-huh. You were supposed to let me back in when I knocked on the window. I practically broke the damn window beating on it. Why didn't you open it?"

"It was three o'clock in the morning. I was asleep," Lauren argued.

"Well, mom wasn't. I told her I was helping a friend, but I still lost my allowance for a whole month."

"You probably had it coming. If she knew what you were really doing, you would have lost a lot more than that."

"No shit. You should have heard her the year I told her not to worry about me getting pregnant because I was a lesbian."

"I can't believe you told Gaylin about having sex in a store window."

"She thought it was great."

"What did you ask her next?" Lauren was dying to hear Gaylin's sexual escapades.

"I wasn't going to ask her about her sex life. She seems so private, I figured she'd just lie about it. I asked her who she fantasized about having sex with."

"What did she say?"

"She thought about it a minute, blushed bright red, smiled, and said she'd take the dare instead."

"She didn't answer?"

"No. But she gave me this really sultry look. I bet she was going to admit some kind of erotic threeway involving handcuffs and whipped cream."

"No, that's your fantasy, Kelly."

"Not me. My fantasy is way more wicked than that."

"I don't want to know. I'm sure it has something to do with S and M and illegalities."

Kelly gave a lusty laugh.

"And your fantasies don't?"

"Not hardly." Lauren had no intention of admitting her fantasies to her sister.

"I don't believe you, sis." Kelly climbed out and collected her towel and suit. "Not for one minute do I believe you. On that note, I am going to bed. And I won't be surprised if I have a wet dream about Gaylin tonight." She looked back and winked.

"Could you at least cover up before you go upstairs?"

"Prude." Kelly stood in the doorway and opened her towel. She struck a pose then went inside.

"Good night, Kelly."

How did this happen, Lauren asked herself. She's doing it again, taking whatever she wants.

Buckeyes

Kenna's college roommate Jean Anne's recipe

1 16 oz. package powdered sugar
1 1/2 cup peanut butter (smooth or crunchy, your choice)
½ cup butter softened (or margarine)
1 teaspoon vanilla
1/2 teaspoon salt
1 12 oz. package semi-sweet chocolate chips
2 squares paraffin (optional)

Mix sugar, peanut butter, butter, vanilla and salt. Shape into balls
Melt chocolate chips and paraffin in double boiler (the paraffin
helps the chocolate set up and gives them a shiny look but you
can exclude it if you wish) Using toothpicks, dip into melted
chocolate chips and paraffin (only partially submerged) Place on
waxed paper to cool and enjoy. You'll want to double this one,
they are that good.

Chapter 11

"Quick! Get me some towels!" Kelly ran into the kitchen.

"What do you need them for?" Lauren asked, wiping her hands and heading to the mudroom. "Big ones? Little ones? What?" She opened the cabinet where she kept the extra towels.

"Big ones. No, little ones." Kelly was frantic.

"What happened? Did you spill something?"

"It's Roxie." She pulled down a stack of towels, dumping another stack on the floor. "Oops. Sorry. Can you get that? I don't have time. I've got to get back upstairs."

"What's wrong with Roxie?" She picked up the dropped towels and began refolding them. "Is she sick?"

"She's having her puppies," Kelly yelled as she ran up the stairs.

"Puppies?" Lauren tossed the towels aside and hurried after her, taking them two at a time. "Is she okay? How many are there?"

"One so far."

Roxie was lying in the corner of the bathroom floor in a nest of towels, licking at the wet brown blob lying next to her.

"You're doing so good, sweetheart. Yes, you are." Kelly knelt next to her, petting her head.

"What should we do?" Lauren had never seen a dog give birth before. "Should I heat some water?"

"No," she whispered, stroking Roxie lovingly. "She can do it. Can't you, baby? Here comes another one."

Lauren had never seen this side of Kelly before. Unselfishly caring and gentle had never been one of Kelly's strong points. But here she was, cooing softly to a dog as a blood-covered protrusion oozed from its bottom.

"Shouldn't you help it? Cut the umbilical cord or something?"

"Roxie will do it. This is her first litter, but she's a good mommy. She knows what to do."

Kelly was right. Roxie went right to work, licking and nuzzling her second baby.

"She's awfully rough. She's going to hurt it, Kel."

"No, she's not. That's how she gets it to take its first breath." Sure enough, the little animal began to squeal. Roxie continued to lick her baby all over, cleaning away every trace of afterbirth. Once she seemed satisfied, she lay back down, almost immediately expelling another tiny wet glob.

"That's three," Lauren said, smiling at Kelly. She sat down on the floor, amazed. I never would have thought it, but there's something miraculous, even mesmerizing about watching Roxie give birth.

"That's a big one. Good girl, Roxie. Good girl."

Number three was a strapping puppy with husky legs and a high-pitched, demanding cry.

"That one looks like a baby bulldog," Kelly chuckled. "It's a toughie."

"Is it a boy or a girl?"

Kelly gently rolled it on its side.

"Boy." She checked the others. "Two girls. One boy."

Roxie had not yet finished cleaning number three when a fourth puppy tumbled into the world.

"Look, Kel! Another one. She needs to wash it. Should we help?" Lauren asked with a worried look.

"No." Kelly leaned over and bumped Lauren playfully. "Not unless you want to lick it."

"Ah, no."

"Isn't it amazing how God's creatures know what to do? Even though this is her first litter she acts like she's done it a hundred times."

"How many do you think she'll have?"

"The vet said it could be up to six, but probably more like three or four. That might be the last one."

Roxie worked tirelessly over her four babies, licking them clean and dry.

"Kel, is that afterbirth?" Lauren said, noticing a small bulge extending from Roxie's vagina.

Roxie folded her ears back and whimpered. She sniffed at her opening and gave it a lick. One more contraction and puppy number five slid out onto the towel.

"Wow! Five puppies, Roxie. Good job, sweetheart."

"She isn't cleaning it," Lauren said. "Roxie, look. You've got another baby. Fix it." She pushed it in front of Roxie's nose. But Roxie ignored it, continuing to lick and nurture her other babies. Finally, she turned to the newborn, but it lay limp at her side as she licked at it, rocking it back and forth. When it didn't move, Roxie sniffed at it, pushing it with her nose.

"Oh, God, Lauren," Kelly gasped. "It isn't breathing."

Lauren's instincts told her she had to do something. She began rubbing the tiny animal's back. Roxie continued to lick at it as Lauren administered crude CPR.

"It's okay, Roxie. I won't hurt your baby," Lauren said.

"Is it dead?" Kelly's eyes filled with tears.

Lauren held the puppy head down, massaging its back vigorously. Suddenly, a tiny squeak came from the baby, the sound of life. Lauren gently set the puppy next to Roxie, who began to nuzzle it.

"It's not dead, Kel." Lauren patted Kelly's leg. "You're still the mother of five puppies."

"Thank you, sis," Kelly said, hugging her. "I panicked. I didn't know you knew anything about being a midwife for dogs."

"I didn't know I did."

Kelly spread out the clean towels and made a new home for Roxie and her babies. She carefully moved each one of the litter, snuggling them against each other. Roxie circled in the new nest, sniffing at her young before settling down to nurse them for the first time.

"Sorry about the towels, sis."

"That's okay. I'll toss them." Lauren bundled the dirty towels together.

"Thanks for helping." Kelly looked up at her with a smile.

"I'm glad I could. They're adorable. Just don't tell Cleo I said so." Lauren couldn't resist petting one of the fuzzy brown puppies before going downstairs. Tallie was standing at her desk, talking on the telephone.

"Here she is. One second." Tallie handed her the receiver. "It's Gaylin."

Lauren smiled. "Hello, Gaylin. I thought you were going out of town today."

"I am. I'm in Little Rock. Tallie said there was a problem upstairs. Is everything okay?"

"Roxie had her puppies. Five of them."

"Wow, five. Is that normal for a small dog like that?"

"According to Kelly, that was about what she expected."

"I bet they look like furry little hot dogs."

"Yeah, they're so cute! Their tiny little ears are no bigger than your fingernail and they stick straight out. Just the tip flops over."

"You sound like a dog lover."

"Not me. Cleo is enough of a pet for me. She does her own thing and we co-exist under one roof. AKC registered dogs are too high maintenance for me. I wouldn't have time for one of those. Do you have pets?"

"Nope. I'm never home long enough to have pets. That's why I called. I don't think I'm going to get back this evening. If I do, it won't be until very late. This is turning out to be a bigger job than I thought. I have to drive down to Pine Bluff. Could you tell Kelly I'm sorry, but I don't think I'll make it for the tree trimming party?"

"I'm sorry to hear that. She will be, too."

"I should have let her know when she mentioned it last night that I might be late. It was nice of you to include me though."

"If you'll wait a minute, I'll go get her. She's upstairs acting like a proud grandmother."

"Could you tell her for me? I'm pulling into the parking lot. I'm already late for a meeting."

"She'll be sorry she missed you."

"Tell her I appreciate the invitation. It sounded like fun."

Lauren hung up just as Kelly came down the stairs.

"Tallie said Gaylin was on the phone."

"She was. She had to go."

"Why didn't you come get me?"

"I tried, but she couldn't wait."

"She couldn't wait one minute? God, Lauren. You should have told her I needed to talk to her."

"I didn't know you did. But she had to go. She was late for a meeting. She is in Little Rock and called to say she probably wouldn't be back this evening. She has to go to Pine Bluff."

"Ahg," Kelly groaned. "But what about the tree trimming party tonight?"

"She said to tell you she was sorry but she didn't think she was going to make it."

"What?" Kelly screeched.

"Don't blame the messenger. I'm just relating what she said."

"She should have waited. I wanted to talk to her."

"Maybe she'll call after her meeting."

"If she does, come get me." Kelly grabbed Lauren's arm. "Tell her I need to talk to her."

"I didn't do it on purpose, Kelly. She said she was late and had to hang up."

"Why did she call you anyway? She should have called me. I gave her my cell number."

"I have no idea. You can ask her when you see her. Maybe she forgot your number. Maybe mine was handy. After all, she is doing my appraisal."

"Don't remind me. That's all you two talk about." She rolled her eyes. "Give me a break. There's more to life than computing income potential."

"I never said there wasn't. But this is important to me. It could mean hundreds of dollars a month in interest payments. I know you don't want to hear about it, but Gypsy Hill is my business, like singing is yours. I take it very seriously."

"I know. God, I know. You and your spreadsheets and bottom line. Look, sis. I know this is important to you but the next time Gaylin comes over, do us all a favor. The only bottom line anyone wants to hear about is this one." Kelly smacked Lauren on the rear.

"I'm sorry if I've bored you and Gaylin."

"That's the trouble. All you have to do is mention that damn appraisal and she's turned on like a five-dollar hooker. That's all she talks about. She acts like she's on a crusade or something. It took me an hour to get the conversation away from you and your property value. She was consumed with it. You'd think she was consumed with you."

Really? Lauren thought. Interesting.

"All right. I won't mention it in your presence. How's that?"

"Fine," Kelly snapped.

"Fine. Now if you'll excuse me, I'm going to the store."

"Fine."

"Kelly, I'm sorry if I've embarrassed you in front of Gaylin. I certainly didn't mean to."

The telephone rang before Kelly could reply.

"Good afternoon. Gypsy Hill," Lauren said.

"Hi, Lauren," Carly said, tentatively.

"Hello, Carly." Lauren looked over at Kelly. Kelly glared at her, shaking her head adamantly.

"Is she there?"

"Yes, she is. She's right here. Just a second." Lauren grabbed Kelly by the wrist and thrust the telephone at her.

"No!" Kelly tried to yank her wrist away. "I told you I don't want to talk to her."

"Then you tell her."

"No."

"Kelly, this is the third time she has called. One way or the other, you owe it to her. Talk to her. I'm going to the store." She placed the receiver in Kelly's hand and headed up the hall.

"Lauren!"

Lauren shook her head and kept walking. She returned an hour later to find Kelly staring into the refrigerator.

"Well, how did it go?" she asked, carrying an armload of groceries.

"Okay."

"Just okay?"

"Yes. Why ask me? You seem to know everything anyway."

"Come on, Kelly. Don't be like that. I just thought you could at least talk to her."

"Why?" Kelly smirked and continued to study the contents of the refrigerator.

"I don't know. Maybe because once you two were lovers."

"This may come as a shock to you, sis. But not everyone retains contact with their former lovers. For most people, when it's over, it's over. End of story."

"Not everyone ends a relationship like snapping their fingers. You even admitted that it ended too quickly."

"What I said was I didn't have time to go through all the details of breaking up. It is easier to end a relationship in one quick break instead of a long, drawn-out scene where everyone says things they will regret later."

"Maybe Carly needed to hear why your two years together ended so abruptly."

Kelly closed the door and turned with a dramatic flourish.

"Well, she's going to get her wish. Carly wants to come over and talk. So I invited her over this evening to help trim the tree. I told her about seven."

The last time Carly had been at Gypsy Hill to help trim the Christmas tree was when she and Lauren were together. Lauren always suspected that was the night Kelly's flirtatious ways and coy smile lured Carly away from her.

"But it's not a date," Kelly added quickly. "Not a date at all."

Queso - Spinach Cheese Dip

Kenna's daughter Beth's recipe
(This is similar to restaurant recipe Queso.)

1 1/4 cup white American cheese
1 cup half & half
1 cup heavy whipping cream
1/4 cup chopped frozen spinach (1/4 to 1/2 package)
1/4 cup jalapeno peppers (optional)

Cook spinach as per package instructions. Drain well and strain. Add all ingredients in Crock Pot and heat until cheese melts, stirring frequently. Serve warm with tortilla chips and it's party time!

Chapter 12

Christmas was Lauren's favorite time of year. The house had been decorated for weeks with everything from garlands on the banisters to lights on the roof. Truth be told, she could live in the Christmas season year round.

She had made six dozen assorted cookies to go with the homemade double rich hot chocolate and the mulled cider. And like every year, she would cut buttered toast into inch-wide strips and sprinkle them with cinnamon sugar, just like her mother had done when she and Kelly were kids. Cinnamon crisps were a childhood treat and she couldn't imagine trimming the tree without them.

Decorating the Christmas tree was the one time her strict business sense was tempered by the joy of the season. By early afternoon, Tallie and Lauren got the ten-foot Scotch pine mounted in the base and placed in front of the living room windows. The boxes of lights and ornaments were piled on the floor, waiting to be added. She knew it would be easier to use a pre-lit artificial tree that she could put back in the box after Christmas, but there was no way she was going to hang her handmade treasures on a fake tree. It had to be live and it had to be big.

"Are you and Sasha coming over this evening?" Lauren asked, centering the tree in front of the windows.

"I don't think so. She wants to rent a movie."

"Which one?"

"I have no idea. It's her turn to pick so it will probably be something shoot 'em up, blow 'em up. How many are you expecting tonight?"

"Not many. Kelly invited someone, but I haven't heard if any of the guests want to come down and help."

"Who did Kelly invite? Anyone I know?"

"Carly."

"You're kidding? Carly Benson?" Tallie gave a doubtful scowl. "How do you feel about that?"

"I don't mind. She's not coming to see me. She wants a chance to talk to Kelly."

"I'm sure she does, but here? Tonight?"

"I appreciate your concern, Tallie, but it really doesn't bother me. I don't mind."

"Carly has a lot of guts to expect you to take her in after what she pulled."

Tallie was being protective but Lauren didn't need it. *I might have felt differently about Carly two years ago, but I'm over it.*

"Don't worry. Everything will be fine. I don't have a problem with her in my house. You know, Carly and I never had the forever kind of love anyway. I certainly didn't want her to stay with me if she was in love with someone else."

"At least you wouldn't be alone."

"Believe me, Tallie, I would rather be single. I'm over it."

"If you're so over it, why aren't you dating again? You need someone in your life, honey. Someone who loves you and you can love back. I wish you'd let me set you up with Sasha's cousin. You two might hit it off."

"Absolutely not. I do not need you making blinds dates for me. I don't have time for that."

"You never have time for that."

Lauren glanced up at Tallie. "I am doing just fine."

"If you're waiting for Santa to bring you someone down the chimney, forget it. It never happens. Take it from me. Happiness isn't going to fall into your lap. You have to go out and find her yourself."

"Thanks for the advice, Dr. Freud." Lauren opened the drawer to her desk and took out an envelope. "Here. This is for you. But only if you promise not to set me up on any blind dates, ever."

"I promise." Tallie laughed, opened the flap, and gasped.

"Oh, honey." Tallie put her hand to her throat. "Are you sure about this?"

"I'm sure. Merry Christmas. I just wish it could be more." She hugged Tallie warmly.

"Thank you so much," she whispered. "I love you, honey."

"I love you, too."

"Sasha is going to get the earrings she wants."

"Get something for yourself, also." Lauren winked at her.

"Oh, I will. Trust me." Tallie slipped the check back in the envelope and headed home. It gave Lauren a good feeling to know Tallie truly appreciated her gift. It wasn't for the practical things but for the little extras Tallie and Sasha couldn't afford. That's what Lauren wanted for them.

"Is that Tallie leaving?" Kelly asked, bouncing down the stairs.

"Yes."

"Are they coming tonight?"

"No. Sasha wants to rent a movie. I think that's Tallie's way of saying she is too tired to spend her evening decorating a Christmas tree."

"I ordered a pizza for dinner. One thin crust pepperoni and

one thick crust mushroom olive. Is that okay with you?"

"If I don't have to cook it, it's great. One would probably have been enough for just the two of us, though."

The doorbell rang. Kelly paid for the pizza and carried it into the kitchen.

"Paper plates?" she asked.

"In the pantry, bottom shelf." Lauren picked a slice of pepperoni off the pizza and ate it.

The doorbell rang again.

"Can you get that? The pizza boy probably didn't like the two-dollar tip I gave him."

"Two bucks is enough, isn't it?" Lauren said, going to answer the door.

"In California they want tens and twenties."

Lauren opened the door and saw Carly standing there.

"Hi, Carly," Lauren said. "Come in."

"Hi, Lauren. I know I'm early but I wasn't sure how long it would take me to get here. I heard the weather might get worse tonight." Her hair was damp and her parka was splattered with raindrops.

"That's okay."

"I hope you can use this." She handed Lauren a large poinsettia plant wrapped in gold foil.

"Thank you, Carly. It's gorgeous. We're in the kitchen. Want some pizza?" Lauren led the way. "We were just talking about you. Kelly, look who's here."

"Who?" Kelly said, standing in the doorway to the pantry.

"Me." Carly's eyes began a slow, almost hungry, scan over Kelly's body. "Hi, Kelly." She smiled broadly.

"Carly, hi." Kelly, too, let her eyes roam down Carly's lean frame and back up again. "You're early."

"I know. I hope you don't mind."

Kelly shrugged.

"See what she brought?" Lauren said, setting the poinsettia on the counter. "Isn't it gorgeous?"

"I thought maybe you'd want to put it in your room," Carly

offered. Her eyes never left Kelly as she pulled off her coat. "You look good, Kelly. Really good."

"God, in this?"

"No one wears low-rise jeans as well as you do."

Even Lauren could see Carly's eyes move from Kelly's crotch up to her tight-fitting top. Kelly seemed to drink up the attention her augmentation was providing her.

"What kind of pizza do you like, Carly? Thick or thin?" Lauren asked, nibbling on her slice.

"Thick," Carly said, her eyes drinking in Kelly's beauty.

"No, you don't," Kelly chuckled. "You like thin crust pepperoni."

Kelly put two slices on a paper plate and handed it to Carly. When their eyes met, Kelly blushed, looked away, and then back again.

Lauren took a slice of pizza and went to her office, leaving Kelly and Carly to visit. From her desk she could hear only muttered voices and occasional giggles from the kitchen. No arguments. No screaming. No loud voices. That's a good sign, Lauren thought. She worked on the computer while Cleo sat on her lap, purring and rubbing against her chest. She clicked on the weather site to check the forecast and was surprised to see a storm warning for southern and eastern Arkansas. Several inches of snow were predicted to cover the bit that had fallen earlier in the day.

Little Rock and Pine Bluff were smack-dab in the middle of the storm area. Right where Gaylin said she had to go.

Lauren clicked on the video weather update. The newscaster was reporting from downtown Little Rock. Ice hung from the trees and power lines, casting shadows on the deserted streets. He warned motorists to stay off the streets, then showed several car accidents. "There have been three confirmed deaths and many injuries have been confirmed, with conditions threatening to get even worse in the overnight hours."

Lauren checked the radar image. Sure enough, the middle of the state was cut off. There was no way around the storm.

Shaking her head, she got up and left her office.

"I checked the weather. Looks like things are pretty bad south of us," Lauren said, entering the kitchen. Kelly and Carly were sitting on the counter, eating pizza and drinking wine coolers.

"That's what I heard," Carly replied absently.

Lauren tried to raise Kelly's attention about Gaylin possibly being caught in the storm but she didn't pick up on it. Lauren returned to her office and opened another Web Site to listen to more weather updates. Whenever they showed an accident or an overturned vehicle, she zoomed in on the screen to see if it was a silver Honda Pilot. Finally, she could wait no longer and called Gaylin's cell phone.

"Hello. This is Gaylin Hart of Hart Appraisal. I'm sorry I can't take your call. Please leave your name, number and a message and I'll return your call as soon as possible. Have a nice day."

"Hi, Gaylin," Lauren said. She wasn't sure what to say. That she was worried? That sounded strange coming from her and not Kelly. "We were just checking on you. Kelly wanted me to call and make sure you weren't out driving in the storm. It looks very bad. Please take care of yourself and call when you can."

Lauren clicked on the weather video for the latest update.

"This just in, we have a report of a multi-car accident twelve miles north of Little Rock on highway forty. Ice and sleet are being blamed for the three fatalities and numerous injuries in the northbound lane of the interstate. According to authorities, a tractor-trailer lost control on the ice-covered bridge and plowed into an SUV, a mini-van and two cars. All five vehicles overturned and landed in the ditch where emergency crews are on the scene."

The camera shots of the accident were too far away to make out what type of SUV it was. Frustrated, Lauren turned off her computer. She was worried enough without listening to more reports. She picked up Cleo and went out to the front porch. The air was full of the smell of burning fireplaces. It was the season for roaring fires but Lauren didn't feel like enjoying one.

She couldn't stop thinking about Gaylin. What if she was one of the victims in that horrific accident? What if she was lying in the bottom of a ditch, bleeding and hurt, waiting for someone to rescue her?

"Oh, Cleo," she whispered, hugging the cat as her eyes filled with tears. "What if it is Gaylin?" Lauren swayed back and forth, trying to comfort herself. "It can't be. It just can't be Gaylin." Her chin quivered. She felt her knees go weak as tears streamed down her face. She sat down on the step, hugging Cleo against her as she cried.

"Hello."

Lauren looked up to see Gaylin striding up the walk.

"Oh, my God," Lauren said. She pushed Cleo off her lap and ran to give Gaylin a hug. "I am so glad to see you."

Gaylin returned the hug. "Wow. I didn't know I was missed."

"Are you all right? Any scratches? Broken bones? Anything?" Lauren looked her up and down.

"Should I have any?" Gaylin teased.

"No, no," she replied, reclaiming her composure. "I mean I'm glad you got home okay. I was afraid you got stuck in that terrible snowstorm down south."

"Yeah, I heard about that. That's why I came home early. It took me three hours to go forty miles."

"But you're all right?"

"I'm fine. How about you? You look upset about something. Everything okay with you and Kelly and the new puppies?"

"We're all fine." Lauren suddenly remembered who was inside with Kelly.

"Are you still going to decorate the tree?" Gaylin asked, walking Lauren up the steps and holding the front door for her. "Hello, Cleo." Cleo meowed and went in first.

"Yes. You are just in time." Lauren knew this was going to be interesting. She was glad Gaylin was back and safe but the wreck that was about to happen when Kelly realized she had two dates for the same evening? Well, this has the potential to be a doozie.

"Have you had dinner? We've got pizza."

"No, thanks. I ate before I came over."

"Who are you talking to?" Kelly called as Lauren led the way into the kitchen.

"Look who's here," Lauren announced.

"Gaylin?" Kelly said, her eyes widening. "Lauren said you wouldn't be back this evening."

"I know. I didn't think I would, but the weather threw a kink in my plans. So here I am, ready to trim a tree."

"Isn't that great?" Lauren said.

Kelly hopped down and gave Gaylin a hug and a kiss on the cheek.

"I'm glad you made it back in time. Gaylin, this is Carly Benson. She's an old friend of ours. Carly, this is Gaylin Hart. She's Lauren's real estate appraiser."

"Hello, Carly," Gaylin said. Carly climbed down and shook her hand.

"This tree trimming thing is a big deal for Lauren. She always has to have a real tree. You'd think she'd get tired of the mess and just buy a fake one," Kelly said.

"Not me," Lauren replied. "I'm not hanging my hundred-year-old lace angels on a plastic tree.

"I remember when we did this four years ago. Remember, the tree kept tipping over. It had a crook in the trunk and wouldn't stand up straight."

"Yes, I remember that," Carly said. "We finally had to cut a foot off the bottom."

"That was also the year we accidentally melted mother's homemade fudge because we had the package too close to the fireplace." Kelly laughed.

Lauren's memories of that Christmas were somewhat different. That was the year she found Carly and Kelly in the hot tub together. Carly had the look of someone in love. The funny thing was, she still had that look. The two years since she and Kelly had broken up hadn't diminished her adoration. Lauren had never seen that look in the two years she and Carly were

114

together.

"What do you do, Carly?" Gaylin asked.

"I'm a nurse practitioner."

"A nurse? That sounds very exciting."

"Sometimes it is. I bet doing real estate appraisals are more exciting than treating runny nose kids with colds."

"I think we both come in a pale second to Kelly's career," Gaylin said, wrapping an arm around her. "I'm envious of anyone who can sing like she does."

"Are you going to sing for us tonight," Carly asked.

"Maybe," Kelly said, obviously enjoying the attention. "If everyone sings with me."

"I hope you'll sing a few Christmas carols, Kel," Lauren said, adjusting the burner under the hot chocolate. "Shall we go see if we can get the lights strung?"

Jill and Debbie, the women from the Rose Room came down to help. While the five women worked at stringing the lights and hanging the ornaments, Lauren shuttled back and forth to the kitchen, refilling the cookie tray and keeping the cider and cocoa mugs full. She noticed that although Jill and Debbie were younger and shy at first, Gaylin wasted no time in including them in the conversation and the fun. Kelly was clearly the center of attention, laughing and joking with everyone. On one of Lauren's trips back from the kitchen she noticed Jill and Debbie had gone.

"Where did they go?" she asked.

"Where do you think?" Kelly said, rolling her eyes upstairs and smiling coyly.

"What happened? Weren't they having a good time?"

"They went upstairs to have a better time." She cackled.

"I hope it wasn't the cocoa. Not everybody likes it so rich."

"That isn't what they wanted to taste," Carly said with a laugh.

"How do you know that?" Lauren finally realized what they meant.

"Jill said so. She said Christmas trees make her horny."

The three women laughed, leaving Lauren with a disapproving expression.

"She actually said that?"

"Yes, she did," Gaylin offered.

"I think they *really* liked decorating the tree." Kelly and Carly laughed again.

"Did this come with the house or does someone play?" Gaylin asked, plinking a note on the piano in the corner.

Carly and Kelly both pointed at Lauren.

"Really? A singer and a pianist in one family."

"I can't play nearly as well as Kelly sings. I'm pretty much a chopsticks kind of pianist."

"You are not," Kelly said, sitting down at the piano. She played a few notes. After a moment, she played the first few chords of "Ave Maria."

"Sing, Kelly," Carly said, sitting on the arm of a nearby chair.

Kelly sang the hymn softly with a pure and intense sincerity, accompanying herself with only a chord or two. Gaylin and Carly watched, enjoying every note. Lauren had heard her sing it before but Kelly's voice never failed to amaze her. When Kelly finished she closed her eyes, savoring the moment.

"Wow." Gaylin applauded. "That was amazing."

Carly went to Kelly and kissed her on the cheek.

"You've still got it, babe."

"Very nice, sis."

"Thank you."

"Can you play that one about mommy kissing Santa?" Carly asked.

"I can try. God, I can't remember." She played a wrong note and made a ghastly face. Lauren reached in and played a few notes to show her.

"You play, Lauren," Gaylin encouraged.

"Yeah, you play." Kelly stood up and steered Lauren onto the bench. Lauren played the first few chords and Kelly began to sing.

It took Lauren a few bars to find the key and the chords to accompany her but soon she was playing like she had been doing it all her life. Carly wrapped her arm around Kelly's waist and joined in singing. Kelly leaned into her, harmonizing. Gaylin tapped her foot and grinned as she watched. Once they were finished, Gaylin applauded and cheered.

"And why aren't you singing along?" Kelly asked, pulling her over to the piano. She sat her down next to Lauren and stood behind her. "Your turn to pick. What shall we sing?"

"I have no idea. Anything."

"It doesn't have to be Christmas."

"Yes, it does," Lauren exclaimed. "We just decorated a Christmas tree."

"Do you always do this on Christmas?" Gaylin asked.

"I never have time. I wish I did." Lauren thought a moment then began to play "White Christmas."

"How about *this one*, Kel?"

"Oh, yes. I love this one," she said and began to sing along. Lauren could hear Gaylin humming along. She nodded her encouragement but Gaylin wouldn't sing.

"I don't sing," she whispered. "I'd sound like a reindeer stuck up the chimney."

Lauren laughed so hard she played wrong notes.

"You couldn't sound any worse than I do," she said, finishing the song with a flourish.

"Hey, look what I found," Carly held up a sprig of mistletoe.

"Where did you find that?" Kelly asked.

"In my pocket." She grinned and held it over her own head. "What do you say, Kelly?"

"I say you're nuts."

"That isn't very nice, sis," Lauren joked, but she knew Carly was pushing her luck to think Kelly would kiss her.

"Yeah, that isn't very nice. It's Christmas. You have to kiss anyone standing under the mistletoe or you'll have bad luck all year."

"Who said that?" Kelly frowned.

"I don't know. One of the wise men. But do you really want to chance it?" Carly waved the sprig over her head.

"Go ahead, Kel. Kiss her and bring us all good luck. We could use it," Lauren spun around on the bench to watch. Gaylin turned also, staring up at them.

Kelly looked down at Gaylin as if seeking permission. Gaylin just smiled.

"Okay, I will. But no tongue, Carly," she warned. She leaned over and kissed her lightly on the lips then pulled away before Carly could become involved with the kiss. "There. Mission accomplished."

"That wasn't a kiss," Carly complained. "You aren't supposed to peck under the mistletoe. You're supposed to kiss." She pulled Kelly to her and kissed her full on the mouth, pouring herself into it. Kelly didn't fight her. She didn't put her arms around her but she didn't pull away either. "Now, *that* is how you kiss under the mistletoe."

Gaylin had watched, nearly expressionless, finally lowering her eyes as they ended the kiss.

"Give me that," Kelly demanded, holding the sprig over Gaylin's head. She then sat down on her lap and kissed her. Gaylin held her on her lap as they kissed. It was obvious Kelly was French kissing her. "Two can play at that game," she said and giggled.

"How about Lauren?" Carly said. "Don't leave her out."

"That's okay." Lauren didn't need a kiss from Carly, but Kelly had already lofted the sprig over Lauren's head. Before Carly could respond, Gaylin leaned over and kissed her, parting her lips just enough to make Lauren moan. When Lauren opened her eyes, Gaylin was still just inches away, her mouth and lips within reach. Lauren couldn't help herself. She leaned into her and kissed Gaylin again. She felt Gaylin's hand caress her back, holding her close.

"Hey, you're going to melt the mistletoe," Carly said, chuckling at them.

"It was your idea." Gaylin took the mistletoe from Kelly and

118

tossed it up to Carly.

"Do you want to come up and see the puppies?" Kelly asked Gaylin.

"Sure."

"I do, too," said Carly.

"Come on." Kelly led the way. "They are so cute. You're going to love them."

"You coming?" Gaylin asked Lauren as she stood up.

"No. I've seen them. You go ahead. I need to load the dishwasher."

"Want some help?"

"No, you go ahead. Kelly is dying to show off her new family."

"Come on, Gaylin," Kelly called from the stairs. "Last one up is a rotten egg."

Lauren carried the dishes to the kitchen and began rinsing them. It didn't take long before she heard footsteps in the hall.

"Little, aren't they?" Gaylin said, coming into the kitchen.

"That was quick. You aren't impressed with Roxie's puppies?"

"Yeah, I am. They are very cute. But the bathroom is a little crowded with three people, a blue puppy pad sprinkled with doggie doo, and a basket full of dogs." She handed Lauren one of the dirty cups from the counter. "Kelly sure is proud of them, isn't she?"

"Lord, yes. You'd think they were her own kids."

"Where does Carly come into the picture, if you don't mind me asking?"

"We've know her for five years."

"That's it? Just a friend? I somehow get the feeling there is more to her story than just a friend." Gaylin handed her the last cup. Lauren rinsed it and set it in the dishwasher before she answered.

"Actually, I've known Carly for five years. I met her right after I bought the inn. Kelly has only known her for four years."

"And?"

Lauren wiped off the counter, dried her hands and hung the towel on the hook.

"Carly and I lived together for just over a year before Kelly met her. Then Carly and Kelly lived together for a little over a year." She took a deep breath and went to snap off the lights in the living room. When she returned, Gaylin was leaning against the counter with her arms crossed.

"I see."

"I doubt you do."

"Carly was in love with you and you were in love with Carly. Then Kelly entered the picture and stole Carly's heart away, leaving Lauren with an ex and Kelly with a new girlfriend."

"Something like that. But I don't harbor any ill feelings anymore."

"What happened? You fell out of love with Carly and Kelly came along to rescue you?"

"No, nothing like that. After seeing Carly with Kelly, I knew we never had that kind of love. We'd never admit it but I think we both were just biding our time until the right person came along."

"What happened with Kelly and Carly after that?"

"After that, I'm not sure. I just know they broke up. Kelly went to LA for a while then moved back to work in Branson. Carly left right after they split up but she recently moved back."

"So they are just friends, right?"

"Yes. More or less."

"Damn. That sounds very civilized. I wasn't sure what was going on. That was a very interesting kiss they shared."

"Someone might say the same thing about our kiss."

"Kisses. We had two."

"I'm sorry about that," Lauren replied.

"I get the feeling it has been a long time since anyone really kissed you."

"I wish I hadn't done it." Lauren walked away. She didn't want to lie to her.

"Are you really?"

Gaylin grabbed her arm and turned her around. She pulled Lauren to her and kissed her again, wrapping her in an overpowering embrace. Lauren gasped and arched her back as if she didn't approve of the kiss. Suddenly, she melted into it, folding her arms around Gaylin's neck. She could feel Gaylin's warm tongue, probing and teasing the inside of her mouth. Gaylin backed her against the counter as she devoured her mouth. She pressed her thigh firmly against Lauren's crotch, holding it there as they kissed. It was a luscious kiss, full of suggestion and possibility.

"Is that what you really wanted?" Gaylin whispered breathlessly.

Lauren was unashamed. She was ready to kiss Gaylin again when they heard Kelly's and Carly's voices coming down the stairs. Gaylin released her, her hands flowing down Lauren's back before she stepped away.

"Kelly is the grandmother of five fur balls," Carly said as she came into the kitchen.

"Yes, I am," Kelly joked. "They are starting to get Roxie's red color."

"Aren't they adorable?" Lauren said, lowering her eyes and then looking up at Gaylin.

"That little one is so cute, sis. She doesn't take shit from the others. She wiggles right in there and latches on to a tit, sucking like crazy. She's going to be a lezbo for sure. By the way, the couple in the Lavender Room wants to know if you have any more blankets. They like to sleep with the window cracked. I told them I'd ask."

"Yes, I do. I'll get them one." Lauren was relieved to have something to bring her mind back from where it had been. Gaylin's lips had taken her halfway to paradise and left her dangling.

"Need some help?" Gaylin asked.

"No, I can get it." She hurried up the stairs, her heart pounding in her chest. *Wow. Now that was a kiss. Bring on the mistletoe.*

121

Christmas Coffee Cake

Kenna's childhood neighbor Betty B's recipe
You'll receive lots of compliments on this easy-to-make breakfast treat.
Freezes beautifully. The aroma while it is baking is amazing.

Serves 6-8

1 cup flour
1/2 cup butter or margarine
1 tablespoon water
Mix together as if for pie crust
Press on cookie sheet in 2 long strips 3 inches wide.

Heat to boiling 1 cup water
And 1/2 cup margarine or butter

Take from heat and stir in 1 cup of flour until smooth
Stir in 3 eggs, one at a time
Add 1 teaspoon almond flavoring
Spread on first mixture strips
Bake at 350 degrees for 50-55 minutes

Frosting
When cool, mix together:
1 cup powdered sugar
1 tablespoon butter
1 teaspoon almond flavoring
Enough cream for frosting

Frost and enjoy.
Serve or freeze. Optionally, you can sprinkle the finished coffee cake top with chopped or sliced maraschino cherries, raisins, almonds or walnut pieces.

Chapter 13

"Good morning, Gaylin. Come in," Lauren said, answering the knock at the front door. Gaylin had her laptop under her arm and a folder in her hand. "If you're looking for Kelly, I'm afraid she isn't here. She went to the store to get dog food."

"No, actually I'm here to see you."

"Me? What can I do for you?" She led the way into the living room.

"I think I've found an issue with the original appraisal done for your mortgage."

"What kind of issue? Is there a problem?" Lauren couldn't stop a twinge of anxiety.

"No, no. It's nothing major. But I think it should be corrected, or at least revisited."

"Now you have my complete attention." Lauren was too

nervous to sit down. Even a small problem was still a problem. Her stomach was tying itself in knots.

"Lauren, really, it isn't anything to get concerned about." Gaylin set her laptop on the coffee table and took Lauren's arm. "Sit down. Relax. You look like you are going to pass out."

"I look like it because I feel like it." Lauren eased down on the sofa, perching on the front edge. "Tell me what's wrong with my mortgage." She rubbed her sweaty palms on her knees and waited while Gaylin's computer booted.

"I was looking at the square footage they listed on your appraisal when you bought the house five years ago. From what you showed me, you haven't increased the footprint of the structure, right?"

"No. I've just redecorated and remodeled."

"Okay." She opened two files, placing them side by side on the screen. "This really isn't something I correct but this is what the county has as your square footage. That is exactly the same figure as the appraisal, to the foot."

"Yes." Lauren leaned in to read it.

"Using this amount, I'm not sure Gypsy Hill will appraise for as much as you need because of the comps I'll have to use."

"I hate to sound dumb but what are comps?"

"I'm sorry. Comps are comparables. I establish value to this bed-and-breakfast by comparing it to other B and Bs of similar size and condition that have sold recently. That's just the way it works. I can't completely pluck the figures out of my head. There are standards I have to use. I can include some variables but my report is based on value by comparison."

"And you think the square footage used for my mortgage is wrong?"

"I don't want to say it's wrong until I remeasure but I have my suspicions. Would you mind if I take a look around?"

"No, I don't mind. Why would I?"

"Because, as you know, the size of the house helps determine your tax base. If we find the figures are wrong and have them corrected, it might cost you more in property taxes. I don't want

124

to do anything without your permission."

"You mean it's a double-edged sword. If they did make a mistake and used a smaller square footage then I've been paying less taxes. If we leave it that way, the house doesn't have as much value because according to the county, it is smaller than it actually is, right?"

"Exactly. This is your decision. I work for the mortgage company. All I am legally obligated to do is research the statistics and make a report based on what I see. An appraiser would assume if you haven't changed the overall footprint of the house or added to the usable living space, the square footage listed is still accurate. I think the first appraiser used the information he found on the books. The old information was probably just eyeballed in the first place and no one ever bothered to check it for accuracy. If you want me to, I can help with this or I can forget it. I'll do whatever you want me to do. It's your call."

"There's really nothing to think about. Please, remeasure. I'll pay the extra taxes, but I want the county records to be accurate. And if it is wrong, what do we do about the appraisal for my original mortgage?"

"Nothing. I can show the correction in my report, justifying the difference in my findings but it will be up to the mortgage company to notify the previous appraiser of any mistake. It all depends on how much of a discrepancy I find."

"Is it possible that a mistake in that first appraisal had anything to do with the higher interest rate they charged me?"

Gaylin shrugged.

"I don't know. Possibly. If they thought the selling price was too high for the appraised value, they might have."

"Will you help me get it corrected?"

"I'd be glad to." She smiled and nodded.

Lauren felt a trust growing with Gaylin, one that reassured her.

"What can I do?" she asked.

"Relax. You look like you're being sent to the principal's office. Trust me. It isn't that bad. I'll take care of it. Let me do some measuring and we'll know where to go from here." Gaylin patted Lauren's thigh. Lauren thought about last night's kiss and struggled to focus on the issue at hand.

"If you find a mistake, do you think the county will demand I pay the difference in back taxes?"

"They can't do that. After all, it's partially their fault. If it were the other way around, they couldn't reimburse an over payment either. You won't have a big arrears bill, if that's what you're worried about. I don't think it's going to work out to be a huge amount anyway. But it will help with my appraisal."

"Are you saying you weren't going to appraise the house high enough for my re-fi?"

"I hadn't established a value yet. I was still working on it when I noticed this. It just didn't feel right, not after I walked through the house and saw it."

"I'm back," Kelly called, coming in the back door. "Is that Gaylin's car out front?"

"We're in here," Lauren called.

"Hi, Gaylin. I didn't know you were coming over." Kelly sat down next to her, folding her arm through Gaylin's. "You should have called. Have you been waiting very long?"

"I came over to talk with Lauren about her appraisal. I need to do some measuring around the house."

"Work, work, work." Kelly looked up at Lauren. "See, I told you."

"Told her what?" Gaylin asked, shutting down her laptop.

"Lauren has you completely consumed with this appraisal thing."

"Oh, she does?" Gaylin smiled and leaned back on the sofa. Kelly leaned back with her.

"Yes. And I'm jealous of it." Kelly pouted melodramatically, sticking her lip out. "I know what I'll do. I'll have you appraise something for me. That way I'll have your undivided attention."

"What makes you think you don't have it already?"

"Oh, I like that. Very good."

"I've got work to do. I've got a house to measure."

126

Kelly jumped up.

"Can I help? Where do we start?"

"I guess we can start upstairs and work our way down." Gaylin pulled a tape measure from her pocket.

"Let me know if you need anything," Lauren said then headed to the kitchen to finish with the breakfast dishes. She was still reeling from their kiss last night. And Gaylin's hand on her thigh didn't do anything to salve that nor did her kind words. Kissing under the mistletoe could be considered innocent fun but the kiss in the kitchen was anything but innocent. Lauren worried just how far they might have gone if Kelly and Carly hadn't walked in, but she had no intention of coming between Gaylin and her sister, no matter how fascinating that kiss was.

"Are you going to answer the phone?" Tallie said from the laundry room where she was folding sheets. Lauren had been too busy daydreaming to hear it.

"Yes, I'll get it." She hurried up to her office. "Good morning. Gypsy Hill. May I help you?"

"Good morning, sweetheart."

"Hello, Mother. It's good to hear from you." Lauren settled into her desk chair with a relieved smile on her face. Even at her age, hearing her mother's voice made her feel secure.

"Did you get the recipes I e-mailed you?" Noel Roberts's voice was wonderful, melodic and deeply joyful.

"Yes, thank you. I tried the lemon butter scones. They were a big hit."

"You can substitute currants for the raisins, but don't go overboard with the cloves. It can overwhelm."

"I've never thought of trying them with cloves in the first place."

"Try everything, darling. You'll never know what is perfect for you unless you experiment. How's Kelly?"

"She's fine. She's upstairs if you want to talk to her."

"Don't bother her. I spoke with her a couple days ago. I just called to see how your plans were coming for your big Christmas dinner. What are you serving?"

"Perhaps beef béarnaise. Coq au vin with Portobello mushrooms. Maybe a lasagna. At least three main dishes. For dessert, fruit flan and petite fours. Maybe chocolate mousse. I wish you were here to help me decide."

"Since when haven't you been able to create a fabulous dinner?" She laughed. "This is what you do, darling. You're good at it."

"Thank you. But this year, I don't know. It seems harder to decide."

"Well, what you have planned sounds exquisite." She sighed. "But you are right. I wish I was there to enjoy it with you."

"I'm sorry you have to work on Christmas, Mother. I miss our Christmases when we were young." Lauren leaned back and closed her eyes. "I miss those times."

"Kelly's there to celebrate with you. You girls should savor these Christmases together. You won't always have them."

"I know."

"What's wrong, sweetheart? I hear something in your voice. I'm a mother. I know when you are upset."

"I'm not upset, Mother. We were just talking about Christmas."

"Are you and Kelly getting along all right?"

"Sure."

"I know you two have had some problems in the past but whatever it is, remember, you will always be sisters. Cherish that, sweetheart."

"I know mother. I know. Kelly and I are having a great time together. I'm glad she is here for the holidays." Lauren could hear someone arguing in the background.

"Sweetheart, I have to go. The hollandaise is curdling. I will talk with you again soon." She hung up.

"Yes, Mother. Kelly and I are getting along just dandy," Lauren muttered as she hung up.

"Lauren?" Gaylin called, looking in from the hall. "Kelly said she needs you upstairs." She had a pad of paper covered with figures.

128

"Did she say what she wants?"

"I'll let her tell you. You didn't hear it from me, but she isn't a happy camper."

"I'll go see." Lauren slowly went upstairs, expecting Kelly to lecture her about letting the appraisal come between her and Gaylin, but when she knocked and opened the door, Kelly was sprawled on the floor, looking under the bed.

"Did you need me?"

"Yes!" Kelly jumped to her feet and took Lauren by the arm, pulling her into the bathroom. "Look at that!" she demanded.

"Look at what?" Lauren saw Roxie curled up in her bed with her nursing puppies crowded around her.

"What do you see?"

"It's feeding time?"

"Count the puppies," Kelly said gruffly.

"Okay." Lauren squatted next to the dog bed and counted. She looked up at Kelly and frowned. "Where's the other one? Is she sitting on it?"

"No, Roxie is not sitting on it. It's gone. I've looked everywhere."

Lauren ran her hand along Roxie's back, feeling for the fifth puppy.

"I already did that. Someone stole it."

"How could someone steal a puppy? No one should even know they're up here."

"Well, they did. The puppies are too small to climb out of the box. It's too deep. One of your fucking guests stole one of Roxie's babies. And I want it back. Look at poor Roxie. She's traumatized." Kelly squatted next to the box, petting Roxie affectionately. "I know, baby. I know."

"You've looked everywhere in here," Lauren asked, checking the edge of the box. "Maybe one got stuck under the blanket."

"That's the first place I checked. I took the blanket out and unfolded it. I checked under the bed, behind the dresser, in the closet. I've checked every inch of this room and no puppy. All five of them were here this morning. I'm absolutely sure of it. You know what really pisses me off? The thief took the littlest one. She was so small, Lauren." Kelly had genuine emotion for the lost puppy glistening in her eyes. "She'll never survive without Roxie nursing her. She was so sweet." Tears began to run down Kelly's cheek. "And I want her back."

"Ah, honey, we'll find her." Lauren squeezed her hand. "I can't very well put out an APB for a puppy though."

"Call them and tell them to bring her back. I'm not fooling around. I'm calling the cops if they don't."

"Wait, call who?"

"The shithead guest that checked out with my dog. Who do you think? Or they are still here and she is hidden away in their room. I want every room searched. Every piece of luggage, every tote bag, every closet. You should start by calling the ones that checked out. That's probably who has her. I'm sure of it."

"I am not calling anyone. You don't know who or even if someone took the puppy and I'm certainly not going to accuse one of my clientele."

"Then give me the phone numbers and I'll call them."

"Absolutely not! Kelly, you can't accuse someone like that."

"The hell I can't. I want Roxie's baby back."

"I'm not giving you the phone numbers and you are not calling my guests. You are not Dirty Harry and this isn't a drug heist. You have no idea where that puppy is." Lauren held up a cautionary finger at Kelly. "And don't you dare say one word to any of the guests. You hear me? Not one word."

"Lauren, do you know how much that puppy is worth?" Kelly looked like the veins on her neck were about to explode.

"Calm down. Let's reexamine what happened. Are you positive you saw *all* five puppies this morning?"

"Positive."

"Okay. Where were they?"

"Right there in the box. I put each one back before I locked the door."

"Put them back from where?"

"I was playing with them on the bed."

"You had them on the bed?" Lauren resisted the urge to roll her eyes. "Kelly, I asked you not to do that."

"Get over yourself, sis. That has nothing to do with the stolen puppy."

Lauren went to the bed and checked along the edge of the headboard then pulled back the bedspread.

"I told you I already looked there. And under the bed, too."

Lauren believed her but she conducted a cursory search of the room anyway to satisfy herself that she had exhausted every possibility.

"Now do you believe me?" Kelly said, leaning on the doorjamb with her arms crossed. "Can we quit wasting time and go check the other rooms?"

"I'll check the empty rooms but we are not searching the occupied ones. That would give my guests the impression that I think one of them is guilty. And how do I explain that pets aren't allowed in Gypsy Hill but oh, by the way, we've misplaced a puppy?"

"Fine. I'm calling the police." Kelly pulled her cell phone from her pocket.

"Kelly, NO. You are not calling the police and accusing anyone. And besides, what makes you think anyone would steal one of your dogs? I've got antiques sitting around the inn and the most I've ever had stolen was a salt shaker. Unless that puppy unlocked the door and crawled downstairs all by herself, no one could have taken her."

"How do you know that?" Kelly snapped. "You weren't up here."

"No, but you were the last one to come down to breakfast and the first one to leave. Everyone else was already seated."

"How do you know someone didn't sneak upstairs when your back was turned? You were in and out of the kitchen. Someone could have gotten by you in all the confusion."

"I doubt it. But I'll ask Tallie if she saw anything. She came in early this morning."

"Ah-ha. Tallie!" Kelly's eyes flashed. "Where is she? She had access to the room."

"Kelly, no. Tallie would never do that. I trust her implicitly. Besides, she already has three dogs, big ones. Why would she want a miniature Dachshund?"

"I don't know but I'm going to ask her."

"You are not! You are not accusing anyone, especially not Tallie. Maybe Roxie did it. Maybe she hid it somewhere.

"Then why didn't she hide them all? And why didn't she bring it back to feed it? No, Roxie didn't do it."

"Well, I'll tell Tallie to keep an eye out for it, and I'll tactfully ask around but you have to promise to let me handle this. I don't want to ruffle anyone's feathers."

"How about Roxie's feathers? Who is going to tell her one of her babies has been puppy-napped?"

"I think she already knows, Kel." She nodded toward Roxie sitting in the doorway, looking up at them with sad eyes. Kelly picked her up and cuddled her, stroking her coat.

"That tiny puppy isn't old enough to be out on its own." Kelly swallowed hard as tears once again filled her eyes. "She won't survive. She'll starve, Lauren."

"Maybe she'll turn up. We can always hope." Lauren rubbed Kelly's arm.

"The poor little thing," Tallie said when Lauren told her what happened. "It won't last very long without its mother."

"It was the runt of the litter. She was barely a handful." Lauren felt a twinge of sorrow. Kelly and Tallie were right. The puppy didn't stand much of a chance without its mother. She was afraid if it wasn't found soon, it wouldn't be found alive.

"Poor little thing."

"Keep an eye out for it. I don't want a guest to find it, especially if it's dead."

"I will." She fished her key ring from her apron pocket. "I'm going to check all the rooms."

Lauren scowled.

"You can't accuse anyone of anything."

"I'm not. I'm just checking to see if I left enough towels." She gave Lauren a devious little wink.

When Lauren got back downstairs, Gaylin had completed her measurements and was entering them on her laptop.

"Did she tell you what happened?" Gaylin asked, copying from her pad.

"Yes. I can't imagine where that puppy could be. I can't believe anyone would steal it. They would have to know it is too young to be taken from its mother."

"I mentioned that to her. But she was positive someone broke in and took it. We looked everywhere."

"Me, too. You don't suppose Roxie did something with it? You know, if it hadn't survived. It was awfully little."

"I don't know. But you'd think there would be some trace of it. I mean where could she bury it in a bedroom?" Gaylin said, trying to sound delicate.

"I'm going to be a nervous wreck until we find it. I don't want someone to open a closet and find a dead puppy."

"I hope the puppy turns up." Gaylin smiled at her, closed her computer, and tucked it under her arm. "I think I'm done here. I have more calculations, but right now, I've got to run by my office." She touched Lauren's arm affectionately. "Don't worry. I'll let you know what I come up with."

"Thank you."

"I'm glad I could help."

She strode out to the car and pulled away. Lauren stood at the window in her office until the sound of her SUV had faded. She should be worried about the appraisal, but the thought that Gaylin was taking care of the problem reassured her. However, the puppy was another story.

Basic Crepe Recipe
Kenna's family recipe

Makes 8 crepes

2 eggs
1 cup flour
1 cup skim milk
2 tablespoons melted butter (or vegetable oil)
1/8 teaspoon salt

In mixing bowl, whisk together flour and eggs. Gradually add in milk. Add salt and butter (or oil). Beat until smooth. Refrigerate for at least 1 hour. Heat a lightly oiled frying pan over medium high heat. (May use a griddle) Pour or scoop the batter onto the griddle, using approximately 1/4 cup for each crepe. Tilt the pan with a circular motion so that the batter coats the surface evenly. Cook the crepe for about 2 minutes, until the bottom is light brown. Loosen with a spatula, turn and cook the other side. Serve hot with syrup and your favorite topping.

Fruit Topping

Wash fresh fruit and drain. Anything will work—strawberries, blueberries, blackberries, etc. Frozen fruit berries may be used. Place fruit in medium saucepan over medium heat. No water is needed since most fruit makes its own. If you do need moisture, add only a very small amount at a time. Add sugar (or Splenda) to taste, 1 – 2 teaspoons per cup of topping Simmer 15 minutes and serve over crepes.

Chapter 14

"Any word on the lost puppy?" Tallie asked, mopping her way across the kitchen floor.

"Not yet." Lauren stood at the sink, dabbing a towel down her shirt. "And Kelly isn't happy about it. I think she blames me. That's why she has been up in her room all afternoon."

"What happened to you?"

"I spilled my soup."

"Tomato? Soak the shirt in cold water."

"That's a good idea. I'd better go change." She headed for her bedroom.

Once in her bathroom she peeled off the shirt, and ran water over it in the bathroom sink, before going to the closet for a clean one. The closet door was open a few inches but she didn't think anything about it. As she opened it, Cleo, curled among her shoes, meowed up at her.

"What are you doing in here? You're lucky you didn't get locked in. Find someplace else to sleep." Lauren waved at her but Cleo didn't move. Instead, she meowed again. "Come on, Cleo. Get out of the closet. Scoot." When she reached down to shoo her away, she saw a tiny brown fuzz ball curled up next to her. "Cleo, are you stealing socks again?" Cleo winked at her.

The fuzz ball moved. "That's no sock! Cleo Roberts? What have you done? You're the thief!" The tiny puppy was squealing and frantically sucking at Cleo's milkless tit.

"Oh, sweetheart. You aren't going to get anything from that spigot," Lauren whispered, picking it up and cradling it in two hands. She rubbed its warm body against her cheek and scowled down at Cleo.

"You are a bad kitty! Bad, bad!"

Cleo meowed.

"Let's get you back up to your mommy." She set the puppy on the carpet and quickly slipped into a clean shirt. As soon as she put the puppy down, Cleo came rushing out of the closet, snatching the puppy up in her mouth and trotting out of the bedroom, the puppy hanging by the scruff of its neck.

"Cleo, come back here!" Lauren ran after her.

Cleo led her through the kitchen, dining room, around the coffee table, over the sofa in the living room, and down the hall before scampering up the stairs.

"Cleo, stop this instant and put that puppy down," she demanded, racing to keep up with her. But the cat darted around corners just as the door to the Rose Room opened and Cleo ran through. "Stop that cat!"

Before the woman could react, Cleo bolted between her legs and disappeared inside the room.

"Sorry!" The woman jumped out of the way.

"Where did she go?" Lauren peeked inside the room.

"Under the bed," another woman said. She was dressed only in a bra and panties as she came out of the bathroom.

"Oh, gosh. I'm sorry for interrupting."

The woman in the underwear shrugged. "That's fine. You go

under from that side. I'll go around this way. Maybe we can trap them in the middle," she said, immediately going to her knees and pulling back the bed skirt.

Lauren knelt and looked under the bed.

"Come on, Cleo. Give it up, you naughty kitty. Kelly is going to roast your whiskers over this."

"Here, kitty, kitty," the woman called, reaching under as far as she could. "Can you reach her? I can't."

Lauren lay down on her stomach and wedged herself as far under as the bedframe would allow.

"No. She's just out of reach. Come on, Cleo. Cooperate. Bring me the puppy."

Cleo seemed to know the exact middle of the bed where neither side could reach her. She set the puppy down and began washing it.

"What's a cat doing with a puppy?" the woman asked, finding the situation funny.

"It's a long story," Lauren said, muffled by the bed skirt. "Cleo, you are being a real pain in the derriere." She lunged but couldn't reach the puppy. "I'm really sorry about this. Cleo doesn't usually do this kind of thing."

Actually, she had. Last summer she had brought a partially consumed bird into the kitchen. She placed it proudly on the mat in front of the sink like it was a present for Lauren. She just prayed Cleo didn't plan on hurting the puppy, especially right in front of a pair of guests.

"How about sticking something under there? Like a broom or something?" Barb said.

"You don't want to hurt them," her partner scoffed.

"I didn't mean poke them. We could kind of sweep them out or at least over to one side so we could reach them."

"Good idea," Lauren said, hurrying out to the linen closet to find a broom. She returned and inserted the handle, being careful not to scare Cleo or her captive. She pulled the handle up next to Cleo but she stepped over it then grabbed the puppy in her teeth and raced out the open door. "Good grief! There she goes. Thanks for your help."

Lauren took off after the cat. Cleo galloped down the hall and up the stairs to the third floor, the puppy swinging back and forth from her mouth. As soon as Lauren got to the top of the stairs, she could hear Roxie barking from inside Kelly's room. Kelly was scolding her and trying to quiet her.

"Open the door, Kelly," Lauren called as Cleo skulked along the wall, looking for a place to hide with the puppy.

"What?" Kelly said, opening the door and peering out into the hall. Cleo darted inside. "Roxie's puppy!"

"Grab her." Lauren lunged for the cat but missed and fell flat on the floor. Kelly swiped at it too but tripped over Lauren, falling on top of her. Roxie continued to bark, wagging her tail as she chased Cleo and the puppy around the room. Cleo jumped up on the bed, scattering Kelly's sheet music in all directions. Roxie put her front paws on the side of the bed and barked furiously, hopping and jumping as she tried to get up.

Lauren kicked the door shut with her foot, trapping Cleo so she couldn't escape.

"Grab Roxie. I'll get Cleo," she said.

"Come here, Roxie." Kelly tried to grab the dog but she ran back and forth, staying just out of her reach.

Cleo dropped the puppy. She folded her ears back and bared her teeth, hissing at Roxie's frantic barking.

"Get the puppy," Kelly screamed over Roxie's barking.

"I'm trying."

Lauren diverted Cleo's attention with one hand while she snatched the puppy with the other. Roxie immediately came to her side, jumping against her leg.

"I've got her, Roxie." Lauren carried the puppy into the bathroom and placed it in the box so Roxie could examine it. Roxie jumped in the box, began licking it, and lay down so all the babies could nurse. The rescued puppy latched on to a tit and began sucking frantically.

"How did Cleo get the puppy?" Kelly asked.

"I don't know but I bet she snuck in when you weren't

looking."

"Where did she take it?" She looked back at Cleo angrily.

"In the bottom of my closet. She was trying to nurse it. The poor little thing was sucking like crazy but wasn't getting anything."

"Bad cat," Kelly said, wagging a finger at the cat. Cleo hopped down from the bed and came to the bathroom door. "Don't even think about it, fur ball."

"Cleo, I'm ashamed of you. You leave the puppies alone. You are not their mommy." Lauren frowned at her then ruffled her fur. "Roxie can take care of them without your help." Cleo went to the edge of the box and looked in. Roxie kept a wary eye on her, but didn't bark.

"I'm surprised Roxie is letting her that close," Kelly said.

"I'm surprised Roxie didn't stop her from taking one." She smiled over at Kelly. "Well, are you happy now? All your puppies are back with their mama."

"Yes. I am. And you stay out of my room, Cleo." Kelly scowled, then gave a little smile. "I'll have to call Gaylin and tell her Roxie's puppy has been found. I know. I'll run over and tell her in person."

"Have you been to her house before?"

"No. But I think tonight is a good night for it." Kelly winked then went to the closet to change.

Lauren picked up Cleo and headed for the door.

"Don't you think you should call first?"

"No. I want to surprise her. Maybe I can talk her into going out for a drink or something." Kelly had pulled off her shirt and pants and was standing in the open closet door in her bra and panties. "What do you think I should get Gaylin for Christmas? Nothing big, but something."

"I have no idea. By the way, I got an e-mail from mom. She shipped a package to us. She said it should be delivered around noon on Christmas Eve. She wants us to open it together."

"I bet it's fudge again."

"Maybe."

"What do you think of this?" Kelly held up a white fuzzy cashmere sweater with a plunging neckline.

"Nice. But don't you think you might be a little chilly in that? It's cold outside."

"Chilly enough for the headlights to come on." Kelly giggled.

"That too."

"I want to look nice for Gaylin. How about black jeans?" She held up a pair Lauren recognized as her skintight ones that looked like they were painted on.

"Tell Gaylin I said hello," Lauren said, heading out the door.

"Where are you going? I want your opinion."

"I've got a lot of work to do before breakfast tomorrow. You can get dressed by yourself. Come on, Cleo. Let's leave Roxie's puppies alone so they can have their dinner." Lauren had no intention of helping Kelly select the clothes of a seductress.

She returned to her office to finish her work, and then to the kitchen to finish the pre-breakfast prep. By ten o'clock she had turned out the lights and stepped into a hot bath, all the while keeping an ear out for sounds of Kelly's return. Just after three, she climbed out of bed and went to the window. Kelly's parking space was empty. A gentle snow had covered the parking lot. No tire tracks. Kelly hasn't been home. She's still out with Gaylin, *she thought*. Normally, it would be a good night for sleeping, cuddled beneath a warm comforter, but not tonight, not with the image of Gaylin's soft lips and warm embrace keeping her sister warm. Lauren leaned her forehead against the windowpane and felt her eyes well up with tears.

"Merry Christmas, Kelly. And please, take good care of this one," she whispered against the glass before climbing back into bed.

Great Pie Crust

Kenna's Recipe

Makes 2 9-inch pie crusts

This pie crust makes a wonderful base for a Quiche
(Pre-bake the crust to use for a quiche)

3 cups all-purpose flour
1 teaspoon salt
1 1/4 cups shortening
1 egg, beaten
1 tablespoon distilled white vinegar
4 tablespoons water

In large bowl mix flour and salt. Cut cold shortening into mixture with pastry blender until resembles coarse crumbs. In separate bowl, mix together egg, vinegar and ice water. Drizzle wet mixture into dry mixture, cutting it in. Chill dough ball for 30 minutes. Roll out dough, and fit into two 9-inch pie pans. Bake at 425 degrees F for 12 minutes.

Chapter 15

The next morning Lauren stayed busy during breakfast. She served up plates of food and talked to her guests, trying not to think about the fact that Kelly had been gone all night. After all, she was a big girl. She could take care of herself. But Lauren couldn't help scan the parking lot on her way past the window. The grandfather clock was striking ten when Kelly finally roared up the drive. Lauren was in her office when she heard the back door slam and Kelly's footsteps in the hall.

"Good morning, Kel. Do you want some breakfast? I've got biscuits and gravy left over. There might be a little bacon, too."

"No, I'm not hungry," she said wistfully.

Oh, yes. You definitely have an afterglow, sis.

"Did you have a nice time?" She wasn't sure she really wanted to know.

Kelly gave a wicked grin.

"Yes, I did. Very nice." She slowly pulled her scarf off her neck, fanned herself with it, and laughed wildly. "Say, do you have any rooms available? It can be anything. The Crimson Room. The Lavender Room. It doesn't matter. I assume the Rose Room and the cottage are reserved."

"For when?"

"Tonight and tomorrow night."

"If you're talking about for yourself, I told you I didn't want to be moving you all over the house, especially now that Roxie has had her puppies. I don't want anyone else knowing they are here."

"It isn't for me." Kelly took off her coat and draped it over her arm. She was still wearing the white cashmere sweater and skintight jeans from last night. Deep in the valley of her cleavage was a rosebud-shaped hickey.

"Who is the room for?"

"Gaylin."

"What does Gaylin want with a room?" The only thing Lauren could think of was she wanted to be closer to Kelly so they could have sex more often.

"She had some sewer problems."

"Yes, I know."

"Well, they got worse. Sometime during the night her sewer line broke and flooded her backyard. They had to shut off her water to fix it. She can't stay in her house. I told her to come stay with me but she won't do it. She's too proud. Even though it will only be for two nights, she insists on paying for a motel. I said I'd see if you had a room available."

"Wait a minute and I'll check." Lauren allowed her computer to finish its update so she could check her reservations.

"Don't bother to offer a reduced room rate. She said she wants to pay full rate or she won't stay here. God, she is so stubborn. I think it's cute." Kelly smiled. "While you're checking that, I'm going to go take a quick shower."

"If I have something available should I call her?" Lauren's eyes drifted down Kelly's cleavage for a last look at the hickey

Gaylin had given her.

"No. I will. Could you come up and tell me?" Kelly said then went upstairs.

Lauren checked her reservations and hurried up to Kelly's room.

"Kelly, it's me," Lauren said, knocking on her door.

Kelly opened the door and waved her in as she talked on her cell phone. She was dressed in the black jeans and bra.

"I told you, John, I can't wear yellow. It washes me out. No, I want blue lamé for that number. Well, at least a jacket. No, lamé performs by itself. It doesn't need buttons or a belt. Okay. I'll be there tomorrow. Yes, ten o'clock." She hung up and tossed the cell phone on the bed. "He's an idiot. I told him a hundred times no yellow. I can't wear yellow." She rolled her eyes. "What did you find?"

"The Lavender Room is available for both nights. It wasn't but I had a cancellation two days ago."

"That's the smallest room, isn't it?"

"Yes, but it's all I have."

Lauren had mixed feelings about renting to Gaylin. She'd love to have her sleeping under her roof, but knowing she and Kelly might sleep together was a bitter pill to swallow. Gaylin may have insisted on her own room but Lauren knew her sister. If Kelly set her mind to sharing a bed with someone, nothing was going to stop her. Certainly not a door.

Kelly pulled her hair back and attached a ponytail holder.

Damn, she has a hickey behind her ear, too. Couldn't she leave her hair down so I don't have to see it?

Kelly quickly dialed Gaylin on her cell. "It's all set. You have a room," she said, grinning at the voice on the other end of the line. "Yes, I told her that. I told her you insisted on paying full price." Kelly rolled her eyes. She covered the receiver and whispered at Lauren. "She looked online. She knows how much it is supposed to cost."

"I put the reservation in her name on my Web Site but I'm not going to take her money. She can forget it."

"Lauren said she put the reservation in your name online. You did?" She laughed then turned to Lauren. "She saw it and already paid with her credit card. She'll be over later. She wants to make sure they get started on the trenching first."

"Any time. Her room is ready and waiting for her." Even though she wasn't happy about taking Gaylin's money, Lauren felt a twinge of girlish excitement. Gaylin was coming to spend the night.

It was after dinner when Gaylin finally checked in. Lauren helped her carry her suitcase, briefcase, a box of papers and a tote bag up to the Lavender Room.

"I really wish you would have let me give you a preferred customer rate," Lauren said, unlocking the door.

"Nope. I told Kelly I didn't want any special favors. But thanks for having a room available. I'm sure it will be more comfortable than one of the motels out on the highway."

"Don't thank me. Thank the Emersons from Memphis. They canceled."

"You can put that box anywhere. Sorry I had to bring so much stuff but I do a lot of work from home."

"No problem. A lot of people bring their work with them. I have Wi-Fi if you need it."

"Yes. That would be very helpful."

"You should have everything you need in here," she said, snapping on the light and guiding Gaylin around the room. "Towels, shampoo, conditioner, lotion. There is a robe on the back of the door. Extra blanket in the bottom drawer. You'll find candy and mints in the dish on the desk. Help yourself. I've got drinks in the kitchen. There are always homemade cookies in the cake stand on the counter. I make them fresh daily. Towels for the hot tub are in the cabinet in the mudroom. It is available from nine a.m. to ten p.m. Breakfast is served from eight thirty to nine thirty in the dining room. Let me know if you have any special dietary needs." Lauren rattled off the guest information as she checked the bathroom, adjusted the curtains and snapped on the bedside lamp. Gaylin had set her suitcase on the luggage rack and was watching her with a curious smile.

"Is that the speech you give all your guests?"

"Yes." Lauren chuckled. "It just comes out automatically. Can I get you anything?"

"No, thanks. I'm good. I think I'll unpack and see if I can find my phone charger."

"I'll leave you alone then. I'll be in the kitchen if you need anything."

"Gaylin?" Kelly said brightly, coming in the room without knocking. "I thought I heard your voice. Did you bring your bathing suit like I told you? I checked the hot tub and it's all set. You'll love it."

"I'd love to, Kelly, but I've got a mountain of work to catch up on this evening. I'm two days behind because of that sewer trouble. How about tomorrow night?"

"Promise?"

"Yep, promise."

Lauren went downstairs, leaving Kelly and Gaylin alone. She kept herself busy with preparations for the Christmas dinner. That didn't stop her from noticing that Gaylin and Kelly didn't come downstairs. Later, Lauren hurried through a bath and climbed into bed, snuggling the comforter around her shoulders. It was late and she was tired, but she couldn't help listening for sounds that meant Gaylin and Kelly were sleeping together. The bed in the Lavender Room was directly over her bed. Many a night she had been awakened by the sounds of that bed creaking. She had told herself she should replace it with one that didn't creak and squeak with every rise and fall of the human body. Tonight she wished she had. She didn't want to hear Gaylin and Kelly making love. She held her breath and listened but didn't hear anything. They must be up in Kelly's room, she thought before turning over and going to sleep.

"Good morning. Can I help?" Gaylin said, striding into the kitchen, fresh from the shower. The edges of her hair were still wet.

"Good morning. You're up early. It's only six fifteen."

"I'm usually an early riser."

"I'm afraid Kelly isn't."

"She said she had a costume fitting in Branson this morning. I thought I'd watch the master at work in the kitchen." Gaylin held the door while Lauren collected eggs and a bottle of buttermilk. "What's on the menu this morning? Can I help you with anything? You just have to remember I'm not a very good cook."

"Have you ever made a pie crust?"

"Eat a pie. Yes. Make one? No. Can you make pie crust?"

"I'd like to have a dollar for every pie crust I've made." She pushed up the sleeves of her shirt and set her rings on the windowsill. "Pie crust is the base for my quiche."

"I didn't know that. Your quiche is delicious. I should find a way to include them in the appraisal."

"They aren't hard to make. Would you like to learn?"

Gaylin shrugged fearfully.

"Come on. I'll teach you how to make a pie crust." Lauren patted Gaylin's shoulder. "Wash your hands."

"Are you sure about this? Word may get out your pastry chef is terrible and your business may plummet."

"I doubt it." Lauren laughed. "First, you measure out three cups of flour into this bowl." She set the canister in front of her.

"Three cups of flour." Gaylin measured it carefully like a scientist measuring critical chemicals.

"Okay. Now add one teaspoon of salt." Lauren handed her the measuring spoon.

"One teaspoon salt." She repeated, meticulously pouring the salt into the spoon. She looked at Lauren for approval. "Okay."

"Yes." She took Gaylin's hand and dumped the contents of the spoon into the bowl, trying not to giggle at how seriously Gaylin was taking this. "A few grains of salt one way or the other won't make a difference."

"But you said one teaspoon. Now what?" Gaylin looked over the ingredients spread across the counter.

Lauren handed her a wooden spoon.

"Give it a little stir and then you can cut in the shortening."

"Am I going to sound dumb if I say I don't know how to cut in shortening? Do I use a knife?"

"Nope. You use this." Lauren held up a pastry cutter.

"Oh! I never knew what that was! I think I have one in my kitchen drawer."

Gaylin took it and began smashing the cutter into the bowl. Bits of flour and shortening flew out in all directions.

"Wait, wait! Easy does it, superwoman." She put her hand on Gaylin's to show her the technique. "All you do is rock it through the shortening. You cut it into the flour, don't smash it into oblivion."

"Wasn't I doing that?"

"Almost. Making a pie crust is not a contact sport." Lauren continued to guide Gaylin's hand, gently rocking it across the bottom of the bowl. "You want to make coarse crumbs. You don't want to overwork it." Lauren glanced up and smiled to herself. She's not watching the bowl. She's focused on me. "Are you paying attention?"

"Uh-huh."

"No, you aren't." Lauren gave her hand a playful slap and giggled. "If you want to pass pie crust class, you're going to have to buckle down."

"Yes, ma'am. I do." Gaylin leaned into her work, concentrating intently.

"Okay, now, in a separate bowl you whisk one egg and add one tablespoon white vinegar and four tablespoons of cold water."

"I can do that. I can definitely whisk. I've heard that term before."

"Let me see your technique before I turn you loose with the equipment," Lauren teased, handing her the whisk.

Gaylin broke the egg into the bowl and began whisking it.

"How's this, teacher?"

"Very nice. Good elbow extension. And adequate derriere rotation." Lauren grinned.

148

"Am I doing that butt shake thing?" Gaylin laughed. "My mom did that when she made brownies."

"Yes, you are. It's very cute. All really great chefs have a butt shake when they stir. It goes with the job. The thicker the consistency of what they're stirring, the more radical the butt shake."

"Like this?" She continued to whisk and shake.

"You've got excellent technique. Enough to balance the arm movement and still be a tad naughty."

She wasn't kidding. Gaylin's little butt shake was more than a bit suggestive. It was down right sensuous. It was turning Lauren on big time.

"Now what do I do?" Gaylin asked, still vigorously whisking the egg.

"Huh?" Lauren's eyes were on Gaylin's butt. "Oh, water and vinegar."

"I got that." Gaylin smiled at Lauren as if she knew she had been staring at her bottom. "What else?"

Lauren pulled her eyes away and took a deep breath as a hot flash raced up her body. For a moment her mind went blank. She had no idea what they were doing or what was next. *Focus, girl.*

"Okay. Now we drizzle the wet mixture into the dry mixture."

"Could you show me?" Gaylin's soft voice rang in her ears.

"You just sprinkle it around over the top, a few tablespoons at a time. Like this." Lauren was glad she had something to do to keep her eyes off Gaylin's ass.

"After you get the wet mixed in, then what do you do?"

"If I have time, I refrigerate the ball of dough for about thirty minutes before I roll it. I'll mix the quiche ingredients while it chills." Lauren covered the dough ball with plastic wrap and set it in the refrigerator.

"What goes in the quiche?"

"Eggs, mushrooms, cheese and some chopped spinach. Would you like to mix it?"

"No. I think I'll quit while I'm ahead. I don't want to ruin breakfast for everyone." She leaned her elbows on the end of the counter to watch. "I'll let the master do her thing."

"I don't consider myself a master." Lauren added the ingredients to the bowl, something she could do almost without looking.

"That's not what Kelly says. She thinks you're quite a chef. I have to agree with her. But I'm not much of an expert. I eat peanut butter right out of the jar."

"You don't cook at all?"

"A little. I can make hamburger casserole." Gaylin grinned and flashed her green eyes. "And I can make a mean grilled cheese and pickle sandwich."

"Grilled cheese and pickle?"

"Yep. American cheese and sliced dill pickles. Yum. Someday I'll share my recipe with you."

"Pickles on a cheese sandwich. That I have to see."

It didn't take long for Lauren to have two quiches ready for the oven. She moved on to making oatmeal raisin muffins.

"Can I ask a question? Kind of personal." Gaylin said, absently stacking the measuring cups.

"Shoot."

"Who is older? You or Kelly?"

Lauren thought a minute. This wasn't the strangest question she could ask but it seemed to come out of the blue. She wondered if Kelly had said something.

"Why do you ask?"

"Just curious. Kelly won't tell me."

"Here. Make yourself useful. Put one in each cup." She placed the muffin papers and muffin pan in front of Gaylin.

"So, are you going to tell me or not? What's the big secret? How old can you be? Thirty? Thirty-two?" She placed the papers in the pan.

"I'm thirty-six." Lauren continued to mix with one hand while she added ingredients with the other.

"And Kelly?"

"What did she say?"

150

"Kelly said she was as young as she felt. That's a direct quote. She did say you were her older sister."

Lauren chuckled to herself. Yes, Kelly was still doing it.

"Well, how much younger is she? One year? Two?" She finished the job and slid the pan across the counter.

"Kelly isn't younger. She's older by two years. She's thirty-eight."

"Really? Why the mystique?"

"Her career. She thinks she needs to be as young as possible for as long as possible. A clerk at the DMV made a mistake on her driver's license about ten years ago. She liked being four years younger than she actually was so she didn't have it corrected. She doesn't lie about it, she just allows people to think she's four years younger."

"And you don't say anything."

"If she needs those four years to extend her singing career, I have no reason to stop her."

"You're a good sister."

"How about you? Any brothers or sisters?"

"Nope. I'm an only child."

"Am I being too personal if I ask how old you are?" Lauren asked, pouring batter into the muffin papers.

"Forty-one. Forty-two in February."

"You sound proud of your age."

"I am. I don't need to hide anything. And neither should you. You don't look thirty-six. That's why I ask. I didn't think you were the older sister. If anything, I thought you might be twins."

"Twins?" Lauren laughed out loud. "Now that's funny."

"Why? You are a gorgeous woman, Lauren. Fresh, sophisticated, radiant."

"Thank you." Lauren blushed. "But Kelly is the one who deserves the compliments. She works very hard to look stunning. And she does a good job of it."

"You are very proud of her, aren't you?"

"Yes. Why shouldn't I be? She's talented and she applies it well. You may have heard her sing in my living room but that's nothing compared to hearing her on stage." Lauren smiled proudly at Gaylin. "She's really good. I'm not just saying that because I'm her sister. She has the voice and the charisma to hold an audience like nothing you've ever seen."

"I'm looking forward to seeing that."

"If you're planning on going to the new show this spring, wait until they've had a few performances. Kelly hits the ground running but the others sometimes have a little trouble settling into a new show. She never recommends the first week or so."

"Anything else I can do to help?" Gaylin went to the sink and began washing dishes.

"I'll do that."

"I helped make the mess. You do the creative stuff. I'll do the cleanup."

"You are my guest. You don't need to wash dishes." Lauren pushed her way into the sink. "I'll do it."

"No, you won't." Gaylin picked Lauren up around the waist and set her aside.

"Gaylin, I've got a routine. I'll do it. You get yourself a cup of coffee." She grabbed Gaylin by the waistband of her jeans and pulled playfully. "Now move it, woman."

Gaylin held on to the sink defiantly.

"Nu-uh." She chuckled.

"Uh-huh." Lauren wrapped her arms around Gaylin and tried to move her. Gaylin's rear was pressed against Lauren's crotch. Gaylin wiggled, trying to shake Lauren off but she hung on, tightening her grip. "Let go of that sink!"

"Nope. You can't make me." They were both giggling and tugging, Lauren trying to pull her away, Gaylin holding on for dear life.

"Yes, I can. This calls for drastic measures." She tickled Gaylin's side, who jumped and let go.

"No fair," Gaylin giggled.

"In the kitchen, all's fair in love and war." Lauren pushed her aside and took her place at the sink. "Now, go get a cup of coffee and let me finish."

"What if I did that to you?"

"Do what? Tickle me? Go right ahead." Lauren raised an arm, exposing her side. "Help yourself."

"Okay, I will." Gaylin tickled her but nothing happened, not even a flinch. "Hey!"

"I'm not ticklish."

"That's a bummer. Everybody is ticklish somewhere. Where's your spot?"

"I don't have one. I've never been ticklish. Not my feet. Not my sides. Not anywhere."

"I don't believe you. There has to be someplace."

"Nope, sorry."

"I have half a mind to find out for myself. Everybody has some secret spot that drives them nuts." Gaylin leaned her elbows on the counter and looked up at Lauren. "If I weren't a nice person, I'd find yours."

Lauren wasn't sure if she was joking or not, but the idea of Gaylin searching for that spot made her knees weak. Lauren did have a spot only found in the heat of passion. It wasn't a tickle spot but someplace she loved to have touched. It was a place only a few women had ever found and when they did, it drove her wild.

"I guess I better get going," Gaylin said. "I've got to be in Lone Star by eight thirty."

"Aren't you going to have breakfast? It's almost ready. After all, you helped make it."

"I wish I could but I want to stop by the office. I barely have time as it is." She plucked a banana from the bunch on the hook. "Save me a bite." She started up the hall.

"I'll save you a whole piece," Lauren called after her.

"A whole piece?" Gaylin looked over her shoulder and smiled. "I'll look forward to it."

"Oh, gosh," Lauren stammered as a blush rose over her face. "I didn't mean it *that* way."

"I know you didn't, but it was fun to think about."

Gaylin went to work, leaving Lauren completely flustered.

153

Mushroom Spinach Quiche

Kenna's mother's recipe

Serves 6-8

1 package chopped spinach
2 cups shredded Swiss cheese
1/2 pound chopped, sauteed and drained fresh mushrooms or
1 8-oz can mushrooms (drained.)
1 Tablespoon flour
2 beaten eggs
1 cup evaporated milk
1 Tablespoon parsley flakes
1/2 teaspoon seasoned salt
1 9-inch pie crust (baked)

Preheat oven to 375 degrees. Cook spinach per package instructions. Drain well. Combine cheese and flour. Stir in drained spinach and mushrooms. Spread into cooked pie crust. Combine beaten eggs, milk, parsley and seasoned salt. Pour over spinach and cheese mixture. Bake until set, about 35 minutes.

Chapter 16

Lauren had been chopping and cooking things for the freezer all day. With two days left until the big Christmas dinner, she needed every spare minute to keep herself on schedule. The house was alive with the holiday spirit. Christmas music played softly from the stereo. Pine and cinnamon potpourri lingered in the air. The aroma of sugar cookies, gingerbread and yeast rolls emanated from the kitchen. Even Lauren's attire suggested Christmas. Her earrings were tiny elf shoes and her shirt had candy canes embroidered up the sleeves. Tallie wore a red Santa hat and Christmas sweatshirt under her apron. They'd left candy canes in all the rooms and bright red poinsettias bloomed throughout the house.

"You want the outside lights on yet?" Tallie asked as she returned the vacuum to the laundry room.

"Is it time?" Lauren said, looking up from the pan of petite fours she was decorating. "Oh, gosh. It's almost dark." She wiped her hands on a towel and went to snap off the lights and turn on the Christmas tree lights. When she returned to the kitchen there was a box with a huge bow sitting on the counter. "What's this?"

"I figured I'd give it to you now. Tomorrow will be too hectic." Tallie removed her apron and hung it on the hook behind the mudroom door. "Open it."

"Should I be careful?" Lauren asked, gently lifting the lid.

"Yes. It's breakable." Tallie put on her coat as she watched Lauren fish through the tissue paper.

"A cookie jar! Oh, Tallie, it's adorable." She pulled out a ceramic cookie jar in the shape of a two-story house. It was yellow with white shutters. "It's Gypsy Hill! Where did you find it? I love it." Lauren beamed over the gift.

"Sasha made it in her ceramic class. I told her it had to be yellow with white trim. She made it. I made what's inside."

Lauren lifted the roof and peered inside.

"Is this your homemade Christmas candy?" Lauren gasped and ate one. "Oh, my. These are soooo good." She held the cookie jar out to Tallie. "Want some?"

"No. I've had a ton of that already. I must have gained twenty pounds this week eating all my mistakes."

"Thank you, honey. I love the candy and I love the cookie jar. Tell Sasha I will keep it right here on the counter." Lauren hugged Tallie. "You always know just what to get me."

"I better go. We're having dinner with Sasha's sister. I've got to get home and shower and find something for a salad."

Lauren opened the refrigerator and took out a covered dish. "How about ambrosia salad? Made fresh today. I got carried away and made way too much." She handed it to Tallie before she could say no.

"Are you sure?" Tallie's eyes brightened.

"I'm sure."

"You are a lifesaver. I had no idea what to make and I'm too tired to care. I'll bring the dish back tomorrow."

"Good evening," Gaylin said, coming in the back door.

"Hello," Tallie said and winked at Lauren. "See you in the morning."

"Good night, Tallie." Lauren walked her to the back door and returned to Gaylin. "How was your day at work?"

"Busy but good. How about you?"

"Two words. Marathon cooking. How are things coming with your sewer? Have they made any progress?"

"I hope so. I haven't had a chance to go look. I didn't get back in town until after dark."

"Gaylin, I know it is none of my business but if they don't get it finished before tomorrow, I want you to stay. They won't work on Christmas, I'm sure. I want you to stay with us as long as you need to. Please? No charge. Consider it my Christmas present to you."

"I won't need to. But thanks. He promised he'd have it done and the water turned back on tomorrow night. I took him at his word."

"But if he doesn't, promise me you'll stay."

"Okay, I promise, but I'm sure I won't need to."

"I wasn't very happy you wouldn't let me reduce the room rate."

"I didn't want you to do that. It would put us both in an uncomfortable position."

"I wouldn't have been uncomfortable with it at all."

"Lauren, hurry!" Tallie called from the mudroom door. "Kelly fell on the ice."

Lauren turned off the stove and ran out the back door, Gaylin following her down the steps to the parking lot. Kelly was sitting with her back against the side of her car, holding her ankle and writhing in pain.

"Kelly?" Lauren said, slipping and sliding across the ice-covered gravel. "Are you all right?"

"It hurts!" She screamed as tears rolled down her face.

"What happened?"

"What the fuck does it look like happened? All I did was get out of my car and wham. I fell flat on my ass." She leaned her head against the car and grimaced. "I think I broke my leg."

"Let me see," Lauren said, kneeling beside her.

"Did you hit your head when you fell?" Gaylin asked, squatting on the other side and brushing the hair from Kelly's face.

"I don't think so. It's just my leg." She bent her knee and hugged her leg as she cried. "God, it hurts."

"Come on. Let's get her inside. We can look at it later." Gaylin scooped her up.

"Are you sure you can carry her?" Lauren asked, trying to help.

"I've got her. You open the door." Lauren held the door then ran ahead to arrange pillows on the sofa for Kelly. Tallie followed, carrying Kelly's purse and looking worried. Gaylin eased her down on the sofa and helped her out of her coat.

"What can I do?" Tallie asked, wringing her hands.

"Nothing, honey. You go on home. We'll take care of this. Sasha will be waiting for you. Please be careful." Lauren kissed her cheek and sent her on her way, before sitting down on the edge of the sofa to examine Kelly's leg.

"Show me where it hurts, Kel." Lauren carefully rolled up Kelly's pant leg. She had several red scrapes across the top of her foot and up her shin.

"Right here." Kelly's tears had stopped but her hand shook as she touched her ankle. "I think I broke my leg."

"Should we call an ambulance?" Gaylin asked.

"No!" Kelly groaned. "Don't call an ambulance. It'll cost a fortune."

"I've got insurance, Kel. If you need it, I'll use it."

"No, I don't want a freaking ambulance." She laid her head back and covered her eyes. "God, I feel so stupid. I can't believe I fell on the ice. If I broke my leg, I won't be able to start rehearsals next month. Shit! Shit! Shit!"

"Are you sure it's broken?" Lauren patted Kelly's leg gently. "Remember when I broke my arm when we were teens? It swelled up like a balloon."

"I don't know if it's broken," she snapped, "but it hurts like hell."

"Okay. I'm going to put some ice on it then I'm calling Carly."

"Don't call her. She already thinks I'm nuts."

"She's a nurse. She can tell us if you need to go to the hospital."

"She's going to laugh her head off." Kelly rolled her eyes and groaned.

Lauren wrapped an ice bag in a towel and placed it against Kelly's ankle before dialing Carly from her cell. After explaining what happened, Lauren hung up.

"She's on her way over," she said.

"Why is she coming over? You should have just asked her if I should go to the emergency room."

"I did. She said the hospital is on a skeleton crew because of the weather. You'd have a six-hour wait just to be seen. She was filling in at the clinic. She'll be here in ten minutes."

"How does your leg feel?" Gaylin asked, adjusting the ice pack.

"It stings and throbs."

"The stinging is probably the road rash. You scraped it up pretty good." Gaylin sat on the arm of the sofa making small talk as they waited for Carly. Lauren went outside to watch for her.

"Thanks for coming over. I appreciate it, Carly."

"Where is she?" Carly was carrying a tote bag and didn't wait to be shown inside. "Kelly? Are you all right?"

Kelly was crying again. Carly pushed the coffee table back and knelt next to the sofa, holding her as she cried.

"I'm here, baby. I'll take care of you. Tell me what happened."

"I was just getting out of my car and slipped on the ice. It was gravel. How can you slip on gravel? It isn't even smooth." She sniffled and wiped at her tears.

"It'll be okay," Carly said, smoothing her hair and stroking her face. "Now show me where it hurts."

Kelly pointed to the spot on the side of her foot.

"Here?" Carly touched the spot gently.

"Ouch. Yes."

"Sweetheart, can you pull your toes up for me?"

Kelly wiggled her toes, grimacing in pain.

"Can you bend your foot?" Carly supported her leg and watched. Kelly flexed her foot, sucking air as she did it. "Okay. That's good." Carly looked up at Lauren. "I'm glad you iced it. That made it easier to examine. Honey, I know it hurts but I need to have you stand up on it. I need to see if your ankle can support weight. I'll help you."

Carly helped her up. Kelly set her foot down gingerly, grimacing but able to stand on it. "That's good. You can lay down."

"Does she need an X-ray?" Lauren asked.

"No, I don't think so. It's most likely a sprain and they hurt like hell. If it is broken, it's a minor fracture."

"How the hell can you have a minor fracture?" Kelly demanded. "A break is a break."

"Not always." Carly patted her hand. "You can go in and have an X-ray if you want, but even if your foot is broken, they are going to wrap it and immobilize it in a boot. That's standard procedure."

"I've got rehearsals coming up. How am I going to do that with a broken foot?"

"Relax, baby. These things heal fast. If it is just a sprain, you'll be up and around in no time. I brought an orthopedic boot with me. Let me wrap your foot for support and immobilize it in the boot for tonight. We'll see how it feels in the morning. If you still need an X-ray, we can go in then."

"How am I going to get upstairs?"

"You won't," Lauren said. "You are sleeping in my bed."

"I can't do that."

"Yes, you can. I'll sleep on the sofa. It's very comfortable."

"She'll need to keep her foot elevated. Have you got some

160

extra pillows?"

"Tons of them."

"Good. Kelly, you can take the boot off while you sleep but it would be better if you wore it when you get up to go to the bathroom." Carly pulled a large support boot and several rolls of ace bandages from her tote bag. "I'll give you a pretty good wrap for support. It'll help with the pain."

"How is she going to get her pants off over the wrap?" Lauren asked when she noticed Kelly's slacks tapered at the knee.

"Maybe we should take them off first," Carly said. "Let's take her into the bedroom." Gaylin reached down to pick her up but Carly pushed her aside. "Here. You carry this. I'll carry Kelly." She scooped Kelly up in her arms and headed for Lauren's room. Lauren went ahead, folded back the comforter, and stacked the pillows against the headboard.

"I'll get you some pajamas." She opened a drawer in the dresser.

"I don't want any. I hate pajamas. Have you got a T-shirt?"

Lauren pulled out a white T-shirt; one Kelly had sent her from Las Vegas with poker chips on the front.

"Do you need help with your pants?" Lauren asked, coming to the side of the bed.

Gaylin and Carly were standing on either side of her, ready to help. Kelly unzipped her pants and wiggled them down over her hips, revealing nearly transparent lace panties. She didn't seem to mind she had interested onlookers.

"Can you pull them down while I raise my butt?" she said, sinking her hands into the bed. Carly reacted in a microsecond, grabbing her pants and sliding them down over her legs. Kelly could have waited until later to change her top but she didn't. She pulled her sweater over her head. Carly sat down on the side of the bed and helped her with that as well.

"Bra?" Carly asked.

"Might as well. I'm not going anywhere tonight." She leaned forward so Carly could unhook it. Lauren discreetly watched Gaylin out of the corner of her eye. Her eyes were on Kelly's

161

breasts. It was unmistakable. So were Carly's. But why shouldn't they be? She had great boobs. She had paid a lot of money to attract these kind of looks. Carly and Gaylin look like two kids waiting for the piñata to burst and the goodies to come falling out, she thought.

Carly helped Kelly on with the T-shirt. Lauren assumed even a severely broken foot wouldn't keep someone from putting on their own T-shirt but Carly offered help and Kelly didn't stop her.

"Can you get a little more ice?" Carly asked. "I want to keep it iced for a while to keep the swelling down."

"I'll get it." Gaylin hurried off to the kitchen as if she was glad to finally have a job.

"I bet it'll look gross by tomorrow." Kelly watched Carly wrapping her foot.

"It'll be bruised and a little swollen."

"Blue and purple, right?"

"Yes, I'm sure. But you'll still be beautiful. Now lean back and let me do this."

"Here's the ice," Gaylin said, rushing back into the bedroom.

"You can just leave it there. I'll put it on once I get this wrapped." Carly was in charge. This was her area of expertise and she was good at it. Lauren didn't know if she was this competent with all her patients but with Kelly, she was at the top of her game.

"Can I do anything?" Lauren asked as she looked down at Kelly.

"I've got it," Carly said. "I'm going to sit with her a while. I want to make sure everything is okay."

Lauren watched. What could go wrong? You wrap it and ice it. It's not as if she just had open-heart surgery and needs round-the-clock monitoring. "I'll be in the kitchen if you need me."

"If she needs anything, I can get it." Carly continued wrapping her foot.

"Convenient for her Carly is a nurse practitioner," Gaylin

said, following Lauren into the kitchen.

"Yes, it is. She's very dedicated."

"I'd guess all Kelly has to do is sigh and Carly will be at her side, holding her hand."

"Probably. Does that bother you?"

"No. I think it's great. She has personalized care. We won't have to worry about her. Do you think Carly will spend the night?"

"Oh, I don't think so. She'll just stay a while and make sure the wrap and ice help with the pain."

"Lauren, do you have any Tylenol? Kelly will need something for the pain," Carly said, coming into the kitchen.

"Top shelf in the bathroom medicine cabinet. Do you want me to get it?"

"No, I'll get it. If it's okay with you, I think I'll stay over. I can sleep on the floor or something. She may need help getting up to the bathroom. I don't want her to do any more damage to it."

Gaylin looked over at Lauren and raised her eyebrows.

"That's fine, Carly. I don't mind."

Carly returned to the bedroom, closing the door behind her.

"Okay, so she is staying. That doesn't mean anything."

Gaylin just shrugged. Suddenly, the front door opened and they heard voices.

"It's just us, Lauren." A middle-aged couple came into the kitchen. They were both loaded down with packages. "I'm officially finished with my shopping," the woman said triumphantly.

"Richard and Rene, this is Gaylin Hart. Gaylin, these are the Martins from St. Louis. One of my holiday regulars."

"Hello," Gaylin said, shaking Richard's hand. "If you are finished with your shopping, can I talk you into doing mine?" she joked.

"Don't even mention it," he replied. "Rene loves to shop. We have been in every damn store in this town. I should have just given her the credit card and stayed in the room to watch the ball game."

"Do you have family here in Eureka Springs?" Gaylin asked, making conversation.

"Lots of them. That's why we are staying here." Richard chuckled then turned for the stairs. "I'm going upstairs to soak my feet. Are you coming, Rene?"

"Remember, we are meeting Alice and Frank at seven thirty, so don't get too comfortable." She followed him up the stairs.

"Have fun," Lauren called after them.

"How many guests are still out?" Gaylin asked, going to the window.

"Two, but I don't expect them until late. They'll use their guest key to get in. Sometimes I don't even hear them. The Rubensteins are already upstairs. They have a stack of DVDs and said they might not come out until tomorrow." Lauren grinned shyly. "They are celebrating their fifteenth anniversary. I also have a couple, June and Olivia from Minneapolis, who wanted to get away from Minnesota weather for the holidays. You'll meet them in the morning. Very pleasant gals."

"What do you have on your schedule for this evening? More cooking?"

"No. I think I'm finished in the kitchen for tonight. I was going to make a cheesecake for the freezer but Kelly's fall put a damper on that idea." Lauren made a note to herself on the bulletin board.

"I was going to drive up and check on the progress to my sewer. Would you like to ride along? I don't think they need our help right now." She rolled her eyes toward Lauren's bedroom.

"Okay. Let me tell Kelly where we'll be."

Gaylin ran up the stairs to get her coat and was back before Lauren turned out the lights in the kitchen and found her keys.

"All set?" Gaylin stood at the door, slipping on her gloves and waiting for Lauren.

"All set."

"Are you warm enough? It's a little breezy outside." She wrapped Lauren's scarf once more around her neck.

"I think so." She wiggled her hands into her gloves then

pulled the door shut and locked it.

Gaylin held the passenger door for Lauren as she climbed in. It was only a mile to Gaylin's house but she drove slowly so they could admire the Christmas lights and decorations along the way.

"You really enjoy Christmas, don't you?" Gaylin asked as she turned down Spring Street.

"Yes, I do. I love it. The smells, the decorations, the festive atmosphere."

"You looked like a little kid when we were decorating the tree. All smiles and giggles. It was adorable."

"I'm just a kid at heart, I guess."

"Is Kelly?"

"I think so. She likes Christmas, too. She's probably not as nuts about it as I am but she enjoys the music."

"You'd expect that."

"How long have you lived in Eureka Springs?" Lauren asked.

"Three years. I've lived in Arkansas most of my life, one place or the other. But Eureka Springs isn't like anyplace else in the state. I like the laid-back attitude and acceptance here."

"You mean the gay acceptance."

"Yes." Gaylin stopped at the corner and waited for a car to pass.

"Before Terry, how long had it been since your last relationship?"

"Three years."

"How long did it last, if you don't mind me asking?"

"A few years." She eased out, spinning her tires on a patch of ice.

"Was it an unhappy ending?" Lauren knew she was being nosy but she wanted to know.

"Aren't they all." She sighed and drew a deep breath as if remembering the details. "Here we are." She pulled into the driveway of a brick bungalow. There was an evergreen wreath with a big red bow hanging on the front door. The porch light was on.

"I'm sorry for being nosy, Gaylin."

"That's okay. You weren't." She climbed out and went to unlock the door. Lauren followed. Gaylin reached inside and snapped on the lights. "Sorry, but I don't have heat. I've got a tankless hot water system so when they shut off my water, there went the heat."

"Why did they have to shut off your water when it was the sewer that had the problem?"

"I didn't understand that myself until he showed me where he had to dig. The water line crossed right over the top of the sewer line. He had to cut the water line to get to the sewer." She smiled. "Come on in."

"This is nice, Gaylin."

"Thanks, but it's no Gypsy Hill."

"I like it. I've always loved craftsmen-style bungalows. They have such rich wood tones and detailing."

The living room was lined with a bookshelf along one wall. A pair of overstuffed chairs flanked a fireplace on the other. The dining room had an oak table and chairs centered under a stained glass light fixture. Everything was clean, dusted and well organized. There was no clutter and nothing out of place. The art on the walls was mostly pictures of houses and buildings. As befitting a property appraiser, Lauren thought and smiled to herself.

"I'm sorry I can't even offer you a cup of coffee. I don't have any bottled water."

"That's okay. I don't need anything. Show me around. I want to see everything."

"That won't take long." Gaylin pushed the swinging door and snapped on the lights in the kitchen. "You've seen the living and dining rooms. This is the kitchen. There's a breakfast nook over there."

"Wow. Granite countertops. Did you do this?"

"I picked them out but I didn't install them. Those things are heavy. It took three guys to lift the long one."

166

"Nice appliances, too. I love the stove."

"I have no idea why I put those in. I really don't cook so I could have installed a camp stove and an ice chest."

"You can consider it an investment in the future." Lauren ran her hand down the smooth granite.

Gaylin stood watching while Lauren roamed around the kitchen, admiring the cupboards and appliances.

"Is this a butler's pantry?" Lauren asked, stepping through an archway.

"Supposedly. I was considering making it a wet bar."

"Don't do that. These cupboards hold tons of stuff. Extra serving pieces. Linens. Glasses. Lots of things." Lauren opened one of the doors. The cabinet was filled with extra lightbulbs, tools and cans of paint.

"Or just junk."

"That, too. I've got three cupboards in the mudroom stuffed full of junk."

"What if I just plumb in a small sink and leave the cabinets?"

"That might work but I'd choose a sink that matched the craftsmen décor."

"Good idea. If I find one, I'll show it to you first and see what you think." Gaylin reached in the cabinet and took out a flashlight then headed to the back door. "I hope he at least dug the hole." She stepped out on the back porch and shined the flashlight across the backyard. A small backhoe sat straddling an open trench. The hole was partially filled with water.

"How does it look?" Lauren said, coming out to see. The porch was small and she almost stepped off the edge.

"Watch it. There's no railing back here. I haven't replaced it yet." She grabbed Lauren around the waist and held her against her side as she continued to scan the trench. "It's a hole at least."

Lauren could feel Gaylin's leg against her bottom and her hand was just below her waistband. She couldn't help but lean back into her.

"Are you okay?" Gaylin's fingers were pressing against

167

Lauren's pubic bone.

"I'm fine. You look. I want to call and check on Kelly." Lauren stepped back inside and pulled out her cell phone. She needed something to do or she would have Gaylin's hand inside her pants.

"How is she, Carly?" Lauren asked, her eyes on Gaylin through the back door.

"Better. The Tylenol is helping with her pain and we've got her foot elevated. She's watching television while I fix her a bowl of soup."

"Did you find everything you need? There's salad in the fridge. Crackers are in the pantry, second shelf."

"Don't worry, Lauren. I know where you keep things. Take your time. I've got everything under control here. I'll take good care of her." She hung up.

Gaylin had come inside and was checking the business cards by the telephone.

"How is she?" she asked.

"Carly is fixing her some soup. She's in good hands. Does everything look okay out back?"

"They've got the trench dug but I can't tell if they've done anything else because of the water in the hole."

"That can't be good, can it?"

"I don't know. With the water shut off at the meter there shouldn't be anything leaking into the trench." She took out her cell phone. "Excuse me a minute. I think I need to check on this."

"Go ahead. I'll look around some more and be nosy."

"Help yourself."

While Gaylin talked to the plumber, Lauren wandered back through the dining room and living room. The only Christmas decoration was a small nativity set lining the mantel in the living room. The stable was made of twigs and small pieces of wood. The animals were crude pottery shapes with chipped and faded paint. One of the sheep only had three legs and was leaning against one of the wise men. Joseph had a chip on his face and baby Jesus was missing a foot. Lauren suspected the set was either antique or maybe a family heirloom. Three Christmas presents were wrapped and stacked on the hearth. They had no tags. Lauren scanned the room in case she had missed it but there was no Christmas tree.

She meandered through the archway into the hall, admiring the photographs of historic buildings. She recognized Union Station in downtown St. Louis and the Flat Iron Building in New York City. She didn't recognize the others. Through a darkened doorway she could see a desk and a file cabinet. This must be Gaylin's office, she thought, peeking inside. It was a small room with forest green walls and wide molding. Down the hall were a bathroom and a linen closet. The last door opened into a larger bedroom. The sheets had been stripped from the king-size bed. A clean set was stacked on the foot of the bed, waiting to be made. Lauren remembered Kelly had been here two nights ago. Had their lovemaking been so passionate it required fresh sheets?

"There you are," Gaylin said from the doorway. "Oh, gosh. I forgot to make the bed. Sorry about that."

"What did you find out about the water in the trench?"

"He has to pump it out. The guy he hired with the backhoe nicked the neighbor's waterline. The water is seeping from their line and filling my trench."

"That doesn't sound good."

"It isn't. They have to fix their line first. I guess Mrs. Hewlett is not happy. She has a house full of company for Christmas so she refused to let them shut off her water. It'll just keep leaking into the ground and into the hole in my backyard all night. It isn't completely cut so she can still use her faucets and toilets. The plumber said he would get a pump started at first light to get it drained."

"That'll be a huge mess by tomorrow."

"I bet he gets it fixed pretty quickly. He has to pay her water bill."

"Just remember what you said. You promised you'd stay at Gypsy Hill if they don't finish tomorrow."

"I know but he'll get it done. No problem."

"Can I help you make the bed?" Lauren moved the pillows off the bed. She opened the fitted sheet across the bed.

"Don't do that. I'll take care of it later. Let's head back." Gaylin went out into the hall but Lauren didn't follow. Instead she hooked the sheet under one corner of the bed and moved to the next.

"Lauren, don't bother with that. It's cold."

"I don't mind. Grab a corner."

"Haven't you made enough beds in your time?" Gaylin came to her side of the bed and took her by the arm. "Come on. Leave it."

"It'll just take a minute then it'll be ready for you." She pulled away and continued smoothing the sheet.

"You are not my maid," she said angrily. She took Lauren's face in her hands and kissed her hard on the lips, invading her mouth with her tongue. Lauren closed her eyes and leaned into the kiss but after a moment, Gaylin pulled away and turned for the door.

"We should head back. It's getting colder."

"Why did you kiss me?"

"I don't know." She didn't look back.

"That's the third time you've kissed me. I don't understand what you want from me."

"We better go." She turned off the lights and stepped into the hall, leaving Lauren in darkness.

Lauren knew there was something Gaylin wasn't telling her. But what? In the past she had always been open and friendly. But now she seemed distant, almost ashamed.

"I'm confused, Gaylin. I need answers."

"It was just me being a jackass." She looked back and tried to smile.

"That's it? That's all you can say?" Her flippant answer was like a slap in the face. If that was all there was to it, Lauren felt used. She didn't know what else to say and couldn't stop the tears that trailed down her cheeks. "When you kissed me, that meant something to me. Obviously a lot more than it meant to you."

"Lauren, I didn't mean to make you cry. I'm so sorry. I never meant to hurt you." She came to Lauren's side and hugged her.

Lauren wrapped her arms around Gaylin, struggling to bring her tears under control. But something inside was breaking.

Gaylin kissed her cheek and wiped away the tears.

"I just didn't know if you wanted me to do that."

"I did. With all my heart I did." Lauren's chin was quivering as she placed a kiss on Gaylin's lips. Gaylin responded, filling her hands with Lauren's hair and guiding their mouths together. A sudden and sweet innocence washed over Lauren as Gaylin leaned her back onto the bed, kissing her lips and face. This was exactly what Lauren wanted and dreamed of. There was no going back. Lauren felt a fire begin to smolder deep inside, something she hadn't felt in a long time.

Lauren moaned and wrapped an arm around Gaylin's neck, pulling her closer. Gaylin worked her hand inside Lauren's jacket. In one moment her hand was against Lauren's pants and the next it was inside them. Lauren hadn't worn a skirt in months but she wished she had one on now because she knew it would be up around her neck. She could feel Gaylin's hand where she needed it the most. Lauren quickly unhooked her pants and spread the zipper. She needed to feel Gaylin in her. She had never needed anything so much.

"Touch me," she gasped and pulled at Gaylin's hand. Gaylin's hand found Lauren's crotch and pushed past her panties, bringing on guttural sounds. Gaylin kissed down Lauren's neck as she fumbled up under her shirt for her nipple. With one hand massaging Lauren's wetness and the other bringing her nipple to erection, Lauren was completely at Gaylin's mercy. The moment Gaylin's fingers entered Lauren's opening she shuddered. It was like a shockwave sending pulses through her body, rendering her breathless. The sheer pleasure of it was lost in the need of it.

"Yes. That's what I want. Yes, baby," she uttered helplessly. Lauren arched her back and reached for the orgasm that began to grow within her. Gaylin's tongue licked and flicked at the soft skin behind her ear, bringing her higher. As Lauren's ecstasy smoldered and exploded within her, she screamed and grabbed for Gaylin. She held on as her body shivered. Somewhere in the darkness, Lauren felt Gaylin's eyes smiling down on her, admiring her moment of rapture. Then her lips fell softly on Lauren's.

"You are so beautiful," Gaylin said, her voice cracking. Nothing more was said. They lay together in each other's arms while billows of frost rose from their nostrils.

"Are you cold?" Gaylin finally said as Lauren began to shiver. "God, I'm sorry I don't have heat. I should have started a fire in the fireplace." Lauren snuggled against her, burying her face deep in Gaylin's jacket.

"I'm plenty warm." Lauren's cell phone jingled in her pocket. "I don't want to answer that. I just want to lay here with you."

Gaylin kissed her softly, wrapping her arms around her. The telephone continued to ring. Finally Lauren gave in and opened it.

"Hello," she said softly, holding Gaylin's hand against her chest.

"Do we have any playing cards?" Kelly asked. "There's crap on TV."

"Any what?" Lauren hadn't yet brought herself back to reality. And Gaylin's fingers winding tiny curls through her hair weren't helping.

"Playing cards. We want to play gin. Where are you, anyway?"

"Decks of cards are in the hall table, top drawer."

"Are you okay? You sound funny."

"I'm just a little cold. We're at Gaylin's. She had to call her plumber because of a problem with the trench." Lauren heard herself lie and she hated it. She wasn't a liar.

"Okay, but don't catch cold. Tomorrow is Christmas Eve. You don't want to be sick. Got to go. See you later." Kelly hung up. Gaylin closed Lauren's phone for her and tucked it back in her pocket.

"Everything okay?"

"Yes." Lauren closed her eyes to try and savor the moment, but Kelly's phone call was enough to kill the passion. She sat up and straightened her clothes. "Maybe we should head back."

"Are you okay?" Gaylin asked, rubbing Lauren's back affectionately.

"Yes, I'm fine." She smiled down at Gaylin. "Shall we go?"

The cold brutal truth of what they had done had hit Lauren even before she climbed in the front seat of Gaylin's SUV. She was ashamed. She had done something she swore she would never do. Come between her sister and someone she loved. She couldn't block out how wonderful it had been and how special Gaylin had made her feel, but she hated herself for betraying Kelly. More than that, she hated herself for enjoying it so much. She might never feel Gaylin's sensuous touch again but for this moment, it was perfect. That was how she wanted to remember it.

Oven Beef Burgundy

Kenna's family recipe

Serves 8

4 lbs. stew beef or round steak cut in small cubes
2 cans golden mushroom soup
1/2 package onion soup mix (Lipton envelopes)
3/4 - 1 cup burgundy wine

Mix all ingredients together. Place in ovenproof dutch oven or casserole dish. Cook covered at 325 degrees for 3 hours. (The slow cooking makes even tough meat tender). Serve with rice or crunchy Chinese noodles. This recipe can be doubled or tripled to feed a crowd. Super-simple and wonderful!

Chapter 17

Lauren and Gaylin pulled into the parking lot behind Gypsy Hill as two of the guests were returning from an evening out. Lauren answered their questions about sites of local interest and where to do some last-minute shopping. Before she could stop her, Gaylin said good night and slipped upstairs.

"See you in the morning," she said, leaving Lauren with her guests.

When the couple went up to their room, Lauren thought about checking on Gaylin but stopped herself. She wasn't at all sure she could control herself when it came to Gaylin. It was better to leave well enough alone. She went into her apartment and knocked on the bedroom door.

"Come in," Kelly said.

"Just wanted to see how the foot is doing." Carly was sitting on the bed next to her, shuffling cards. There were two glasses of wine on the bedside table.

"Better. Where is Gaylin?" Kelly looked past her toward the door.

"She went upstairs to take a shower and turn in. She said she was tired." Lauren wondered if she looked as guilty as she felt.

"Where are you going to sleep?" Carly asked as she dealt the cards.

"On the couch."

"In the living room?" Kelly sounded hopeful.

"No. In my sitting room." She motioned out the bedroom door.

"Oh." Kelly picked up her cards and began sorting them but couldn't hide a disappointed smirk.

"Why don't you sleep up in Kelly's room?" Carly suggested.

"Yeah, sis. Why don't you?" Kelly brightened. "That way you'll have a nice comfortable bed to sleep in. And you can check on Roxie and her puppies."

"I'd rather sleep down here in case one of my guests needs something. I wouldn't hear them if I was upstairs. I promise. I won't bother you. You can sleep as late as you want. And if you need help getting up during the night, I'll be right outside the door."

"We won't." Carly sounded confident, even adamant she wouldn't need Lauren's help.

"Good night then." Lauren collected her pajamas, a few toiletries, and a change of clothes. She closed the door behind her and went to make her bed on the sofa. Sometime during the night she heard a few muffled giggles from the bedroom. She sat up to listen in case her help was needed but the room fell silent. She went back to sleep and didn't wake up until well after six.

"Oh, gosh. I'm late." She scrambled out of bed and rushed into the hall bathroom to change. She hadn't overslept in years. Her routine was so ingrained and predictable she didn't need an alarm clock. She hated to bother Kelly and Carly but she had forgotten her hairbrush. She listened at the bedroom door then tapped quietly. When no one answered, she peeked in. Kelly was asleep in Carly's arms, both of them sharing one pillow. Lauren tiptoed through to the bathroom. When she returned, she noticed Carly was awake and watching her cross the room. She held her finger to her lips. Lauren nodded and slipped out, closing the door.

Oh, Kelly. What are you doing? For that matter, what am I doing? How could something so wrong feel so good?

When Lauren went to make coffee she noticed a note from Gaylin taped to the refrigerator door.

Sorry I can't stay for breakfast. I bet it will be wonderful as always. The plumber promised to be at my house at seven and I want to make sure things get done today. Talk with you later. Gaylin. P.S. The bed was great. Slept like a baby.

I wish you would have woken me, she thought while starting breakfast for her guests.

Blueberry pancakes, sausage and scrambled egg casserole were ready just as the first guests came down the stairs. With Christmas Eve just a day away, everyone was in a convivial mood. Try as she might, Lauren had trouble concentrating on what she needed to accomplish. She had a lot on her mind. A Christmas buffet to prepare. A sister with a sprained or possibly broken ankle sleeping in her bed with her love-starved ex at her side. An evening of passion being overshadowed by ominous guilt. A house full of paying customers who deserved her professionalism and congeniality. A cat that refused to stay out of the Christmas tree. And a woman staying under her roof who could talk her out of her clothes and down on the kitchen floor at the drop of a hat.

Carly went to work at the clinic but, due to the weather, was home before lunch. By noon the streets were covered with an inch of fresh snow with more expected. It bottled up traffic and made driving the steep streets of Eureka Springs a nightmare. Lauren wished she didn't have to go out, but she was down to the wire on last-minute items she needed from the grocery store.

"I'll be back as soon as I can," she said, pulling on her boots and gloves.

"Be careful. I hear it's getting slick." Tallie was watering the dozens of poinsettias scattered around the house.

"As soon as I get back, I want you to head home. I don't want you to get stuck."

"Sasha brought me in. She'll come pick me up in the truck. Be sure and take your cell phone in case you need a tow."

"If anyone calls, take the number and I'll call them back. I have my doubts the Jeffersons or the Porters will make it. It's snowing harder in Missouri." She took her list and headed out the back door. As she descended the back steps, Gaylin was pulling into the parking lot. She put her window down and waved.

"Where are you going?"

"The grocery store," Lauren replied, retying her scarf around her neck to keep the snow out. "I wish I didn't have to go but I can't wait. I have a list of things I simply have to have for the buffet."

"Get in. I'll drive you." She reached over and opened the passenger door.

"That's okay. I can drive." She slipped and caught herself as she stepped off the bottom step.

"I've got four-wheel drive. You don't. Hop in." Gaylin's windshield wipers were having trouble keeping up with the snow. "Come on before it gets too bad to drive."

Lauren looked over at her snow-covered car. Gaylin was right. She probably couldn't get out of the parking lot, much less down the street.

"Are you sure you don't mind?" She tapped her boots on the side of the SUV then climbed in. "My car isn't much use in this kind of weather."

"I'm glad I came along when I did." She waited for Lauren to get buckled in then pulled out.

"We're going to have a white Christmas this year. Isn't it great?"

As Gaylin turned the corner, her tires spun before taking hold, snapping their heads back.

"If you say so."

"How is the trench work coming? Did he get it pumped out?"

Gaylin's jaw muscles rippled.

"Not yet," she said, clenching her teeth. "But he's working on it."

"Gaylin, remember, you promised," Lauren warned.

"I know. But I'm an optimist. He still has a few hours of daylight. At least he got the neighbor's waterline repaired."

"That's something. But if he doesn't get yours fixed, you are staying right where you are. The Lavender Room is yours as long as you need it. I don't want to hear a word about it."

The car swerved and slid sideways down the street before Gaylin could correct it.

"Whoa! Hang on." She reached over and braced her arm across Lauren's chest, her hand cupped over her breast as she turned the wheel into the slide and gained control. "You okay?"

"I'm glad you are driving. I love the snow. I just hate to drive in it."

"Don't worry. I've got you covered." Gaylin's hand lingered on Lauren's thigh like it belonged there. When Lauren looked down at it, Gaylin smiled over at her.

The parking lot at the grocery store was full of shoppers stocking up before the holiday. Gaylin dropped Lauren off at the door and went to park. Lauren was weighing apples when Gaylin caught up with her. Gaylin pushed the basket as Lauren made her selections and checked off her list.

"You don't use the herbs in the little jars?" Gaylin said, watching her select bunches of fresh herbs.

"Some of them. But some things are better fresh. There's no comparison when it comes to parsley and basil. Caprese salad with fresh basil. Yum."

"That's good stuff. I had that when I was in Venice last year."

"You were in Italy?"

"Uh-huh. Love the food. Have you ever been?"

"No. But I can imagine it was wonderful. I'd never tell my

179

mother, but I really prefer Italian to French food."

"You'll definitely have to go sometime."

Lauren sorted through the Portobello mushrooms, picking only the freshest ones.

"What are you going to do with those?"

"Sauté them in wine and fresh parsley. It's wonderful with the beef béarnaise. You'll love it."

"Is that what you're fixing for Christmas?"

"Among other things. There will be four main dishes and six or seven vegetables and side dishes. I want you to try a little of everything. Do you like chicken?"

"Sure. Fried?"

"No. Coq au vin. My mother's recipe. It's chicken with a wine sauce. Delicious."

"Sounds like it. You're making my mouth water. One of these days I'm going to have to cook for you. How do you like your grilled cheese sandwich? Rare or well done?" There was a twinkle in her eye.

"Bien cuit." Lauren chuckled. "Well done."

"I'll remember that."

"What kind of cheese do you use, Chef Hart?" Lauren asked as she handed her a bag of onions and a bag of potatoes.

"That will have to be a surprise." Gaylin made room for them in the cart. "All the great chefs never divulge their secrets, especially when it comes to grilled cheese sandwiches." She winked.

There's that dimple. God, it's cute. And a wink to melt your heart. Do you have any idea how much I adore kissing you?

Lauren unzipped her coat. She was getting way too hot and it was Gaylin who was providing the fuel. She needed a cool breeze and a little self-control. She opened a freezer case and stood in the door, pretending she was reading packages as she cooled off.

They finished their shopping and began the arduous trip back to the inn. Lauren noticed several cars stuck in the snow. Some looked like they had been abandoned where they stopped.

"I'd be calling AAA by now. Thank you again, Gaylin."

"I'm glad I could help. I'll pull up out front to unload the groceries. It will be closer for you to get inside."

"I don't mind walking from the back."

"I do." She smiled over at her. "I don't want you to slip on the ice. One sprained ankle at Gypsy Hill is enough."

Gaylin pulled to the curb and helped Lauren carry in the first load of sacks.

"How's the foot?" Lauren asked as Kelly hobbled across the kitchen in her knee-high boot brace.

"Awkward. At least it doesn't hurt when I wear this thing. But I sound like peg-leg Pete when I walk." She demonstrated.

"Are you supposed to be walking around on it?" Lauren hung her coat over a hook in the mudroom then turned on the water to make tea while she began putting away the groceries. Gaylin had gone back to the car for another load.

"Sure. Carly said as long as I keep the boot on, I can be up and around. I hate just lying there. She makes me elevate it whenever I sit down. We're going to use the hot tub. She said hot water will help with the sore muscles. I'll have to ice it again afterward."

"Are you sure you want to trudge through the snow and cold? Where is Carly, by the way?"

"She's out shoveling a path to the hot tub." Kelly grinned. "I think she just wants to see me in my bikini. She said I looked hot in one."

"Hey, Kelly," Gaylin said, bringing in an armful of bags. "How's your ankle? Does it hurt?"

"Not too bad. We don't think it's broken. Just sprained."

"I'm glad to hear it. I better go get another load. Your sister bought out the grocery store." She headed up the hall.

Lauren waited until the front door closed.

"Kelly, are you sure you should be in the hot tub?"

"I'm sure. Carly said so."

"I mean, are you sure you should be in there with her?"

"Why not?"

"I thought you invited Gaylin to sit in the hot tub with you. Why are you now inviting Carly? That doesn't seem right."

"What's the big deal? I'll sit in the hot tub with Gaylin later. This is therapeutic."

"There is a perfectly good bathtub right in my bathroom. You could use that."

"It doesn't have jets."

"The one in your room upstairs does."

"That's two flights up. I've got a freaking boot cast on my foot. What's wrong with you?" Kelly scowled at Lauren but the front door opened before she could reply.

"One more load." Gaylin set the sacks by the pantry door. Her hair was white with snow and her cheeks were pink.

"Want some help?" Lauren offered.

"Nope. I'll get it. You two stay in here and keep warm." She went back out to the car.

Lauren looked down the hall to make sure she was gone.

"I'll tell you what's wrong with me. I don't think what you're doing is fair. You are stringing Gaylin along while you're obviously playing footsie with Carly in my bed. How can you do that?"

"Don't lecture me. I don't need advice from my older sister on who I see and what I do."

"You can't even be honest with yourself about that! I am not your older sister."

"Yes, you are," Kelly snapped. "I'm thirty-four."

"You are thirty-eight! I'm tired of this charade. If you want to pretend you're something you're not, stop including me in your lies. Just because your driver's license says you are thirty-four, doesn't make it true."

Kelly turned her back on Lauren and stared out the window.

"You don't understand how hard it is to make something of yourself. Who am I hurting?"

"No one, so long as you know the truth." Lauren knew this was a touchy subject for Kelly. She desperately wanted to remain young and vibrant. She would sell her soul for a chance to be twenty-five again. "Just be yourself, Kelly."

"I am not in a monogamous relationship with anyone right now. I can go out with whomever I choose." She straightened her posture. "I do not have to apologize to anyone."

"What about Gaylin?"

The front door opened again. Gaylin brought in the last load.

"It is really coming down out there." She went into the mudroom to brush the snow from her hair. "Anything else I can do before I take off my coat?"

"I think that's everything. You were a great help. I've got the water heating. Would you like tea, coffee or hot chocolate?"

"I'm good. I think I'll give Jim a call and see how he's coming on the sewer." She wandered into the living room to make her call. Carly came in the back door, stomping her way across the mudroom floor.

"It's all shoveled. We better get changed and get out there or it'll be covered over again." She followed Kelly into the bedroom to change. A few minutes later they emerged wearing terry cloth robes and shoes. Kelly wore the boot but the ace wrapping had been reduced to a single layer. "Do you want to join us, Lauren?" Carly asked without much sincerity.

"No, thanks. I've got work to do. Have fun." She wanted to tell Kelly to keep her bikini on but that would be just enough incentive to make her take it off.

"Where are they going?" Gaylin came to the window, watching them scurry across the garden. "Hot tub?"

"Yes. Carly thinks it will be good for her foot."

"Probably will. It's too bad she hurt herself and right before Christmas, too." She leaned against the counter and crossed her arms. "I wish there was something I could do to help."

"I think it is just one of those things that needs time to heal."

"I meant help you. You seem to be saddled with all the work. I don't think Kelly's going to be much assistance with that thing on her foot."

Did Kelly tell her she helps? That would be a first.

"I'll be fine. I'm used to it. Besides, Tallie will be here and I've got quite a bit already prepared. I'll do the setup after breakfast."

"After Carly and Kelly are finished in the hot tub, how about you and I use it? They won't be out there very long. I bet it would do you good to sit and relax for an hour or so. How often do you get to use it?

"Not as often as I used to but I've got an angel food cake to make." She shuffled through a stack of recipe cards.

"Couldn't you do that later?"

"Thanks but no. You're welcome to use it though."

"Oh, come on. It will be great. Just think. Hot steaming water. Freshly falling snow." She took the recipe cards from Lauren's hands and set them on the counter as she flashed her dimples.

"Thank you, Gaylin. But no." She picked up the recipes and went back to her search. "I'm way behind. I'll be lucky to have everything ready for breakfast as it is."

"What if I help? How about I set the tables?"

"Gaylin, you go ahead. I need to take care of this."

"Then how about tomorrow? You and me in the hot tub."

"I don't think so." She turned away, trying to bury herself in work.

"All right. No hot tub. How about dinner then? Or maybe lunch? After Christmas." Gaylin followed her to the sink and took hold of her arm.

"No." Lauren turned to face her. "I'd rather not."

"Why?"

"I don't do that."

"Do what? Accept invitations? Or just invitations from me? Did something else happen last night I don't know about?"

"Gaylin, what happened last night isn't something I'm proud of. It was a one-time thing. If I could undo it, I would. I don't accept invitations from my sister's girlfriend. That may be acceptable for some people but not me. Someone always gets hurt. Believe me, I've been there before. I was on the receiving end of a broken heart and I'm not going to be part of it again, especially not at Christmas. I'm sorry. We can be friends but that's all."

Gaylin stared at her with a wounded look on her face.

"God, it's cold out there," Carly said, scurrying through the kitchen. Her bathing suit was wet and she was shivering. "Kelly needs a bottle of water." She retrieved a bottle from the refrigerator then hurried back outside without stopping to talk.

Gaylin's cell phone rang. She took it from her pocket and held it in her hand but didn't answer it as she stared at Lauren.

"Don't you think you should answer that?" Lauren asked as it continued to ring.

Gaylin finally turned and walked down the hall then answered it. It was a short conversation. After she hung up, she went upstairs. In spite of the snow, the house became a buzz of activity. Kelly and Carly spent twenty minutes in the hot tub but came in when other guests came down to share in it. There was a steady stream of guests coming and going, making last-minute shopping trips downtown. An elderly gentleman spent an hour at the piano, playing Christmas tunes from memory. The snow ended just after dark.

When Gaylin didn't come down for dinner, Lauren went up and knocked on her door.

"Gaylin," she said as she knocked a second time. "Time to stop work and come have some dinner." She knocked again but there was no answer. "Gaylin? Are you in there?"

The door across the hall opened.

"I don't think she's there," the woman said, returning a DVD to the cabinet at the end of the hall.

"Okay. I'll catch her later then." Lauren started down the stairs.

"She was carrying a suitcase. I think she made two trips. She looked like she was checking out."

"Checking out?" she mumbled as she pulled her pass key from her pocket and unlocked the door. Sure enough, the room was empty. There was no trace Gaylin had ever been there. Lauren hurried downstairs. Gaylin's SUV wasn't out front or in the parking lot.

"Kelly, have you seen Gaylin?" she asked.

"Not recently. You could have knocked, sis." They were on the bed, watching television. Kelly's foot was elevated on a pile of pillows.

"Sorry." Lauren closed the door and went to the telephone. Gaylin didn't answer her cell phone, her home or her office number.

"Hi, Gaylin. I assume the sewer is fixed," she said to the voice mail. "Why didn't you tell me you were leaving? Call me, please."

"Where is she?" Kelly said from the doorway, having heard Lauren's message.

"I don't know. She checked out. Her room is empty. I thought maybe she said something to you."

"The last time I saw her or talked to her was here in the kitchen." Kelly frowned at Lauren. "What did you say to her?"

"I didn't say anything."

"Carly said you two were talking about something pretty serious when she came in to get the water. What was it?"

"It was really nothing. I just told her I didn't have time to sit in the hot tub with her."

"She asked you?"

"Yes, she suggested it. She was just being polite. She thought I needed a little R&R. I told her thank you for the invitation but I was too busy."

"That's all you said?"

"When I said I wouldn't sit in the hot tub with her, she asked if I'd go out to dinner with her."

"She asked *you* out to dinner?" Kelly propped a hand on her hip.

"Yes. But I told her no. I said I didn't think that was a good idea."

"Why not?" Kelly narrowed her eyes.

"I told her I didn't think it was a good idea for us to go out. I told her I wasn't going to date my sister's girlfriend. I didn't do that kind of thing."

Kelly studied her critically.

186

"Have you fucked her?" she asked bitterly.

"I beg your pardon." Lauren scowled back.

"You heard me. Have you?"

Lauren didn't know how to answer. She didn't want to lie. But she didn't want to admit she had broken one of the cardinal rules of sibling loyalty; that of sleeping with the other's girlfriend. Kelly never respected that rule but Lauren never dreamed she would break it.

"You have. Goddamnit. You have!" Kelly's nostrils flared. "It was last night when you went with her to check her sewer. That was just a damn excuse, wasn't it?"

"Kelly, I'm sorry. Please don't blame Gaylin. It was completely my fault. It'll never happen again. I promise you. Never. You don't know how badly I feel."

"You were lecturing me on cheating and look what you did. God, Lauren. You acted all pious and judgmental, telling me who I should sit in the hot tub with."

"I know. I know. I was wrong. I just wanted you to think about what you were doing."

"I was not cheating."

"Did you have sex with Carly in my bed last night?"

"So what if I did."

"What I did was wrong but what you did was cheating. Don't you see that, Kelly?"

"You can't cheat on someone if you haven't had sex with them," Kelly shot back.

"What do you mean haven't had sex?"

"I'm not cheating on Gaylin because I haven't slept with her."

Lauren didn't believe her. She knew all about her sister's reputation for bedding her dates. Kelly had even admitted sex was her way of judging a girlfriend's potential.

"You want me to believe you and Gaylin haven't been to bed together?" Lauren crossed her arms defensively.

"I don't care what you believe. I'm just telling you there's something wrong with her. Maybe she's a virgin. Maybe she doesn't know how to perform. I've tried but she just isn't interested."

"The other night you went over to her house. Remember? The white sweater. The skintight jeans. The next morning you even told me what a great time you had."

Kelly swallowed and turned to the window.

"Okay, yes. I went to Gaylin's house. And we talked for a while." She looked back to Lauren with a cutting stare. "She was preoccupied with your freaking appraisal. I couldn't get her away from it. She had three phone calls about it."

"You were there all night."

"No, I wasn't. I left about ten thirty. My God, Lauren. I did everything but put her hand down my pants. She didn't want me."

"Then where did you go all night?"

Kelly stared at Lauren, a softness coming into her eyes.

"Carly's," she whispered solemnly. "I called her and asked if I could come over."

"You spent the night with Carly?"

Kelly nodded as she looked to her sister for approval.

"I was upset that Gaylin rejected me. I needed comfort."

"Kelly, you are playing with fire here, honey. Carly loves you. I don't think she has ever been out of love with you. You can't play games with her like this."

"I know. I know."

"Do you love her?" Lauren asked, taking Kelly's hands in hers. "Please be honest with yourself. Do you love Carly?"

"I don't know," Kelly said as her chin began to quiver. She put her arms around Lauren's neck and began to cry. "I just don't know." Kelly crumbled to the floor in Lauren's arms, sobbing uncontrollably.

"Oh, honey," Lauren whispered, holding her and stroking her hair. "It'll be all right. I'm here for you. I'll always be here for you, Kel. I am so sorry about all this."

Kelly cried in her sister's arms. It was the fragile side of Kelly she didn't show very often. Lauren knew she was in deep turmoil over what to do and all she could offer was support. Lauren's own tears streamed down her face. They were a sister's tears, wishing she knew how to take the pain and heartache away. And they were tears for what might have been.

Lauren tried throughout the evening to call Gaylin but got no answer. Once she even considered braving the icy roads to drive to Gaylin's house. Instead, she spent the evening preparing for Christmas and trying not to worry what had forced Gaylin to leave without a word to anyone.

To Lauren's complete surprise, Kelly sat on one of the stools at the end of the counter, and, with her foot propped on the stool next to her, she finished the lettering on the place cards. She then volunteered to frost a cake and spoon cookie mix onto a baking pan. Lauren didn't know if Kelly was helping to show off in front of Carly or because she felt guilty. Whatever the reason, she was glad for the help. When Lauren returned from a run upstairs, Kelly was even singing softly.

"I'll be home for Christmas. You can count on me. Please have snow and mistletoe and presents on the tree."

Carly was watching her adoringly as if every word she sang was magical.

"Did Kelly tell you?" Carly said as she finished the song. "You get your room back tonight. I told her she could climb the stairs, so long as she wears the boot and is careful." Her smile told Lauren she planned on accompanying Kelly up those stairs.

"Are you sure you're ready to do that, Kel?" Lauren looked at her as if asking if she was ready for the commitment it meant to have Carly back in her room and her life.

"I think so. I have to find out if I'm ready sometime," she replied.

It was nearly midnight and the house was finally quiet when Lauren slipped into bed. *I haven't heard from Gaylin. Perhaps I won't. I did a good job of pushing her away. I have no one to blame but myself.*

If she hadn't allowed sex to come between them, Gaylin

might not have left without a word. Lauren felt alone. She had Christmas to look forward to without the one smiling face she longed for under her mistletoe. Not even Santa Claus could bring that present down her chimney.

Rum Balls

Even my teetotaler grandmother liked these

Makes a distinctive gift.

½ cup bourbon or whiskey (instead of rum)
1 cup pecans – ground
3 cups vanilla wafers – ground
1 cup powdered sugar
3 tablespoons light Karo syrup
1 1/2 tablespoon cocoa powder

Mix all ingredients and make into balls approx. 1 inch in diameter.
Roll in powdered sugar. For something different, roll in ground
Oreo cookies (minus the filling).

Chapter 18

Lauren wasn't surprised when Carly spent the night again. Nor was she surprised Carly just happened to have an overnight bag in her car. It looked like she had moved in with Kelly, at least for a few days. Lauren wondered how they would explain it to Gaylin but didn't necessarily mind. This time together might be just what Kelly and Carly needed to find out if there was anything in their relationship left to salvage.

Still, Gaylin was getting shafted. So what if she and Kelly hadn't been intimate yet? Maybe it was just a matter of time before Gaylin laid Kelly on the bed with soft words and passionate kisses. The more Lauren thought about it, the more she couldn't imagine Gaylin hadn't noticed the seductive glances flying back and forth between Carly and Kelly. Could that have been why Gaylin left so suddenly? Or had she just had her fill of the Roberts sisters?

"When did mom say her package was arriving?" Kelly asked, plinking a tune on the piano. "And why do I have to be down here anyway?"

"She said we both needed to be here at noon for delivery. Maybe we both have to sign for something."

"Well, they're late. It's twelve thirty-five."

"The weather may have put deliveries behind."

Lauren finished filling the Christmas tree stand with water then gazed out the front window, looking for Gaylin's SUV.

"Where's Carly?"

"She said she was going to the store, but I think she is shopping for my Christmas present." Kelly played a run across the keys with her thumb then stood up. "Someone is coming up the front walk." There was a knock at the door. "Looks like our package is here. I'll get it." She hobbled to the door.

"Are you Lauren or Kelly Roberts?" the woman asked, leaning a large box against the doorjamb.

"Who is it, Kel?" Lauren asked, coming into the hall.

"Yes, we are." Kelly held the screen as the woman placed the box on the floor in the hall.

"Merry Christmas," the woman said and trotted down the porch steps.

"Merry Christmas," Lauren called after her.

"What do you think it is?" Kelly said, pushing it into the living room.

"It's too big to be fudge, that's for sure." Lauren helped her push it.

"Can we open it now?" Kelly had already run her nail along one seam of the tape.

"I guess so. She didn't say we couldn't." They looked at each other and grinned like two giddy children. They ripped and tore into the box but when they opened the flaps they could only stare in disbelief.

"Why did she send back the presents I sent her? She didn't even open them," Kelly said with a puzzled look.

"Mine, too." Lauren sorted through the box. "What's this?" She pulled out an envelope taped to the inside of the lid. She opened it and read aloud.

Merry Christmas, my angels. Here it is Christmas again and I know you are both busy with the holidays. It seems like only yesterday you were small and we hung your stockings by the fireplace together. I hope we can start a new tradition and spend Christmas together again. I miss those happy times. All my love, Mother.

"What new tradition?" Kelly said, reading over her shoulder. "Our only tradition is that we don't have any traditions."

Lauren read it again.

"Oh, Kelly. It can't be!" She gasped and ran to the front door. When she opened it, a woman in a red wool coat and hat was standing at the gate. "Mother!" Lauren screamed and rushed through the snow to hug her.

"Merry Christmas, sweetheart!" she said, taking Lauren into her arms.

"Mom?" Kelly shouted. She stumped her way down the steps and joined them on the walk, throwing her arms around them both.

"Merry Christmas, my babies. Merry Christmas." She hugged them, kissing their cheeks over and over again.

"Why didn't you tell me you were coming?" Lauren demanded, then grinned. "I can't believe it." She hugged her again.

"How did you get here?" Kelly said, smiling so wide tears squeezed out the corners of her eyes. "You should have told us."

"I flew into Bentonville. And I didn't tell you because I wasn't sure I could get away. I didn't want to say I was coming and have to disappoint you. We've done that too many times. When I heard you hurt your foot, Kelly, and you were so busy with guests, Lauren, I knew I had to come. I can only be here two days but I'm so happy to see you both." Noel Roberts cupped her hands around her daughters' faces and smiled proudly. "This is the first time in twenty years Le Vin Rouge has been run by an assistant manager on Christmas. And you know, it was worth it just to see your faces when you opened that door. I can't imagine opening my gifts anywhere else but right here. Now, let's go inside and have a Merry Christmas."

They walked arm in arm up the steps. The woman in the van deposited Noel's luggage in the hall, collected a generous tip, and drove away.

"Show me to my room, Lauren. I want to get changed and come help in the kitchen. It's been years since we got to cook together. I want to see what you've learned."

"I'm going to put you in my room, Mother. It's the best room in the house." Lauren hated to tell her she didn't have a room available for her. Even the Lavender Room had been snapped up online.

"No, no. I'm not putting you out of your bed. I never do that. Not to friends and certainly not to family."

"She can stay with me," Kelly said, but there was an air of disappointment in her voice.

"Thank you, baby, but no. I'll leave you two to your beds and I'll have one of my very own."

"I really think you should stay in my room. The bed is new. You'll love it and it looks right out onto the garden." All the while Lauren was talking her mother was shaking her head. "I didn't know you were coming. I'm thrilled you are here but I don't have an empty room. You can sleep in my bed. I'll sleep on my sofa. It's very comfortable. I slept there last night."

"Then tonight you will sleep in your bed." She squeezed Lauren's face between her hands and kissed her lips. "Now, show me to the Lavender Room."

"I'm sorry but the Lavender Room is occupied, or at least it will be when the Colemans get here."

"The Robert Colemans?" Noel asked, removing her hat and ruffling her chestnut hair.

"Yes. How did you know?"

"I wasn't very original but I wanted to surprise you, sweetheart. I'm the Colemans." She pointed to her suitcase. "I got the name from the tag on my luggage." She threw her head back and laughed at her daughters' dumbfounded expressions. "I made the reservation late last night. You were booked solid all week then I noticed you had a room available and I grabbed it." She grinned as she picked up her tote bag and started up the stairs.

"You little stinker." Lauren scolded her then laughed and followed her with the suitcase.

"Kelly, go prop up your foot," Noel said over the railing. "I'll be down to hear all the news about your new show. And I want to hear your beautiful voice."

"Yes, Mom." Kelly smiled up at her.

"Tell me all about this meal you've got planned, Lauren. What can I do? What can I stir?"

Noel Roberts was a bundle of energy. She'd been working eighteen-hour days at her restaurant for the last twenty years. She had started as a prep cook in a greasy diner before putting herself through cooking school. She came out with a dream of owning a restaurant in the New Orleans' French Quarter that served authentic European French cuisine and not Cajun French. She had high standards for her restaurant, her employees and her food. The walls of her office were covered with autographed pictures of celebrities and political notables who had flown thousands of miles to eat her flaming Crepes Suzette with Marionberry filling. She had earned many awards for her original variations of time-honored recipes but she seldom had time to sit and revel in them. A hands-on chef and the driving force in her kitchen, she often prepared the delicate dishes herself rather than relinquish them to her assistants. She hadn't always been such a strong-willed woman. It took a failed marriage to an unfaithful husband to show her that if she wanted to succeed in the world she would have to do it for herself. With two small daughters to raise and few skills she could count on, Noel Roberts had transformed herself from cowering divorcee to an elegant and successful restaurateur whose customers were happy to pay forty dollars for Cordon Bleu. From her charismatic personality to the sophisticated swagger in her step, she was a woman to be reckoned with. Unlike many successful mothers, she hadn't excluded her children from her life. Instead, she urged them to achieve their hearts' desires through dedication and hard work. It was only natural Kelly and Lauren found success. Noel couldn't have imagined them doing otherwise.

Lauren sat on the bed and chattered away while Noel unpacked and hung up her clothes. There was still a mountain of work to do before tomorrow's reservation-only Christmas buffet but for now, mother and daughter were having fun just visiting. After Noel changed into something casual, they walked down to the kitchen, Noel's arm locked through Lauren's. It didn't matter if they always spoke on the phone. This was in person, face-to-face. They acted like college chums at a class reunion, trying to squeeze every last moment of conversation out of the visit before they would have to part company.

"What can I do to help, sweetheart?" Noel asked, claiming an apron from the drawer. "Show me your menu."

Lauren pointed to the menu pinned to the bulletin board.

"Let's see what we have here." She read, nodding in agreement as she slid her finger down the list. "Yes, yes. Very nice. Ah, with Portobello mushrooms. Very good. Not too much nutmeg in the apples, sweetheart. Nutmeg should whisper its flavor. Not shout it," she said, looking over her granny glasses at Lauren.

"Yes, Mother." She chuckled to herself. "It's good to have you here to help."

"I wouldn't have missed it."

Noel fit right in. She seemed to know what Lauren needed help with even before she asked. She knew what could be done ahead and what would have to wait until tomorrow. That was good because Lauren's buffet had been sold out for four months. It wasn't a cheap dinner but her food wasn't run of the mill, either. Noel understood her daughter's menu and how special it had to be, everything from hors d'oeuvres to an after dinner aperitif.

While Noel chopped and stirred, Lauren prepared oyster stew. If there was a tradition to be found, it was Lauren's Christmas Eve oyster stew dinner. She had invited Tallie, Sasha, Dee and Trina to join them. She invited Gaylin as well but had a feeling she wasn't coming. The meal included an assortment of cheeses, fruit and homemade croissants. Lauren made small gifts for each guest, something silly and fun. Tomorrow would be all business when it came to dinner. But tonight was family and friends. It was the way Lauren always envisioned it. She only wished Gaylin was there to share in it.

"What do you think?" Lauren held up the spoon for her mother to taste. "More salt?" She knew it didn't need it but she wanted her mother's opinion anyway.

Noel tasted the stew, first smelling the aroma.

"No, no. It's perfect, darling. I love the shallots."

"It's your recipe."

"Mine? It doesn't taste like mine. This is better." She took another taste. "What is your secret?"

"A dash of Tabasco and a half cup of sherry." Lauren winked.

"Why didn't I think of that?" Noel smiled proudly at her daughter.

"Would you like to select a wine for dinner? There should be something in the wine cooler."

"Let me see what would complement oysters," she said, reading the labels through her granny glasses. "It should be something rich and white. Ah, here we are. White burgundy." She pulled two bottles from the cooler. "I understand you and Kelly had a guest in the house. Will she be with us this evening, I hope?"

"Gaylin? No. She was only here two nights while her sewer was being repaired." She didn't know how else to explain it that wouldn't require more information.

"Do you like her?" Noel asked as she finished arranging the cheeses on a platter.

"Yes. She is my appraiser. She's very professional. She has spent a lot of time helping me with my refinancing."

"Tallie said she's nice looking. Is she?"

"Yes, she is. She's also very charming." Her mother was on a fishing expedition. Like Kelly, her questions were never subtle.

"Would you like to call her and invite her to join us?"

"No, I don't think so. I'm sure she is with family this evening. We can call everyone to the table. The stew is ready."

Lauren served the steaming stew from a soup tureen while her guests sat around the dining room table enjoying each other's company. Sasha, Dee and Trina were all easy conversationalists. Dee and Trina had been together for fifteen years and spent all of it touting one cause or the other. This month, they wanted to save the forests of eastern Tibet. Sasha and Tallie sat next to each other at the table, discreetly holding hands under the long tablecloth. Carly and Kelly sat across from each other but that didn't stop them from exchanging little smiles and winks. Noel sat at one end of the table like a conductor of a symphony, capturing everyone in conversation. Lauren sat at the other end, closest to the kitchen although her mother offered to take that chair, knowing it meant trips to the kitchen for refills.

Noel waited for all the bowls to be served before standing.

"With your permission, Lauren, I'd like to make a toast." The women raised their wineglasses. "To my beautiful daughters and their friends. The spices of life couldn't be sweeter than here with you on this Christmas Eve. May God bless you and bring each and every one of you true happiness." Smiling, she held her glass in salute and sipped.

"Thank you, Mom," Kelly said.

"Yes, thank you, Mrs. Roberts," Tallie agreed, kissing the back of Sasha's hand.

Lauren stood and held up her glass.

"I want to toast my mother for all she has taught me. Through all the good times and all the rough times, and even all those times we didn't agree, I can't imagine anyone having a better mother."

"Here, here." Kelly sipped again then stood up. "And here's to my mom for putting up with me and my crap for all these years. I don't know how the hell she does it, but she stills loves me. God, she is one tolerant woman." Everyone laughed.

"Here, here, to that." Lauren grinned at her sister. Something was happening to Kelly. She was becoming less self-absorbed.

Her conversation didn't constantly revolve around herself. Carly had brought out a softer more generous Kelly and it looked good on her.

After dinner was finished and the dishes were loaded in the dishwasher, everyone gathered around the counter in the kitchen to watch in fascination as Noel prepared flaming Crepes Normande for dessert.

"That looks so complicated," Tallie said, watching in awe.

"It's easy," she said with no more effort than stirring a saucepan. "It's all in the wrist."

"Don't let her kid you, Tallie. It's harder than it looks. She's been doing it for twenty years," Lauren said, watching her mother at work.

"Can you do that, Lauren?"

"Not nearly as well."

"I will teach you, darling. It's simple." She raised the pan and allowed a column of flaming sauce to drizzle across the plate of rolled crepes.

"I bet Gaylin would enjoy this," Kelly said.

"Probably so." Lauren forced a smile as her thoughts drifted back to Gaylin. "She is probably with her family for Christmas."

"No, she isn't. She told me she didn't have any family. At least not any she saw at Christmas. Her mother died several years ago and her dad lives somewhere in Idaho. They aren't very close."

"I'm sure she isn't spending it alone."

The telephone rang. It was the guests in the cottage needing more towels.

"No problem. I'll be right over." Lauren hung up and went to get a stack of towels. "You all go ahead and enjoy mother's crepes. I'll be right back."

"Would you like me to take them over?" Tallie asked.

"I'll do it. You enjoy." As she was going out the back door, there was a knock at the front door. "Can you get that? Somebody probably forgot their key."

"I'll go," Tallie said.

Lauren hurried through the garden and up the hill to the

200

cottage. She stayed a few minutes, listening politely to Mr. and Mrs. Ramsey tell about their new grandchild and the gifts they bought her.

She was finally able to excuse herself and slip away, rushing back through the snow. When she came through the kitchen she saw Kelly standing at the front door holding a brown envelope. She looked confused.

"Who was it?" Lauren asked.

"Gaylin." Kelly held out the envelope. "She brought you this."

"Gaylin? Where is she?" Lauren pushed her aside and opened the front door. But Gaylin was gone. "Why didn't you invite her in? I said I'd be right back."

"She didn't want to stay. I asked her to come in but she said she had someplace to go. Don't blame me she wouldn't stay. She said she wanted you to have this before Christmas. It's a copy of your appraisal report. She said she mailed it this afternoon. Thank God. She's finally finished with that damn thing." She smirked.

"Oh, grow up, Kelly. What else did she say?"

"Then she said—" Kelly hesitated as if she was bewildered, "—she said she was sorry."

"Sorry for what?" Lauren suspected she was apologizing to Kelly for having sex with her sister.

"All she kept saying was she was sorry. It was a mistake and she was ashamed of herself. She was practically in tears." Kelly pulled Lauren into her office. "She didn't say it in so many words but we both know what she was apologizing for. I could see it in her eyes. So I told her I reconsidered. I told her she was nice and all but I just didn't see us together."

"Did you mention Carly?"

"She did. She actually kissed me on the cheek and hoped Carly and I were happy together. Then she left. So here." She slapped the envelope against Lauren's chest. "Take your appraisal. You can have it. You can have Gaylin, too." Kelly returned to the kitchen.

Lauren quietly dialed Gaylin's cell phone.

"You've reached Gaylin Hart of Hart Appraisals. Please leave a name and number and I'll return your call as soon as I can."

She closed the phone and slipped it back in her pocket without leaving a message. How could she offer comfort and support for Kelly's decision to end their relationship in a fifteen-second message? She wiped the tears that welled up in her eyes and turned to join the others in the kitchen. When she did, she saw her mother standing in the hall, studying her. Noel intercepted Lauren, walked her back into her office, and shut the door.

"What is it, my darling? What has you crying on Christmas Eve?" She wiped away the last trace of a tear.

"Nothing."

"I may be just your mother but I get the feeling there is something you're not telling me. Does this have anything to do with this Gaylin person who was here talking to Kelly?"

"There isn't anything to it, really."

"Honey, I'm only going to be here two days. We don't have time for me to pry it out of you inch by inch. Just tell me." Noel squeezed her daughter's hand.

"All right." Lauren heaved a resolute sigh. "Gaylin is more than just my appraiser. She and Kelly have been out a few times. Kelly's the one who talked Gaylin into staying here while the work was done on her sewer."

"So she is more than just a friend?"

"Yes."

"A lover?"

Lauren nodded though she didn't want to admit exactly who that lover was.

"But what about Carly? My mother's intuition tells me there is something going on between those two again. Is Carly the reason Gaylin isn't here tonight?"

"A little." Lauren fiddled with the seam of her slacks nervously.

Noel studied Lauren for a moment before wrinkling her brow at her.

"Are you involved in this, Lauren?"

Lauren hesitated then nodded.

"Have you had sex with her?"

"Mother?!"

"Don't look at me like I don't know these things. You may be gay but you do have sex. And remember, we are French." Noel grinned. "We may not have invented it, but we certainly perfected it. Now, did you?"

Lauren couldn't believe her mother had read that on her face. Even if she was just guessing, she was very perceptive.

"Yes."

"And Kelly knows?"

Lauren nodded again.

"Oh, sweetheart." Noel frowned at her.

"I know what you're going to say."

"I am not judging you. My concern is that you are setting yourself up for heartache. You know better than to fall in love with someone who is spoken for."

"The trouble is, I fell in love before I knew she was spoken for." Lauren looked up desperately. "I didn't know Gaylin was going to fall for Kelly. It happened so fast."

"Then Kelly is in a relationship with two women at the same time." Noel's eyes flashed. The last time Lauren saw her mother so angry over something Kelly did was when she skipped school for a whole week her senior year to avoid gym class. "I'm shocked she would do that."

"No, she isn't. Not anymore. She ended it with Gaylin tonight. Oh, mom. I'll never forgive myself if I came between them."

"You give yourself too much credit, dear. I know your sister. If she wanted Gaylin, you couldn't have stopped her. Have you told Gaylin you love her?"

"No. How could I?"

"And why not? If you are sure Kelly and Gaylin are no longer together, don't you think you should tell her how you feel?"

Lauren went to the window and watched the last few flakes

of falling snow.

"I don't want to be the sister she settles for." She lowered her eyes then turned back to her mother. "I'm tired of being the afterthought."

"I have news for you, Lauren. No one settles for someone. They choose them. Your only regret should be you didn't confess you loved her the moment you knew it. If you still love her, you have to tell her. If she turns you down, then you will always know you tried. You don't want to be sixty years old and sharing your long lonely nights with a refrigerator full of leftovers. I know what I am talking about, sweetheart. Believe me. If there is a chance for happiness, please, don't throw it away."

"But what if she doesn't love me?" Lauren said as a tear trailed down her cheek.

"She seems to think a lot of you to come out on Christmas Eve in the snow to bring you this." She patted the envelope.

Lauren looked down at the writing on the envelope. She traced her finger over Gaylin's signature.

"Mother, can you take care of things here for a little while?"

"I'd be happy to, sweetheart." She stroked Lauren's face and smiled. "You do what you need to do for yourself."

Lauren grabbed her coat and hurried out to her car. She roared up the driveway, spinning and sliding through the snow-packed streets. As she rounded the corner, she could see the porch light on at Gaylin's house. She was relieved to see her SUV in the driveway. Lauren climbed the steps and knocked on the door but no one answered. She knocked again. Gaylin finally opened the door. She had a bottle of beer in her hand and an indifferent gaze. She didn't invite Lauren inside.

"Why didn't you wait so I could talk to you?" Lauren asked.

"The appraisal was pretty self-explanatory. I only brought it over because I thought you'd like to see my report."

"That isn't what I'm talking about but thank you."

"The square footage was wrong by five hundred eighty square feet. That made the difference. Five hundred eighty square feet is equivalent to two whole rooms. It doesn't seem like a lot but when it comes down to comparisons, it is. That is as accurate and as fair an appraisal as I could make. I didn't want anyone to say I had a conflict of interest."

"To tell the truth, I haven't looked at it yet. I had other things on my mind. Can I come in? It's cold out here." Lauren pulled her coat collar around her chin as a shiver raced up her body.

"I guess so." Gaylin shoved her hand in her jeans pocket and leaned back against the open door so Lauren could slide through. "Shouldn't you be home with your dinner guests?"

"You were supposed to be one of those guests, too. I came to find out why you aren't there." She stood in front of the crackling fire to warm herself. "The fire is nice and cozy."

Gaylin shut the door and leaned her shoulder against it then took a swallow from her beer.

"Did the plumber get the trench all filled in and the sewer repaired?" Lauren asked, searching for a topic of conversation.

"Partially."

"Do you have sewer and water?"

"Yes."

"And heat?"

"Not yet. He said tomorrow."

"No heat?" Lauren scowled at her. "You promised you'd stay at Gypsy Hill if it wasn't finished. How can you stay here if you don't have heat?"

"I have heat," Gaylin said, motioning toward the fireplace.

"But you promised."

"I am not staying at Gypsy Hill," she said adamantly. "I'll be fine. And you shouldn't be out in this weather, not in your car."

"It wasn't too bad. The roads have been sanded and the snowplows are out. If you had stayed so I could talk to you I wouldn't have had to come out tonight." Gaylin just stared at her. "Gaylin, are you all right? You look like something is bothering you."

"Nope, I'm fine. How about you?" Gaylin seemed flippant.

"If you really want to know, I'm furious with you. If you had a problem, you should have come and talked to me instead of checking out without saying a word to Kelly. Or to me. Why?"

"I apologized to Kelly. And I'm apologizing to you. I thought under the circumstances it would be better for all concerned if I checked out."

"Under what circumstances? The fact I wouldn't go out with you? Or because you made love to me when you were involved with my sister? Gaylin, I'm the one who needs to apologize. I am deeply ashamed of myself. Kelly told me what she said to you tonight. If I came between you and my sister in any way, I am truly sorry."

"It was my fault. Not yours."

"No, I'm the one who encouraged it. I was being selfish. I should have respected your relationship with Kelly."

"Stop apologizing, Lauren. You don't understand," Gaylin shouted. "I knew exactly what I was doing and I hate myself for it. You know what I'm going to do tonight? I'm going to get drunk. I'm going to get myself plastered. And you want to know why? So I can forget." She finished her beer. "It shouldn't take much since I'm not a drinker. But I can't think of a better night to learn."

"Gaylin, please don't do that. You're making a mistake."

"Mistake?" Gaylin threw her head back and laughed out loud. "Oh, yeah. I definitely made a mistake all right."

"I don't think what you and I did had anything to do with Kelly's decision to give Carly another chance. That was going to happen regardless. Carly is one of those unstoppable forces in Kelly's life. Maybe I should have warned you about my sister."

"I'm not blind. I saw what was going on with those two. And you know what? I don't care. If they are happy together, I say go for it. I wish them well."

"I definitely should have warned you about Kelly."

"You don't understand, Lauren. I don't care. I never cared. Lauren, I wasn't interested in Kelly."

"Then why did you go out with her?"

"I didn't go out with her. We happened to be at the same places a couple times. Eureka Springs isn't that large. I was finishing a business meeting when she came into Heston's and sat down. And Jolene's coffeehouse? I was pulling into the parking lot to deliver some paperwork to a client when she pulled in next to me. She was going in so we sat together."

"Kelly sure made it sound like there was more to it than that." Lauren wasn't sure she believed Gaylin's excuse. Kelly could be very persuasive.

"Don't get me wrong. I loved it. Who wouldn't love all that attention? Kelly has a way of making you feel very special. Carly is a lucky woman."

"Are you saying you didn't want anything to do with her? You just saw her on a lark?"

"Oh, I wanted something from her all right." Gaylin came to stand next to Lauren, staring into the fireplace. "And for a little while, I got what I wanted."

"What? Attention from a beautiful woman? You didn't have sex with her."

"Yes, I did," Gaylin said softly, turning her eyes to meet Lauren's. "I did have sex with the most beautiful woman I have ever met. For one special night, I was in heaven."

"But…" As their eyes met, Lauren instantly knew what she meant. "Me?"

"Yes." Gaylin held Lauren's gaze with tenderness so real it took her breath away. "You were what I wanted from Kelly. I wanted to be near you. I wanted to know everything there was to know about you. I wanted to see you smile and hear you laugh. Kelly was my excuse. She made it so easy. I used Kelly and I hate myself for it." She threw the empty beer bottle into the fire. It exploded, sending broken glass across the hearth. "I've never done anything like that in my life. I was just your appraiser. One businesswoman to another. I knew you weren't interested in me. So I used Kelly to get close to you. How could I do that to someone?"

"Oh, Gaylin," Lauren gasped. "You are so very wrong. I've been in love with you from the first day we met." Lauren took Gaylin's face in her hands and kissed her. "I thank God for the rain that made you crash into my mailbox."

Gaylin pulled away. She went to the door and opened it.

"I don't need your sympathy. I finished your appraisal. Gypsy Hill appraised high enough for your refinance. You got what you needed. I think you better go."

"Please, Gaylin. Talk to me."

"I'd rather not. I've got an appointment with the rest of a six-pack," she said callously. Her eyes had gone cold and Lauren knew nothing she could say would soften them.

"My mother was right. She said I should stop being a businesswoman and just be a woman. I came here tonight as a woman. My visit has absolutely nothing to do with the appraisal or with Gypsy Hill. I wish you could see that. We've got something very special here, Gaylin. We may not have been honest with each other but do you really want to throw it all away because of how we got here? Maybe you're right, maybe you did make a mistake with Kelly. But it pales in comparison to the mistake you're making now."

"Some things just aren't meant to be, Lauren."

"You seem bent on flogging yourself over this. When you finish, I hope you realize what you missed. I love you, Gaylin." Lauren placed a kiss on Gaylin's cheek and walked out onto the porch. She wrapped her scarf around her neck and descended the steps without a backward look.

Holiday Wassail - Traditional

Yields about 3 quarts

6 cups apple cider
2 1/2 cups apricot nectar
2 cups unsweetened pineapple juice
1 cup orange juice
4 whole allspice
1 teaspoon whole cloves
3 (3-inch) sticks cinnamon

Combine all ingredients in a Dutch oven and bring to boil. Reduce and simmer 15 minutes. Strain and discard spices. Serve hot.

Chapter 19

Christmas breakfast was only sparsely attended. Many of the inn's guests left the house early to spend Christmas morning with family and friends in the area. In spite of her frustration over Gaylin, Lauren needed a smile on her face as she prepared breakfast for the guests who did come down to eat. With her mother's help, they made crepes with strawberries, scrambled eggs Florentine and rum raisin coffee cake.

"How many more crepes do we need?" Noel asked as she dipped the batter into the pan and gave it a swirl. Cleo sat next to her feet purring loudly as if she knew something wonderful was going on in the pan.

"Just two. Everyone else is finished." Lauren carried dirty dishes to the sink. "Why don't you let me take over, Mother?" She wrapped an arm around her mother's shoulder and watched. "Let me make your breakfast. You haven't eaten yet." Cleo meowed loudly, weaving her way between Lauren's legs.

"No. I'll do this. You have other things to do." She kissed Lauren's cheek. "Don't deprive a mother of her fun."

"All right. Have it your way. And yes, Cleo loves crepes. But not too much. Her eyes are bigger than her stomach."

Noel dropped a bite to her.

"You didn't even notice my Christmas present." Noel flipped her hair, revealing her new earrings. "I'm wearing the necklace, too."

"You've got them on. Let me see." Lauren looked closely. "Do you like them?"

"I love them. Thank you, darling. I will treasure them." She enjoyed jewelry and would wear the pearl earrings and necklace Lauren gave her with pride. Noel was one of those mothers who could receive a sack of rotten bananas for Christmas and say *oh, good, I can make banana bread*. She loved any gift. Small or large. Expensive or handmade.

"Do the slacks fit? I can exchange them if you need a different size."

"They are perfect." Lauren turned, showing off her gift. "They are so comfortable."

"You inherited your father's cute little ass. He was an asshole but he had a great body." She rolled her eyes. "How about the sweater? Did it fit?"

"Yes. I love it, too. I just didn't want to wear it in the kitchen. How did you know I wanted a cashmere sweater?"

"Every woman should own at least one cashmere sweater." Noel rolled her shoulder seductively. "Nothing is sexier than a well-fitting sweater that begs to be touched. You should wear it for Gaylin." She tossed her a suggestive gaze. "I didn't see you come in last night. How did things go?" She smiled at Lauren as if she expected her to admit a night of passion that didn't end until they were both sweaty and exhausted.

"It could have been better," Lauren said and went back to the breakfast room for another load of dirty dishes. When she returned, Kelly was hobbling into the kitchen.

"Good morning, everyone," she yawned.

"Merry Christmas, sweetheart," Noel said, coming to give her a hug. "How is my baby this morning? Is the ankle doing better?"

"I think so. It's ugly purple but Carly thinks I'll be ready for rehearsal in a week or two." Kelly dropped a piece of bread in the toaster.

"Don't you want a crepe?" Lauren asked.

"No. Just toast. Carly will be down in a few minutes. She's taking a shower. She'll probably want something. She said she was starving."

That meant they had sex last night. Carly was always ravenously hungry the morning after sex. Lauren remembered that. The more times they did it, the hungrier she was.

"How did it go with Gaylin last night?" Kelly asked.

"Are you sure you don't want crepes? Toast isn't much breakfast. I don't plan on fixing anything else before dinner."

"No. I want toast. So, what happened with Gaylin?"

"She said it could have been better." Noel volunteered when Lauren didn't answer.

"We can talk about it later," Lauren said and went back for another load of dishes.

"I want to know now," Kelly demanded when Lauren came back through the doorway. "Tell me."

"Don't nag your sister, dear. Maybe she'd rather not talk about it in front of her guests."

"No one can hear."

"Breakfast was wonderful, Lauren," a woman said as she cut through the kitchen on her way to the stairs. "I loved the coffee cake."

"Thank you, Jean. Would you like a little more? I've got plenty."

"No, but thanks. I'd just eat it." As soon as she went up the stairs, Kelly was at Lauren for an explanation.

"What happened, Lauren? Did you spend the night with her?"

212

"No, I didn't." Lauren busied herself with the dishwasher.

"Why not? Isn't that why you went over there?"

"Kelly!" Lauren frowned at her. "I did not go over there to spend the night."

"You shouldn't pry into your sister's personal life, Kelly," Noel interrupted.

"Why the hell not? She pries into mine," Kelly said then folded her toast in half and took a bite.

"It seems your sister has had a crush on Gaylin from the start."

"You're kidding. Really?" Kelly leaned against the counter, chewing her toast. "Why didn't you say something?"

Lauren just shrugged and kept filling the dishwasher.

"You two may discuss this alone. Call me when the fur has settled." Noel took her plate of crepes into the breakfast room.

"Lauren, you never said anything. I thought you weren't interested in her. You talked about her doing your appraisal but I thought that was all there was to it. You just wanted her to submit a report that would get you your re-fi. If there was more, you should have told me."

"I wasn't going to say anything, not when you were going out with her. I thought you two were getting along."

"I thought so, too, at first." Kelly finished her toast and opened the refrigerator. "Funny how sometimes it doesn't matter what you say or do. Some people just aren't into you. Gaylin and I never clicked. You definitely should have said something."

"Why should I have told you I was interested in Gaylin?"

"If I knew you were interested in Gaylin for more than just the appraisal, I might not have said some things, is all." Kelly suddenly looked uncomfortable.

"What things?"

"I honestly didn't know you were interested."

"What things, Kelly?"

"I might have said something about you and the appraisal."

"Such as?" she demanded.

"I told you she was always preoccupied with that damn thing.

That's all she talked about. It was driving me crazy."

"What things did you say, Kelly?" Lauren came closer.

"All she talked about was you. Lauren this. Lauren that. She was obsessed. I wanted her to pay some attention to me. I might have said you were only interested in her for the appraisal."

"You told her that?"

"I might have." Kelly backed up against the counter. "I didn't know. You never said anything."

"How could you do that?" Lauren shot back.

"You don't understand. She wouldn't even kiss me, Lauren. The only time we ever kissed was under the mistletoe that night we were on the piano bench. She kissed you longer than she kissed me. She wouldn't even French me."

"So you told her I wasn't interested?"

"Sort of."

"Sort of what?"

"I didn't exactly tell her you weren't interested." Kelly hunched her shoulders defensively. "I kind of told her you didn't like her. At all."

"Kelly!" Lauren shouted. "How could you do that?"

"I'm sorry."

"No wonder she said she didn't want my sympathy."

Lauren was so furious she couldn't look at her. She stormed into her room and slammed the door.

Kelly followed, opening the door without knocking. "I said I was sorry, Lauren. I didn't mean to make you mad."

"I'm not mad, Kelly. I'm hurt." She sat down on the bed, holding her forehead in her hands. "I can't believe my own sister would say something like that."

"Please don't hate me. I didn't know how you felt."

"So you stabbed me in the back," she replied bitterly.

Kelly sat down next to her, wrapping an arm around Lauren's back.

"I'm sorry. I just wanted her to like me as much as she seemed to like you. You are so smart and successful. You've got a thriving business. You can do anything. My sister, the entrepreneur." Kelly leaned her cheek against Lauren's shoulder. "How am I supposed to compete with that?"

"Me?" Lauren straightened and looked over at her. "You're the one with the great voice and the fabulous body. You attract women like candy in a store window. All I ever do is cook for strangers. I'm nothing more than a glorified maid."

"You are not. You are the owner of Gypsy Hill. You know where your next meal is coming from. I have to sing for my supper." Kelly went to the window and pulled back the curtain. "I have no idea what I'm going to do when I can't sing anymore."

"You'll always be able to sing. And if you can't, you'll teach singing. Or you'll be a stage manager for a show someplace. You've got a gift, Kelly. You can entertain."

"I'd trade it all to be like you." Kelly looked back at Lauren. Her chin began to quiver. "I know I am older, but you are my big sister. You are my rock. I can always count on you. Even when I do stupid things, I know you will be there for me." Lauren came to hug her as she began to cry. "I am so sorry, Lauren. I never meant to hurt you. I love you."

"I love you, too, Kel." Lauren held her and swayed back and forth. "You know what's funny? You want to be like me. But I've always been jealous of you. You are beautiful and energetic. You have a gorgeous voice. I'm so proud of you." She could feel Kelly's tears against her cheek. "I forgive you, honey."

"Are you sure?"

"Yes, I'm sure. Now, go wash your face and dab on some of that great lipstick you wore last night." Lauren brushed the hair from Kelly's face. "It's Christmas. And I've got a Christmas dinner to prepare."

"I want to help."

"You're kidding. You?"

"I mean it. I want to help."

"Good. I could use it. I think this is the best Christmas present you ever gave me."

"Better than the Donna Karin watch?"

"Even better than that." Lauren winked and headed for the door.

"What are you going to do about Gaylin?"

"Nothing. I'm not sure she wants anything to do with the Roberts sisters right now. Or ever, for that matter. We haven't been very honest with her."

"Should I call her and explain?"

Lauren wrinkled her nose. "No. I'd rather you didn't."

"Did you invite her to dinner tonight?"

"Yes. Three times. I even sent her an invitation."

"Maybe she'll come," Kelly said with a hopeful smile.

"Maybe."

"Are you going to be all right, Lauren? Did I ruin your Christmas?"

"No. You didn't."

"I don't want anything to come between us ever again."

"Sisters are forever, Kel. I still love you. We've just got to stop competing for the same woman," Lauren said with a wry smile.

"I promise. Never again." Kelly held up her hand.

"Before I forget, I have something for Roxie and her family." Lauren went to the closet and pulled out a wrapped package. Kelly grinned and tore into it.

"Oh wow! Gourmet puppy treats from Pet Paws! She'll love them."

Lauren smiled. "I didn't think I'd like having them here but they were fun."

With that, Lauren went to work on dinner and spent the entire day consumed with it. The dinner guests began arriving at five. They enjoyed appetizers and mulled cider as they congregated in small groups waiting for the feast to begin. By five thirty the buffet line was open.

"Do you have horseradish sauce?" Carly asked, hurrying into the kitchen. "The guy in the green shirt wants to know."

"Yes. It's in the red dish that looks like a Christmas ornament. The lid might still be on it." Lauren peeked at the pan of rolls in the oven. As Carly went back into the dining room, Kelly passed her in the doorway.

"Hey, sis. Is the rectangular dish butter or margarine?"

"Butter. The round dish is whipped honey butter." She handed Kelly a bowl of mashed potatoes. "Can you replace this for the one on the table that's almost empty? Wait." She sprinkled fresh parsley flakes on top. "Okay. Go. Bring back the empty one."

"The Blanchards forgot their reservation card. Do they need it?" Carly stuck her head around the corner.

Lauren scrunched up her face as she thought.

"Vivian and Jack? No, that's fine. Tell them not to worry about it."

"Don't back up, sweetheart," Noel said, checking the rolls. "These need two more minutes."

Lauren and Noel worked like chickens in a barnyard, checking this then doing that. Dinner was on and the guests had begun to file through the dining room. Dozens of bowls, chafing dishes and artfully garnished platters covered the walnut buffet interspersed with sprigs of greenery and red bows. Relishes, salads and baskets of steaming hot rolls filled every space. The tables in the breakfast room and the card tables scattered around the living room were set with red tablecloths, gleaming silverware, stemmed goblets and greenery-and-pinecone centerpieces. Just as Lauren had hoped, Christmas had brought out the merriment in everyone, even in a house full of strangers. Cooking and time management was the easy part, but it was the last-minute details that had her pulling her hair out. Regardless of how hard she tried, there was always something she missed or someone who needed help.

"How do you do this every day, Mother?" Lauren asked, adjusting the burner under the extra gravy.

"Do what?" She laughed as if she knew exactly what she meant. "Practice, honey. Just practice. You'd be surprised. By the five hundredth time, it seems easy. And you have to wear comfortable shoes."

"That must be it." Lauren picked a carrot from the pan and ate it. "Why don't you go get a plate? I can handle the rest."

"No, no. I'd rather wait. I've learned to eat later." She pulled the pan of rolls from the oven and began filling a basket.

"I really appreciate your help. This year seemed to be more of a chore. I don't know why."

"I do. You have more on your mind. You're preoccupied with Gaylin. I'm sorry it didn't work out for you, sweetheart."

Lauren forced a small smile. She knew if she tried to justify it she would cry.

"More coffee?" Kelly asked, carrying the coffeepot.

"Sure." Lauren refilled it and took it back herself. She needed something to do. The crowd around the buffet table had thinned and the guests seemed to be enjoying their meal. Lauren's menu was a big hit, from the beef béarnaise and coq au vin to the corn pudding, pecan squash and scalloped apples. She kept a small fire burning in the fireplace for ambiance as well as soft Christmas music playing in the background. The Christmas tree received its share of compliments, its sweet pine aroma adding to the festive mood. As the guests returned for seconds, Lauren began setting out desserts on a separate table. The pies, cakes, cookies and petite fours made selection difficult. Most people chose a small piece of several. Carly, Kelly and Noel finally filled their plates and sat at the table in the kitchen Lauren had set especially for them.

"Grab a plate, Lauren," Carly said. "Come eat with us."

"You go ahead," Lauren said, resting her hand across Carly's back as she placed a basket of rolls on the table. "I want to check the coffee." She wasn't hungry. As the dinner wore on and she realized Gaylin wasn't coming, she had little interest in food or conversation.

The first guests left just after seven. By eight o'clock only the bed-and-breakfast guests still milled around the living room, visiting and enjoying a last cup of mulled cider. Lauren bid Merry Christmas and good night to the last guest and closed the front door. She stepped out of her shoes and began the arduous task of packaging the leftovers. Noel was sitting on the couch with Kelly, sipping a glass of wine and hearing all the news about Branson's upcoming season. Carly brought the last load of dirty dishes to the sink.

"That's it. Everything is here."

"Thanks, hon." Lauren filled the detergent cup and closed the dishwasher door.

"Anything else?" Carly looked around for something else she could do to help.

"Could I talk you into folding up the card tables and chairs in the living room?"

"Done. I already put them away."

"The tablecloths can go in the laundry room."

"Done. I set the centerpieces around the living room."

"Wow. You are efficient," Lauren said, smiling at her. Carly had always been a good helper.

"Lauren, I'm really sorry about you and Gaylin," she said softly.

"Gosh, does everyone know about my failure?"

"Kelly told me what happened and she feels really bad about it. She had no idea you had any feelings for Gaylin."

"Can we just forget it?"

"Sure. So long as you know Kelly is really sorry."

"I know, Carly. And I appreciate your concern." Lauren cocked her head and studied Carly for a moment. "You know, Kelly is very lucky to have someone who cares so much about her."

"Kelly is very lucky to have a sister who is so understanding about everything."

"I'm glad you two got another chance. Be thankful for that."

"Oh, I am." The doorbell rang. "I'll get it," Carly turned for the hall. "I found a pair of leather gloves on the sofa table. Someone is probably back to claim them."

Lauren poured the last of the coffee into a cup and sniffed it. It was strong and probably bitter but she zapped it in the microwave anyway.

"Lauren, have you got a minute," Carly said from the hall.

"If it involves cooking, no," she said, retrieving her cup.

"You've got a visitor."

When Lauren turned around, Carly stepped aside. Gaylin was standing in the hall, holding the stack of presents that had been on her hearth.

"Gaylin," Lauren gasped, spilling the coffee on the floor.

"Have I come at a bad time?"

"No, come in." Lauren set the cup on the counter, dropped a towel on the spill, and crossed to her. She didn't know if she should smile or cry. "Merry Christmas." That was all her brain could come up with.

"I wanted to bring these over."

"I'm glad. Can I fix you some dinner? I've got tons of leftovers." She pulled Gaylin into the kitchen.

"No. I've already eaten. I thought it was only right that I bring Christmas gifts on Christmas but I can't stay."

"Did I hear Gaylin's voice?" Kelly said, hobbling into the kitchen. She had taken off the boot brace exposing a thick ace bandage wrap.

"Hello, Kelly," Gaylin said with a reserved smile. "Merry Christmas."

"Merry Christmas," she said, giving her a hug. "I wish you had come for dinner. It was super and I even helped, for a change." She grinned as if this was big news.

"How's the ankle?"

"Better. I hate the damn boot. I only wear it when I want attention." She laughed and winked at Carly.

"Did I hear we have company?" Noel said, striding into the kitchen. "Hello, I'm Noel Roberts."

"Mother, I'd like you to meet Gaylin Hart. She's a friend of mine who happens to be my appraiser. Gaylin, this is my mother."

Gaylin shook her hand warmly.

"Hello, Mrs. Roberts. I've heard a lot about you."

"How do you do, Gaylin? I'm very pleased to meet you." Noel looked her up and down politely. "I've heard a great deal about you, too."

"I hope at least some of it was good."

220

"Very good. We had hoped you would be here for dinner. I know Lauren did."

"She stayed away because she is mad at us," Kelly quipped.

"I'm not mad at you, Kelly."

"Ladies, I'm going to bed," Noel said, stiffening her posture. "It's getting late and I'm tired. If anyone needs me for anything, I hope it can wait until morning. Good night, everyone and Merry Christmas." She kissed Lauren, Kelly and Carly on the cheek then turned back to Gaylin. "It was very nice to meet you, Gaylin. I expect to see more of you."

"It was nice to meet you, too, Mrs. Roberts."

"By tomorrow morning I expect you to call me Noel." She smiled, patting Gaylin's face knowingly. She started up the stairs, carrying her shoes in her hand, before turning around. "Behave yourself, Kelly. You've done enough damage for one year. If you don't, I'll be back down here to paddle your bottom."

"Or I will," Lauren muttered caustically.

"I'm really not mad at you, Kelly. In fact, I brought you a present." Gaylin handed her a package. "Here. Santa Claus thought you'd like to have this."

"What is it?" she said, tearing into the wrapping paper. "Oh, wow. The Patsy Cline Collector's Edition! This is fantastic. This set has every song she ever recorded. I love it." She clutched it to her chest and grinned happily.

"I believe there are some old radio interviews on there, too."

"Thank you, Gaylin. This is so sweet of you." Kelly kissed her cheek sweetly. "I have something for you. It isn't much but I hope you like it." She found a package she had placed on top of the refrigerator and handed it to Gaylin. "At least we are thinking along the same lines."

Kelly leaned against Carly's side while Gaylin opened the package.

"This is you, isn't it?" Gaylin smiled at the picture on the cover of the case. "I didn't know you had a CD out."

"It didn't exactly sell millions."

"And you even autographed it. To Gaylin. World's best

221

appraiser." She chuckled. "Thank you, Kelly. I'm sure I'll enjoy listening to this. You have an incredible voice."

"Thank you."

"And this is for you, Carly," Gaylin handed her a small package.

"Me? You shouldn't have done that." Carly was hesitant to take it. "I didn't get you anything, Gaylin."

"I didn't expect you to. Here. Open it." Carly finally gave in and opened it then burst out laughing. It was a date planner. "You'll need that if you want to keep up with Kelly."

"You're right. I'll definitely need one of these. Thank you."

Gaylin had one present left in her hand but she didn't hand it to Lauren. Instead, she set it on the counter.

"Come on, Kelly," Carly said, taking her arm. She seemed to know it was time for them to excuse themselves and leave Lauren and Gaylin to talk. "Santa Claus has something for you upstairs."

"It's about damn time you gave me my present. I'm not showing you yours until you show me mine." She giggled and headed for the stairs. "Good night, Gaylin."

"Good night."

"Good night, you two," Lauren said, walking them to the stairs. "And thanks for your help this evening. I appreciate it."

"Merry Christmas, sis." Kelly smiled over the railing at Lauren. "I hope Santa brings you what you really want for Christmas." She and Carly went upstairs, leaving Lauren and Gaylin to the kitchen, which was empty and quiet for the first time since early morning.

"Why don't you take your coat off?"

"I really can't stay very long," Gaylin said, unzipping her coat.

Just then the mudroom door opened and a woman burst through, looking frantic.

"Lauren. Oh, good. I'm glad you're here."

"Hello, Mrs. Ramsey. What can I do for you?"

"The lock on the cottage is stuck. Rick tried and tried but it just won't open."

"I'll come take a look at it. Let's try my master key. Gaylin, will you please excuse me?" Lauren hated to leave her but this was business. When a guest had a problem, she had to deal with it, not ignore it. If Gaylin had a problem with that, it was better to know it now. "I'll be right back." She took the master key from the drawer and followed the woman out the door. It only took a minute to fix the problem. The corner of the curtain had gotten closed in the door latch. When Lauren finished, she hurried back to the house, worried Gaylin might not be waiting for her. But thankfully she was sitting on a stool at the end of the counter, her coat folded across her lap.

"I'm sorry about that. It seems like there is always something when you least expect it."

"Did you get it fixed?"

"Yes. A shoulder to the door frame works wonders." Lauren poured the remainder of a bottle of wine into two glasses and set one in front of Gaylin.

"How did your dinner go? I'm sure it was a big success."

"It seemed to go well. Everyone ate and had a good time. I wish you had been here."

"I thought it would be better if I came afterward. I knew you wouldn't have time to talk while you had a house full of company."

"Probably not. I'm only sorry you didn't feel comfortable enough to be with us. By the way, I have a little something for you." She rushed into the living room and returned with the last gift from under the tree. "I hope you like it."

"What's this?" Gaylin asked, holding the box and staring down at the card. It read *To Gaylin. Thank you for all you did. Merry Christmas, Lauren.*

"Go ahead. Open it." Lauren pulled off the bow.

Gaylin tore off the paper and opened the box.

"Oh, Lauren. This is gorgeous. A leather case for my laptop."

"I never saw you carry your laptop in anything so I thought

you might need one."

"I love it," she said, smiling wide enough to show off her dimple.

"It's monogrammed," Lauren said, turning it over.

"This is beautiful. Thank you." She ran her fingers over the monogram. "I didn't expect this."

"Look inside."

Gaylin unzipped it and found a postcard with a picture of Gypsy Hill on the front.

"Read the back."

"This entitles Gaylin Hart to a free night's stay at Gypsy Hill in a room of her choice. I hope you can find it in your heart to stay with us again. Merry Christmas. Lauren and Cleo."

"It can be extended," Lauren said softly.

"Thank you."

"You're welcome. After last night, I wasn't sure I should give it to you. A laptop case looks like a business gift and I wasn't sure you'd appreciate that."

"I love it. And this is for you." She slid her last package across the counter to Lauren.

"For me?" The gift had no tag. Just a red bow over gold paper. She carefully removed the bow and released the tape. For Lauren, opening the present was half the fun. She wasn't a ripper. Gaylin propped her elbow on the counter and leaned her chin in her hand as Lauren unwrapped the present.

"Do you always open presents like this?"

"Sure. It heightens the anticipation."

"It's like watching a stripper in slow-motion," Gaylin joked, sipping her wine.

"What is it?" She parted the sheets of tissue paper and gasped. "Oh, Gaylin. It's beautiful." She lifted out a carved wooden box and opened the lid. It began to play music. "Secret Love?" she said, smiling at the tune.

Gaylin nodded.

"This is wonderful. I love music boxes. How did you know?" She leaned over and kissed Gaylin on the cheek. "Thank you."

"You're welcome."

Lauren wound it and set it on the counter to play again.

"Music is a big part of your life, isn't it?"

"Mother has always loved music. She insisted we learn to appreciate it as well. When we realized Kelly could sing, Mother had her take singing lessons. I took piano. She couldn't afford to pay for lessons so she traded cooking lessons with a lady who gave music lessons after school." Lauren wound it again. "So, am I your secret love?" she asked, letting her gaze drift up to Gaylin's.

"I think we need to talk." Gaylin closed the music box.

"All right."

"This is a little awkward for me." Gaylin took a sip then drew a deep breath as she ran her finger around the rim of the glass. She was clearly uneasy.

"Don't let it be. We'll just talk and see where it goes. Start by telling me what you did with your Christmas."

"I didn't do much. At least not like you do. I saw the crowd of cars around Gypsy Hill. You had a house full."

"To tell the truth, I would have traded it for a quiet Christmas dinner with you. Do you like Christmas?"

"Yes, I do."

"Did you have a big tree and lots of decorations when you were growing up?"

"No. It wasn't a big deal when I was a kid. My dad wouldn't allow a Christmas tree in the house."

"For heaven's sake, why not? Was he allergic to them? Or was it his religious beliefs?"

Gaylin shrugged.

"It was money. My folks spent a lot of time arguing and most of the time it was about money. She was a waitress. He was an out-of-work mechanic."

"The nativity set you have on your mantel. Where did that come from? Is it an antique?"

"No. It isn't that old." Gaylin finished her wine in one gulp and set the glass aside.

"Where then?"

"I made it. I was about twelve. Our neighbor invited me to go to vacation Bible school at her church one summer. They had a craft table and we were allowed to make whatever we wanted. It took me all week to make the stable and all the figures. It's made from twigs, papier-mâché and clay. The legs on the sheep are wooden matches. There are a few popsicle sticks in there, too."

"You made it? It's adorable. I bet your folks loved having it out during the holidays."

"Mother didn't tell him about it. She packed it away until that next Christmas then just set it up. We were going to surprise Dad with it."

"I bet you were proud."

"Yeah, well."

"What did your dad say? Did he like it?"

"No. He thought she spent money on Christmas decorations. Money they didn't have. They had a big argument so I ran off to my room. When I came out, my baby Jesus set was in the trash."

"Oh, Gaylin. Is that how it got broken?"

She nodded.

"Why didn't you tell him you made it? Or why didn't she?"

"I don't know. She was intimidated, I think. Sometimes it was just easier to give in and let him have his way. He wasn't always like that. Sometimes he was agreeable."

"So you rescued it from the trash?"

"Mom did. She wrapped it up in newspaper and put it in a shoe box. When she died six years ago, the box was on the shelf in the back of her closet right where she put it. It was covered in dust. I don't think she ever opened it again. Dad was throwing stuff out and I told him I wanted it."

"He knew you made it, didn't he? I mean, after all that time, surely she told him."

"No, he didn't know and he wasn't going to give it to me. He said it was just trash."

"How did you talk him out of it?"

"I gave him fifty bucks for it. That's the last time I talked to

226

him." She looked away, as if resigning herself to it, then looked back at Lauren with a smile that didn't mask the pain in her eyes.

"I am so sorry, Gaylin."

"I envy your Christmases. Is it like this all the time at Gypsy Hill? Big dinners. Lots of people."

"No. Thanksgiving, Christmas, Mother's Day and Easter. Those are my big buffets. The long winter months after Christmas can be pretty slow so I have to take advantage of the profitable seasons when I can. Like I said before, there are times when I'm the only person in the house."

"What do you do when the nights are long and the days are cold?"

"I catch up on my reading and wish I wasn't alone. How about you? What do you do during our dismal cold winters?"

"Work. Mostly I do commercial appraisals in the winter. People normally don't sell houses during the winter unless they are forced to by finances or a move. Of course, there are always a fair number of refinances just like yours, thanks to sub-prime mortgages. I do a little reading of my own, waiting for spring."

"By the way, Kelly told me what she said to you. About me and the appraisal. That I didn't like you. No wonder you didn't believe me last night. She was wrong, you know. She had no idea how I felt."

"I think I knew it wasn't true. I was just too embarrassed. Or maybe I was being stubborn. I should have been more direct with you all along. And you with me."

"You're right. We should have. But we can move past it."

Gaylin shook her head. Her normally dimpled smile had changed to a frown.

"I don't think we can just pick up from where we were and go on as if nothing happened. I think too much has been said and done for us to do that. Too many games have been played by too many people."

That wasn't what Lauren wanted to hear. She felt a lump rise in her throat.

"Gaylin, you're wrong," she said desperately. "We're adults. We can get past this. I know we can. I love you. And you said you loved me. Isn't that all that matters?"

"Sometimes love isn't enough. I worry there will always be a shadow of deception hanging over us. You will always harbor bad feelings against Kelly and Carly."

"No, I won't."

Gaylin touched Lauren's face and smiled through what looked like a tear.

"You say that now but what about next week or next year?"

"I promise. I harbor no bad feelings against anyone." She held Gaylin's hand against her cheek. "Kelly is my sister and I love her. And Carly is part of my past. That's all."

Gaylin pulled her hand away and put on her coat.

"Gaylin, please don't go," she said, tugging at her sleeve. "Talk to me. Don't walk away again. I love you. I've loved you from the first moment we met. You were covered in mud and smelled like a sewer. I couldn't see your face and I didn't even know your name. But I knew we were meant to be together. I know we can work this out."

"I don't see it, Lauren. I don't see us able to move past it." She started down the hall. Lauren hurried to keep up with her, holding on to her arm.

"I do. Give us a chance. Remember that night you made love to me? It was wonderful. I know it meant something to you. I could tell it did."

Gaylin put her hand on the doorknob and looked back at Lauren, a pained look on her face.

"I don't think we can ignore what has happened between us." She opened the door and stared out into the darkness, a deep frown on her face. Then she looked back at Lauren. "Unless we start over, from scratch."

"Start over?"

"Yes. We have to erase everything as if it never happened."

"I can do that," she agreed instantly.

"From now on, we have to be honest with each other.

228

Say exactly what we mean. No deception. No assuming. No secrets."

"Yes. That's what I have always wanted. We say what we feel." Lauren nodded and held on to Gaylin's sleeve, hoping to dissuade her from leaving.

"Are you sure you want to do this? Are you certain you want to start over?"

"Absolutely. I do."

"It may be a rough road," Gaylin warned.

"That's okay. I do. I want us to start over."

"Then come with me." Gaylin took Lauren by the arm and led her out the front door into the darkness.

"Where are we going? I don't have a coat."

"We are going to start over," she said, walking her through the gate.

"I don't understand and I'm cold."

"I've very sorry to bother you on Christmas, Ms. Roberts, but I seem to have crashed into your mailbox."

"What?" Lauren looked and sure enough, the front bumper of Gaylin's SUV was parked over her broken mailbox post, again.

"The road must have been slick and I couldn't stop. But I'll be glad to fix it for you."

"You ran over my mailbox again? How could you do that? The pavement isn't even wet. The snowplows scraped it dry," Lauren groaned as she looked under the front of the car.

"You said you wanted to start over. Well, this is the place it all started." Gaylin's frown slowly changed to a smile. "And this is the place we first met." She opened the bent mailbox and pulled out a red rose. "My name is Gaylin Hart. I'm forty-one years old. I'm an appraiser and I'm gay." She handed Lauren the rose and kissed her softly. "One more thing. I love you with all my heart. Would you be interested in going out with me?"

Tears immediately began to stream down Lauren's face.

"Yes, I certainly would." She threw her arms around Gaylin's neck and kissed her.

"I want to know everything there is to know about you," Gaylin whispered as she laced her fingers through Lauren's hair. "Every detail. I want to know what brand of toothpaste you use. What flavor ice cream you like. What kind of pajamas you wear."

"Colgate. Strawberry. And I don't wear pajamas, not anymore. Not since I found you." Lauren held on to Gaylin as if she would never let go.

"I was wondering if I could redeem my gift certificate tonight. Do you have any rooms available?"

"Yes, as a matter of fact, I do." Lauren smiled lovingly. "Mine."

"The best room in the house." They strolled up the walk toward the porch, Gaylin's arm around Lauren's waist.

"Wait. Give me your little finger."

"What for?" Gaylin asked as she held out her hand.

"I've always wanted to do this." Lauren hooked her little finger through Gaylin's.

"Me, too." Gaylin brought Lauren's hand to her lips and kissed it. "Me, too." They walked down the hall and into Lauren's bedroom, their little fingers hooked together. Lauren would never let Gaylin forget just how special she was.

Publications from
Bella Books, Inc.
The best in contemporary lesbian fiction

P.O. Box 10543, Tallahassee, FL 32302
Phone: 800-729-4992
www.bellabooks.com

WARMING TREND by Karin Kallmaker. Everybody was convinced she had committed a shocking academic theft, so Anidyr Bycall ran a long, long way. Going back to her beloved Alaskan home, and the coldness in Eve Cambra's eyes isn't going to be easy. $14.95

WRONG TURNS by Jackie Calhoun. Callie Callahan's latest wrong turn turns out well. She meets Vicki Brownwell. Sparks would fly if only Meg Klein would leave them alone! $14.95

SMALL PACKAGES by KG MacGregor. With Lily away from home, Anna Kaklis is alone with her worst nightmare: a toddler. Book Three of the Shaken Series. $14.95

FAMILY AFFAIR by Saxon Bennett. An oops at the gynecologist has Chase Banter finally trying to grow up. She has nine whole months to pull it off. $14.95

DELUSIONAL by Terri Breneman. In her search for a killer, Toni Barston discovers that sometimes everything is exactly the way it seems, and then it gets worse. $14.95

COMFORTABLE DISTANCE by Kenna White. Summer on Puget Sound ought to be relaxing for Dana Robbins, but Dr. Jamie Hughes is far too close for comfort. $14.95

ROOT OF PASSION by Ann Roberts. Grace Owens knows a fake when she sees it, and the potion her best friend promises will fix her love life is a fake. But what if she wishes it weren't? $14.95

KEILE'S CHANCE by Dillon Watson. A routine day in the park turns into the chance of a lifetime, if Keile Griffen can find the courage to risk it all for a pair of big brown eyes. $14.95

SEA LEGS by KG MacGregor. Kelly is happy to help Natalie make Didi jealous, sure, it's all pretend. Maybe. Even the captain doesn't know where this comic cruse will end. $14.95

TOASTED by Josie Gordon. Mayhem erupts when a culinary road show stops in tiny Middelburg, and for some reason everyone thinks Lonnie Squires ought to fix it. Follow-up to Lammy mystery winner Whacked. $14.95

NO RULES OF ENGAGEMENT by Tracey Richardson. A war zone attraction is of no use to Major Logan Sharp. She can't wait for Jillian Knight to go back to the other side of the world. $14.95

A SMALL SACRIFICE by Ellen Hart. A harmless reunion of friends is anything but, and Cordelia Thorn calls friend Jane Lawless with a desperate plea for help. Lammy winner for Best Mystery. #5 in this award-winning series. $14.95

FAINT PRAISE by Ellen Hart. When a famous TV personality leaps to his death, Jane Lawless agrees to help a friend with inquiries, drawing the attention of a ruthless killer. #6 in this award-winning series. $14.95

STEPPING STONE by Karin Kallmaker. Selena Ryan's heart was shredded by an actress, and she swears she will never, ever be involved with one again. $14.95

THE SCORPION by Gerri Hill. Cold cases are what make reporter Marty Edwards tick. When her latest proves to be far from cold, she still doesn't want Detective Kristen Bailey babysitting her, not even when she has to run for her life. $14.95

YOURS FOR THE ASKING by Kenna White. Lauren Roberts is tired of being the steady, reliable one. When Gaylin Hart blows into her life, she decides to act, only to find once again that her younger sister wants the same woman. $14.95

SONGS WITHOUT WORDS by Robbi McCoy. Harper Sheridan runaway niece turns up in the one place least expected and Harper confronts the woman from the summer that has shaped her entire life since. $14.95

PHOTOGRAPHS OF CLAUDIA by KG MacGregor. To photographer Leo Wescott models are light and shadow realized on film. Until Claudia. $14.95

MILES TO GO by Amy Dawson Robertson. Rennie Vogel has finally earned a spot at CT3. All too soon she finds herself abandoned behind enemy lines, miles from safety and forced to do the one thing she never has before: trust another woman. $14.95

TWO WEEKS IN AUGUST by Nat Burns. Her return to Chincoteague Island is a delight to Nina Christie until she gets her dose of Hazy Duncan's renown ill-humor. She's not going to let it bother her, thoug $14.95